A Hand to Hold

A Hand to Hold

A Hearts of Middlefield Novel

KATHLEEN FULLER

Love Inspired

Recycling programs
for this product may
not exist in your area.

LOVE INSPIRED BOOKS

ISBN-13: 978-0-373-78707-4

A HAND TO HOLD

First published by Thomas Nelson, Inc. 2010

Copyright © 2010 by Kathleen Fuller

Scripture quotations are from the King James Version of the Bible.

www.LoveInspiredBooks.com

Printed in U.S.A.

To Jimmy, for always
giving me a hand to hold.

Pennsylvania Dutch Glossary

ab im kopp—crazy

appeditlich—delicious

boppli—baby

bruder—brother

bu—boy

buwe—boys

daed—father

danki—thank you

Dietch—Pennsylvania Dutch

dochder—daughter

dumm—dumb

dummkopf—dummy

familye—family

frau—wife, Mrs.

fraulein—unmarried woman, Miss

freind—friend, friends

gaul—horse

geh—go

geh die nacht—go tonight

glee—little

grossdochder—granddaughter

grosskinn—grandchild

grosssohn—grandson

grossvadder—grandfather

gut—good

gut nacht—good night

haus—house

hees—hot

Herr—Mr.

kapp—an Amish woman's prayer covering

keenich—king

kinn—child

kinner—children

lieb—love

maed—girls

mann—man

mami—mother

mei—my

mudder—mother

nee—no

nix—nothing

obsenaat—obstinate

onkel—uncle

rumspringa—the period between ages sixteen and twenty-four, loosely translated as "running around time." For Amish young adults, *rumspringa* ends when they join the church.

schulhaus—schoolhouse

schee—pretty

schwester—sister

schwoger—brother-in-law

seltsam—weird

sohn—son

wunderbaar—wonderful

ya—yes

Yankee—a non-Amish person

yung—young

Chapter One

Ruth Byler picked up a fresh piece of chalk and, with precise strokes, wrote her name on the blackboard in both cursive and print. She took a step back and smiled, admiring the letters, stark white against deepest black. This was her blackboard. Her classroom. Her dream.

She turned to look at the empty desks filling the room. All twenty of them were aligned in five rows, four to a row, with equal space between them. Tomorrow, the first day of school, they would be filled with her students, from first through eighth grade, for whom she had spent the last two hours finishing her preparations.

On each desk sat a pencil and a brand-new spiral notebook. She had purchased them with her own money, had sharpened each pencil, and had written her students' names on the inside cover of each notebook in the upper left-hand corner. Her favorite time of year had been the day her mother purchased school supplies. She remembered the crispness of notebook paper, the snap of that first binder ring, and the thrill she felt when she looked at her unused colored pencils. She imagined her students' eager expressions when they walked into the classroom tomorrow morning, how pleased they would be with their gifts.

Ruth walked to the back of the classroom to check the four posters on the wall—a map of the world, the alphabet in print and in cursive, a list of classroom rules, and a basic grammar guide. After ensuring they were well secured, she went back to her desk, slipped on her reading glasses, and opened her planning book. Every minute of the day was scheduled, and she'd prepared lessons for the first four months, all the way up to Christmas break. After reviewing tomorrow's plans, she thought to rework a lesson but resisted. She was already pushing it by being here on the Lord's day. She closed the book and put it in its designated spot in her desk.

She started for the door, then stopped. "Almost forgot," she said and pulled a wooden apple out of her satchel. Her brother Lukas had made it in her family's woodshop, Byler and Sons, as a congratulatory present for getting the teaching job. She rubbed her fingers against the slick, red-lacquered surface, admiring the smooth curves and the grain of the wood. She set it on the desk, her fingers lingering on it for a second longer.

As she lifted her hand, a loud roar sounded in her ears. She whirled around, her mouth gaping open, and saw the back wall of the classroom explode. Wood splintered and boards flew in the air. Instinctively she put her arms up to shield her face from a wood plank hurtling toward her. But she was too late. Darkness enveloped her.

Zachariah Bender moaned as he lifted his head from the steering wheel. He reached for his forehead, his right arm moving as if in slow motion. A bump had started to form. Pulling his hand away, he expected to see blood, but let out a long breath when he didn't. He carefully released his white-knuckled grip from the steering wheel, then checked his arms and legs. Everything moved okay, and other than the bump on his head, he wasn't in pain. Thank God he wasn't seriously hurt. But he couldn't say the same for the truck.

Through the windshield, he stared at the hazy sight of splintered wood and debris scattered around the gray four-by-four. He fought the urge to vomit. The last thing he wanted to do was ruin the interior too.

Zach put his hands on top of his head and shut

his eyes. He had done plenty of stupid things in his life. Up until now, he'd considered the time he'd lit a stack of newspapers with a cigarette lighter in his *daed's* repair shop as the dumbest. Twelve years old at the time, he had found the lighter on the side of the road and nearly burned down the shop. But driving a truck into the schoolhouse? This was definitely worse. Much, much worse.

Zach gingerly pushed open the door, wincing at the loud clacks of debris hitting the floor. The dust outside floated inside and filled his lungs, making him cough and increasing the ache in his head. When he stepped out of the vehicle, his foot hit something hard. A bookshelf lay facedown on the floor, and books and magazines were spilled everywhere. He turned and looked back at the truck, and his stomach turned 360 degrees. *Oh man.* Rick was going to kill him. And if Rick didn't, Zach's father would. He didn't even have a driver's license.

He'd told Rick he could handle driving a couple miles to the convenience store. The entire trip would take ten minutes tops. They had been rebuilding a four-wheeler in Rick's parents' garage, and they couldn't find anything to drink in the house—at least nothing they wanted. He'd driven the truck just fine before, with Rick sitting in the passenger seat, but this time Rick had let him go by himself. Then halfway to the store, two deer ran out in front of the truck. He'd cut the steering wheel hard to the right, then tried to straighten out, but he overcorrected. The last thing he remembered was the schoolhouse coming up on him. He'd slammed on the brake pedal—a bit too late.

Zach shut the door, and several pieces of wood slid onto the hood. A hot breeze slammed into him, and he turned around to see a cavernous hole in the school wall, with the truck parked halfway through it. A huge board dangled above the bed, then dropped, causing the vehicle to bounce on its shocks. Among all the clatter, he thought he heard a soft moan. Was someone here? He jumped over two damaged desks, scanning the room as he made his way to the front. Near the teacher's desk, a petite female lay on the floor, struggling to sit up. He knelt down beside her. "Are you all right?"

She put her hand on the floor and pushed herself into a seated position. Her round, silver-rimmed glasses sat askew on her face, and her dark blue eyes shone from behind the lenses. Strands of dark blond hair had pulled loose from her white head covering, hanging limp against her cheeks. His stomach lurched at the blotch of blood on her forehead. A thick strip of jagged wood lay in her lap, probably the cause of her injury.

The blood began to trickle beneath the bridge of her glasses and over her nose. He patted his pockets for a rag, cloth, something to stop the bleeding. Nothing. He untucked his light blue shirt from his pants, ripped part of the bottom off, then wadded it up and put it against her head. "Don't move."

"What?" She turned her head and looked at him, her eyes unfocused.

"Be still. You might have a concussion." *And it would be my fault.* Not only had he knocked out part of the schoolhouse, destroyed the furniture inside it, and crashed his friend's truck, but now he might have seriously injured someone.

The young woman ignored his warning and straightened her glasses. Then she reached up and touched her head. Her finger slid against the blood. She jerked her hand away and stared at the red smudge on her skin.

He braced himself, waiting for her to pass out, or at the very least get hysterical. To his relief and surprise, she did neither. Instead she calmly said, "I'm okay."

"You're bleeding."

"Just a little bit." She took the cloth from him and looked at the round, red stain on the fabric.

"See. Not that much." She started to stand, but when she got to her knees, she began to sway.

He put his arm around her slim shoulders to steady her. "You need to see a doctor."

"*Nee.* I'll be all right in a minute." She gazed at him, her brows sliding into a V shape. "Don't I know you?"

He looked directly at her face. Then he recognized her. Ruth Byler. He'd gone to school with her, although she was a couple of years behind him. But who could forget Miss Perfect, straight-A, teacher's pet Ruth?

"I do know you. Zachariah Bender, *ya?*"

"*Ya.* That's me." Right now he wished he were someone else. And someplace else. He glanced at the board behind the big teacher's desk. It had been spared from the flying debris, and he saw letters on the board in print and cursive. "You're teaching here?"

"Tomorrow's my first day." She moved to a standing position, keeping her gaze on the floor. She placed the bloody piece of his shirt on her desk and looked up, adjusting her glasses again as she faced the wreck. Her body froze, her fingertips remaining on one corner of the frames. Her lower lip began to tremble.

Uh oh. Her body began to sway, and he popped to his feet to steady her again.

"What…happened?"

Aware that his arm was still around her shoulders, he stepped away, but stayed near in case she started to swoon again. "I'm really sorry. It was an accident."

Ruth brushed past him toward the truck. "The desks...the floor." The words sounded like they were stuck in her throat. Turning slowly, she fixed her eyes on him, her expression a meld of shock and confusion. "What have you done?"

"Now, hold on. It's not as bad as it looks." The words sounded dumb, but he needed to reassure himself almost as much as he needed to reassure her. He was grateful that he hadn't gone through the window-side of the schoolhouse. If he had, there would have been flying glass everywhere. And who knows what would've happened to Ruth then. He walked away from her and wove through the debris toward the truck. He pulled a couple of broken boards away from the front. The truck only had minimal damage. The silver bumper hung by a screw, the front grille had a large dent, and there was an impressive crack dividing the front headlight. The windshield also had a crack that stretched across two-thirds of the glass, but from what he could tell, everything could be easily fixed.

He couldn't say the same for the schoolhouse. He turned back to Ruth and saw her bend down and pick up a spiral notebook. She brushed off the dust and stared at it for a long moment. Her forehead had started to bleed again, but she stood there, staring at the mess, unmoving as the blood trickled down her face. Zach returned to the front of the room, retrieved the rag from her desk, and without thinking, walked over and dabbed her forehead. To his surprise she didn't resist, probably too shocked to do anything but gape at the disaster surrounding them.

"You've got to get this checked," he said. "You might need stitches."

She pulled away from him and shook her head, placing the notebook on one of the desks that hadn't been struck. "There's no time for that. School starts tomorrow. I have to clean all this up."

"Ruth, school won't be opening tomorrow… or…for a while." Guilt nearly suffocated him as he spoke.

She didn't respond. Instead, she picked up pieces of a broken desk, setting them in a pile. When she stood up, her body swayed again. He scurried behind her, ready to catch her if she fell. "That's it. You're going home."

"*Nee*, I've—"

"What in the world happened here?"

Zach looked up to see a Yankee man looking through the hole in the wall. He scooted his way around the truck, stepping over the rubble carefully, then looked at them with concern. "I was driving by and I saw the truck sticking out of the building. What a disaster. Are you two okay?"

"I'm fine," Zach said, but he didn't say anything about Ruth. He'd never seen this man before, and while he was probably a well-meaning stranger, Zach didn't want him involved.

The man rubbed his salt-and-pepper goatee as he scanned the room. Zach caught a glimpse of the round bald spot peeking through his gray hair on top of his head. He glanced at Ruth, then Zach. "Is this your truck?"

Knowing it was useless to lie, Zach shook his head.

"You mean someone drove in here and then took off?"

Pausing for a second, Zach shook his head again. "Um, not exactly."

The man reached into the pocket of his khaki shorts and pulled out a cell phone. "I better call the police."

"Nee." Zach stepped away from Ruth, pausing a moment to make sure she was solid on her feet. He strode toward the man, almost slipping on a spiral notebook. He could only imagine all the laws he'd broken today. The last thing he needed was a ticket. "This is my fault. I was driving my buddy's truck and lost control. But we're both all right. You don't need to call the police."

Doubt crossed the man's features. "Are you sure?" He peered around Zach's shoulder and scrutinized Ruth. "Is that blood on her forehead? I could call an ambulance. Or don't you people use regular doctors?"

Zach realized the man wasn't from around here. "We don't need a doctor, but thanks for the offer."

Ruth stepped forward and stood next to Zach. "It's only a scratch." She dabbed the bloody cloth on the wound, then pulled it away. A few drops clung to the pale blue fabric. "See? I'm fine, really. You don't have to call anyone."

The man frowned. "All right, but it's against my better judgment. I can give you both a ride home at least. You're not going anywhere in that truck."

Ruth shook her head. "My buggy and horse are here." She kept her gaze focused on the Yankee.

The man didn't answer for a long moment, and Zach thought he might call the police anyway. Finally he said, "Guess there's nothing I can do then." He looked toward the hole in the wall then back at Zach and Ruth. "As long as you're sure you're okay…"

"We are." Ruth nodded, still not looking at Zach.

"Then good luck to you. Looks like you'll need

it." The Yankee took one more glance over his shoulder before disappearing outside.

Ruth immediately started picking up several textbooks off the floor, hugging them close to her small frame. Her glasses slipped down her nose, but she didn't bother to push them up. She also hadn't bothered to listen to him when he'd told her to stay still.

Putting his hands on his hips, Zach looked at her. "Ruth, *halt*. There's nothing else we can do, at least not today. Come with *mei*. I can drive you home in your buggy."

Now she looked at him. "I'll drive myself home."

"*Nee*. You don't need to be driving with that bump on your head. I'll take you."

"I'll drive myself home." Her voice had a slight edge that hadn't been there before. "I feel fine." Squaring her shoulders, she removed her glasses and tucked them in her free hand while setting down the textbooks she'd picked up a moment ago. Any trace of confusion or anger in her expression had disappeared. "But I feel I must inform you that I will be stopping by my *schwoger's haus*. Gabriel is on the school board. It's appropriate he be notified of…" She paused, her lower lip quivering for a second. "Of what happened here."

Zach's shoulders hunched forward. "*Ya*, you're

right. I'll have to let my *daed* know as soon as I get home. He'll probably call an emergency meeting."

Ruth's delicate eyebrows arched. "Your *daed's* on the school board?"

"Has been for years. You have him to thank for hiring you."

She stiffened, but her emotions were controlled. The complete opposite of how he would have reacted if their situations were reversed. He appreciated the way she kept her cool.

"From what I understand it was a *group* decision."

Ouch. Maybe she wasn't as calm as she seemed.

Ruth looked around the schoolhouse again. "It took me two weeks to get everything in order." Her voice was barely above a whisper. She turned toward the hole in the wall. The remnant of a poster clung to it, fluttering in the summer breeze.

Zach wanted to seep through the cracks in the floorboards—well, through the ones that weren't splintered or destroyed already. His gaze followed her as she walked through the obstacle course to her desk and gathered her belongings into a navy blue tote bag. She slung it over her shoulder and started for the front door, clearly intending to leave without saying anything to him. She stopped just before walking outside and picked something up off the floor. A wooden apple, stained a rich red color. She brushed her tiny fingers over the glossy surface, then put it in her bag and walked out of the door.

He couldn't let her go just like that. He jumped over the mess, slid past Rick's truck, and left the schoolhouse through the new exit he'd made. He rushed to her buggy.

Standing behind her, he said, "Look, I'm really sorry." His hat had fallen off in the accident, and he pushed back his damp bangs with the palm of his hand. It was a hot one today, the air surrounding them thick and heavy like a damp wool blanket. "I didn't mean for this to happen, honest. And I didn't mean to cause you trouble. The least I can do is take you home. I'm serious about you not driving with your head all messed up like that."

She placed her bags on the bench seat of the buggy before facing him. Her expression blank, she said, "As I told you, I'm perfectly fine to drive myself home. I only live two and a half miles away." She turned from him and walked over to unhitch her horse.

For some reason, her attitude rankled him. He'd rather she yell at him than behave as if everything was okay. That's what a normal person would do. But Ruth was acting anything but normal. Giving up, he stepped to the side, then watched her back up her horse and buggy and ride away.

After the *clip-clop* of her horse's hooves faded, he turned and faced the nightmare in front of him. Dread filled his gut and made him temporarily forget about Ruth. He clenched his jaw. How was he going to explain all this to his *daed*? He and his father had disagreed for years over everything from his choice in friends to the way he drove his buggy. But that wasn't the end of his problems. He'd also wrecked his friend's truck and destroyed an entire schoolhouse, not to mention making Ruth Byler really mad, even though she refused to show it.

How was he going to fix all that?

Chapter Two

"Ow!" Ruth winced as her oldest sister wiped her forehead.

"You're lucky it's just a small cut," Moriah said, dipping the wet rag back into a bowl of cool water. "You could have been seriously injured. What were you doing at the *schulhaus* today? It's Sunday. You're not supposed to be working."

Ruth grimaced again. It wasn't the cut that bothered her but the knot her sister kept touching. "I wasn't working, per se. I was just making sure everything was ready for tomorrow."

"Knowing you, I'm sure everything was perfect a week ago." Moriah dabbed a little more. "You shouldn't have been at the *schulhaus*, Ruth. You know that."

"It doesn't matter if I was there or not. Everything would still be ruined." She closed her eyes, fighting her bubbling emotions. Just remembering the destruction in the schoolhouse caused her stomach to twist. It had taken all her mettle not to lose her temper with Zachariah. Yelling at him wouldn't have changed or fixed what had happened.

She had driven over to her sister's house right after leaving the schoolhouse. Now she sat in Moriah's kitchen, trying to keep a logical head about what had happened as her sister continued her ministrations. Moriah had stopped dabbing, so Ruth opened her eyes.

"Sundays are the Lord's days, Ruth. A day for rest. You would do well to heed that from now on."

Unable to take any more of Moriah's hovering, Ruth took the rag from her. *I'm not a* glee kinn *anymore.* As the youngest of six in the Byler household, Ruth had spent her whole life trying to prove that she was capable, that she wasn't the little sister everyone had to watch out for and protect. She'd never liked to be babied, which Moriah insisted on doing, even now. She was almost seventeen years old and could take care of herself.

"I need to use the restroom," Ruth said, standing up. She made her way to the bathroom, flipped on the battery-operated lamp her sister kept on the vanity, and closed the door.

Looking in the mirror, she examined her forehead, noting the slightly off-center bump made by the flying piece of wood. Gingerly she cleaned off the rest of the blood dotting her skin, then rinsed the dust from her face with cold water from the sink. She dried her cheeks, then released a deep breath. Moriah was right; she was lucky she hadn't been seriously injured. The wood plank could have struck her in the eye or hit her head with enough force to give her a concussion. She didn't want to admit it, but both her sister and Zachariah had a right to be concerned.

Her head throbbed, but the pain didn't compare with the fury rising inside her. Maybe she shouldn't have been at the schoolhouse in the first place, but Zachariah shouldn't have been either. She took a deep breath, fighting to tamp her anger down. Zachariah Bender. It would figure he was the one to do something like this. Who could forget such a troublemaker?

She hadn't realized who he was at first, which could have been due to getting hit on the head. Or it could have been because he had changed since they had been in school together. She remembered him as a short, stocky boy who was always disrespectful to authority, annoying the teacher and everyone around him, except for the few boys he hung out with who laughed at his juvenile jokes. To Ruth, he'd been the most irritating person she'd ever met, and she had been jubilant when he finally graduated.

But he had grown since then. He still had the same deep red hair, light-green eyes, and pale freckles on his face. But he'd grown several inches and lost some of his youthful girth. Now he was lean, muscular, and at least a head taller than she was. Well, his body may have changed, but his penchant for being irresponsible obviously hadn't.

Guilt pricked at her. She was judging him. But it was hard not to when faced with what Zachariah had done. When she gained sufficient control, she left the bathroom and entered the kitchen. From the smile appearing on Moriah's face, Ruth surmised she had been successful in masking her internal struggle.

The kettle whistled, and Moriah went to the stove and turned off the burner. Two white mugs were on the counter, a thin string with a small white tag dangling over the lip of each one. She poured hot water into each cup. Moriah handed Ruth a cup and gestured for her to sit down.

Although she wasn't thirsty, she acquiesced to satisfy her sister. What she really wanted to do was go home and try to figure out what to do about the schoolhouse. But first she had to tell her brother-in-law what had happened. When she'd arrived, Moriah had made such a fuss over

Ruth's injury that she hadn't had the chance. "Where's Gabriel?"

"He's out with the girls in the backyard. I'll *geh* get him."

Ruth shook her head. Gabriel worked long hours in his blacksmith shop, and she didn't want to interrupt his time with his daughters: Verna, who was almost four; Ester, almost three. Baby Leah had just turned eighteen months. "I can wait until he's done."

"I'll get the *maed* and Gabriel will take you home. I don't want you driving yourself."

Ruth suppressed a sigh. Moriah's words echoed Zachariah's. His motives had been transparent, and she could tell he wanted to take her home more out of his guilt than for her safety. Moriah's concern was genuine, though just as annoying. "That's not necessary. I drove all the way over here from the *schulhaus* without a problem."

Moriah frowned. "If you ask me, Zachariah should have offered to take you."

"He did. I refused."

"But why? Ruth, I don't understand you sometimes. It's one thing to be independent; it's another to be foolish."

"I'm not foolish." Her voice rose, and she brought it back down. "I know my own body, and I'm fine." Even if she hadn't been fine, she wouldn't have accepted a ride from Zachariah.

Visions of the wrecked schoolhouse came to her mind. All her meticulous planning, wasted. All her hard work, ruined. School would be delayed until the *schulhaus* could be repaired, and her students would be behind from the start. How would she make that time up? Her head started to pound, and she brought her fingertips to her temples.

"Ruth, it's going to be all right." Moriah came over to her and put her arm around her shoulders. "Maybe the *kinner* can meet at someone's home until the school is fixed."

Ruth tried to shrug her off, but Moriah's grip held firm. The idea was plausible. It would require flexibility on all their parts, but she would be willing to do it as long as the school board and parents agreed to it. Finally, Ruth gave in and accepted Moriah's comforting.

"Stay here and I'll get Gabriel," Moriah said. "He'll be happy to take you home. He was just saying the other day how you two never get a chance to talk."

Ruth nodded, knowing it would be useless to argue with her sister, as Moriah would wear her down with kindness. Ruth was already worn down enough.

Moments later Gabriel came inside the kitchen carrying Leah and Ester, with Verna and Moriah tagging close behind. The tightness around

Ruth's mouth relaxed at the sight of her nieces. Verna ran and jumped in her lap. Ruth's arms went around the small child, feeling the sweat on her niece's skin and dress from playing in the heat outside.

"*Aenti* Ruth, I flipped out of the swing!" Verna grinned, her brown eyes twinkling, her smooth forehead beaded with sweat.

Moriah gasped, but Gabriel chuckled. "First and last time." He handed Leah to his wife and set Ester down on the chair at the table. He took off his yellow straw hat and threaded his fingers through his damp brown locks. "She reminds me so much of Levi. Not afraid of anything."

Ruth looked up at Gabriel's mention of his late twin brother. Levi had actually been Moriah's first husband, and he was Verna's biological father. Ruth had only been twelve when Levi had died in a car accident. She'd seen how Gabriel had helped Moriah during that tumultuous time, supporting her through the pregnancy. Then they had fallen in love, marrying a year later and starting their own family. Verna had never met Levi, so Gabriel was the only father she knew. And he clearly loved her as his own.

Moriah gave her daughter a stern look. "If you're going to be reckless, you won't be allowed to swing anymore."

Verna's grin faded into a pout, and for the first

time since Zach had crashed into the school-house, Ruth had the urge to smile. She didn't dare, though. Her niece might look adorable with her bottom lip poking out, but rebellious behavior wasn't tolerated by any member of the family. Moriah picked up Verna and set her on the chair. "Stay put."

"But—"

"You heard your *mami*." Gabriel stood next to Moriah, unified in their discipline.

Verna nodded and remained still.

Ruth admired her sister and brother-in-law's parenting skills. She planned to apply the same type of calm consistency in her classroom. If she ever had the chance. She gripped the edge of the table.

Gabriel looked at Ruth. If he noticed her stress, he didn't let on. "Moriah said you need a ride home."

"She's insisting."

"Oh, so you don't want to ride with your old *schwoger*?" Gabriel moved toward the back door where the pegboard held a couple of yellow straw hats and Moriah's black bonnet.

"Sorry, that's not what I meant. And you're not old. What I should have said is she's making me accept a ride from you. Which I appreciate, of course."

"Of course." Gabriel gave her a knowing smile.

"I don't mind taking you home, Ruth." He peered at her as he put his hat back on. "From the looks of that bump on your forehead, I don't blame her for being concerned. She told me a little about what happened. I'm eager to hear the rest. Sounds like we have a problem on our hands."

Ruth said goodbye to Moriah and her nieces, thanking her sister for her untouched tea. Once she and Gabriel were on the road, she explained what Zachariah had done to the schoolhouse. The ride was short, only fifteen minutes, and she barely noticed the cars zipping by as she talked. By the time they reached her parents' home, the sun had nearly set, leaving behind faint slivers of light between the feathery clouds.

Gabriel slowed the horse as he pulled in front of the house. His normally placid expression was troubled. "Zach's *daed* is on the board."

"I know. He told me."

"I'm sure I'll be hearing from Gideon about a meeting soon enough."

"I hope so. I don't want the students to be any further behind than they have to be." *No thanks to Zachariah.*

She reined in the thought. *Mercy. Forgiveness.* She was struggling to do what the Bible, and what her faith, directed her to do: apply mercy to him and the situation. But doing that just felt painful, like shards of glass sliding down her throat. She looked at her brother-in-law's profile, his gaze seemingly fixed on the back of his horse's head.

Gabriel was a firm believer in forgiveness and leaving the past behind. He had hired Aaron Detweiler as an apprentice in his blacksmith shop after Aaron had spent time in jail and rehab. When Aaron returned home, he'd floundered around, trying to find his way. Gabriel, who always saw the good in others, gave Aaron a chance. Then Ruth's sister Elisabeth had married Aaron about a year ago. Ruth knew she needed to see the good in people too.

"Ruth?" Gabriel's voice yanked her out of her thoughts. "We're here."

Ruth looked through the buggy's front opening to the white, two-story house where she lived with her parents and her older brother Stephen. Her other brothers, Tobias and Lukas, were married and had their own families. Her mother's flower boxes hung over the banister of the wraparound front porch. Like the flower beds rimming the house, they were filled with vibrant red, white, and pink impatiens and lavender and purple petunias. They had thrived despite the simmering summer heat.

Gabriel angled his body to face her. "Are you okay?"

She wished everyone would stop asking her

that. She wiped the perspiration off her brow with the heel of her hand before picking up her purse and tote bag. "Do you want to come inside for a bit?"

"Sure, but just for a bit. I want to get back and help Moriah with the *maed*." Ruth moved to get out of the buggy, but Gabriel suddenly stopped her. "I know you're disappointed about the *schulhaus*."

"Moriah suggested that we hold school at someone's *haus*."

He ran his forefinger over his bearded chin. "I'll have to see what the school board thinks about that. But don't worry, Ruth. We'll make sure the *schulhaus* is fixed as soon as possible. And if the board decides it's best to delay school for a short while, enjoy the time off."

She didn't want time off; she wanted to teach. But she didn't say that to Gabriel. He wouldn't understand. No one in her family appreciated her devotion to education and learning. She told him what he wanted to hear. "Okay. I won't worry about it anymore."

"Gut."

She and Gabriel walked into the house and found her parents in the front living room, where they usually spent their Sunday evenings reading. Her father, Joseph, was dozing in his chair, his head tilted back and his mouth partly open as he snored softly. Her mother, Emma, was on the couch, thumbing through an afghan pattern book. The only light in the room came from a small lamp on the end table. The windows were open, but it was only slightly cooler in the house than it was outside.

When her mother looked up and saw Ruth's forehead, she stood and went to her. "*Gut* heavens, what happened to you?"

For a third time Ruth relayed the story, her father waking up soon after she started speaking. When she finished, Gabriel reassured her parents, just as he had Ruth, that the schoolhouse would be repaired.

Her father rose from his chair, his knees quietly popping as he stood. "*Danki* for bringing Ruth here. I can drive you home."

Her mother adjusted the silver-framed glasses that she wore all the time. As Gabriel and *Daed* started to leave the room, she said, "Tell my precious *grossdochders* I said hello."

"Verna wasn't acting too precious when we left," Gabriel said with a chuckle.

"Not a bit surprised. But I'm sure she'll be over it in no time."

Ruth touched her mother's shoulder. "You should *geh* with them. That way you can tell them hello yourself."

"Oh, *nee*. I couldn't leave you—"

"*Mami*, I'll be fine. I promise. I'll stay right here on the couch."

"*Ya*, you will, and I'll be right here to make sure that you're okay."

Ruth stifled a sigh. So much for taking care of herself.

After Gabriel and Joseph left, her mother started fluffing the pillows on their sage-green couch. She set her book on the plain coffee table in the center of the room, then gestured to the sofa. "You can lie down here."

Ruth looked at the couch. She was hot, still piqued over the wrecked schoolhouse, and now her head was throbbing. The last thing she wanted to do was lie down. But she did as her mother said anyway.

"Are you hungry? I can make you some soup."

"*Nee*. I'm not hungry," she said, stretching out her legs on the couch. "Or thirsty," she added, knowing her mother would offer her some tea.

Her mother dimmed the lamp on the side table. "Very well. I'll let you rest. If you need anything let me know. *Don't* get up and get it yourself." Her thin gray brows arched over her blue eyes. "Understand?"

Ruth nodded and watched her mother leave.

She let out a deep breath and closed her eyes, forcing herself to at least try and relax like everyone wanted. But she couldn't, not when her mind whirred, going over everything she had to do to salvage her teaching situation. What she really wanted to do was go to her room, which had always been her sanctuary. She'd been lucky as a child to have her own room upstairs in the attic, as her siblings had always had to share. It had become her safe haven, and over the years she had spent many hours there, studying, reading, and dreaming. Tonight, though, she was stuck on the couch.

As she lay there, the ribbon of tension through her body slowly loosened. Closing her eyes, she tried to take Gabriel's advice and let the worry go, but it clung on the edges of her mind. Many of the supplies had been destroyed, including some textbooks and workbooks, her posters and maps, and some of the spiral notebooks she'd purchased for her students. Replacing those would be the easy part. Readjusting her school plans wouldn't. Weeks of lessons, prepared down to the last detail and written in ballpoint pen, would have to be redone. But she couldn't even do that, not until she knew when the repairs would be completed so school could begin. Earlier this afternoon, everything had been organized, planned, and prepared to her specifications. Now, it was all in shambles.

Tears of frustration threatened to spill, but she refused to give in to them. She'd learned early on to hide her emotions and remain in control. Because only when she was in control could she convince everyone else that she was okay.

Chapter Three

Paradise, Pennsylvania

"*Gut* tea."

Deborah Coblentz looked at the man seated across from her in her aunt's living room and tried to muster a smile. "*Danki*, Thomas." She forced a little more enthusiasm into her words. "I'm glad you like it."

Thomas nodded and took another noisy slurp from the amber-colored tea glass. Her own untouched glass sat on the coffee table between them. She hadn't expected Thomas Smucker to stop by her aunt's house on a Sunday afternoon. He'd been here nearly half an hour already, and she still didn't know what he wanted. But for some reason she suspected it wasn't just to say hello.

"Where's the *bu*?"

She didn't care for the way he always called her son "the *bu*." "*Will's* upstairs taking his afternoon nap. He's usually exhausted by this time of the day."

Thomas didn't reply. Instead he drained the tea glass, then let out a quiet burp. When she first moved to Paradise, Pennsylvania, almost two years ago, she didn't make much of an effort to become a part of the community, Amish or Yankee. It had been easier to hide from everyone at her Yankee aunt's house, not to have to explain the circumstances that brought her here from Middlefield. But she couldn't live in isolation forever, so she began to attend church services. She soon learned that her fears of rejection were unnecessary, and she planned to join the church in a few weeks, taking another step in forging her new life.

Thomas hadn't paid any particular attention to her until recently, when he started talking to her after services. She was shocked he'd acknowledged her at all, considering she had a child and had never been married. Before then she hadn't known him very well, only saying hello in passing during church services. From what she could tell he seemed nice enough. The fact that he was interested in her, despite her past, reinforced her first impressions.

He set down the glass and brought a beefy

fist to his mouth, clearing his throat. A success-ful carpenter, he owned his own business, some-thing he'd mentioned to her at least five times since they'd met. His chest resembled the side of a barrel, round and protruding, with broad shoulders and strong arms that strained against the confines of his white Sunday shirt and black vest. She expected him to say something, but he remained silent, his silvery eyes straying to Roy, the colorful stuffed parrot perched inside a tall, metal birdcage in the corner of her aunt's living room. "Is that thing real?"

Deborah raised her eyebrows. Roy sported at least seven colors not found in nature. "*Nee. Mei aenti's* late husband won it for her at the Geauga Fair nearly thirty years ago. She brought it home and put it in the cage, which has been Roy's home ever since." She couldn't help but smile at her aunt's humor.

"I see." He turned and stared at her for a long moment, not a hint of amusement in his eyes. Deborah couldn't tell what he was feeling or thinking by looking at his expression.

She shifted on the couch, the skirt of her dark blue dress wrinkling as she moved. She smoothed it out. "Would you like something to eat?"

He shook his head. "I had a big meal at *Mamm's*. Pot roast. She makes the best pot roast in Paradise. Do you know how to make pot roast?"

The question caught her off guard. "Um, *ya*. I do."

"What about apple pie? Can you make a decent apple pie?"

"I haven't made one in a long time. *Aenti* Sadie doesn't care for apples—"

"And mashed potatoes? Do you use real butter or that fake margariney stuff?"

"Real butter. Thomas, I—"

"Glad to hear it. Because any *frau* of mine has to be a real *gut* cook."

Deborah's mouth dropped open, and her body tensed. *"Frau?"*

"Right. *Mei frau* will need to be a *gut* cook, sewer, and keep a spotless *haus*." He looked directly at her. "She must also be able to have *kinner*. Preferably *buwe*."

Deborah shifted on the couch, crossing one leg over the other, trying to hide her surprise and the sudden unease his words triggered. "Thomas, are you asking me to marry you?"

"I'm asking you to consider it. I believe you're the kind of *frau* I need, Deborah." For the first time, she saw a hint of a smile.

"But we hardly know each other."

He leaned forward, his lips curving into an almost-grin. "I think we know enough."

She jumped up and walked to the opposite end of the room, her thoughts jumbled. "I'm not ready for marriage, Thomas."

"What about the *bu*?" He settled back in the chair, surprise entering his eyes. "Have you thought about him? About his future?"

"Of course I have. I think about that all the time."

"Then getting married should be the first thing on your mind, not the last. The *bu* needs a *daed*."

Deborah didn't answer. She knew Will would eventually need a male figure in his life. But he was only a year and a half old. There was plenty of time to think about finding a husband…wasn't there?

Thomas's brow furrowed. "He needs a *mann* to guide him. Someone to teach him the ways of the church and of God. You can't do that. But I can. I own my own business and it makes a lot of money. I can buy us a large *haus* without borrowing a cent. I have the best and largest buggy available. And I have a legacy I can give to the *bu*. He'll never want for anything. In return all I ask is that you take care of the *haus*, bear *mei kinner*, and be a proper *frau*."

Her mind reeled, and the words popped out of her mouth before she could stop them. "What about love?"

"Love will come, if God wills it."

"If?"

His gaze narrowed slightly. "Did you love the *daed* of the *bu*?"

She thought about Chase, the Yankee she'd

worked with at Mary Yoder's Amish Kitchen. He had noticed her sadness after her boyfriend broke up with her. He'd paid attention to her, said all the right things. Then their one night together had changed her life forever. And had given her Will. But had she truly loved Chase? She knew now she never had.

He must have taken her hesitation for the word *no*, because his expression relaxed. He leaned one arm over the back of the chair. "See? Love only complicates things. Marriage should be approached logically, based on what two people can offer each other."

Deborah couldn't disagree more, but she didn't say it aloud.

"Deborah, have you seen my tweezers?" Sadie entered the living room, holding a copy of the *National Enquirer* under her arm. "I can never find those things when I need them." Her thin brows rose when she saw Thomas. "Oh, I'm sorry, I didn't realize you had company."

Thomas rose from the chair. "It's fine. I was just leaving."

"You don't have to go on my account." Sadie pursed her bright lips and turned to leave. "I can make myself scarce. Just pretend I wasn't even here."

Deborah thought that a little difficult to do considering her plump aunt had on a fuchsia tube top with a neon orange shirt layered over it and lime green shorts. But if Thomas thought anything of her aunt's garish attire, he kept it to himself.

He picked up his black hat from the coffee table and put it on. "Think about what I said, Deborah. When you do, you'll realize I'm making sense." He looked at her expectantly.

Realizing he was waiting for her to respond, she said, "I'll walk you out." They went outside, and she blinked against the bright sunshine as she stood in her aunt's small front yard. "*Danki* for stopping by, Thomas."

He looked down at her. They were nearly the same height, with him only about an inch taller than her five-foot-seven frame. "I'll give you some time to think about my proposal."

Deborah didn't respond right away. What she really wanted to do was tell him no. She had never considered marrying for anything but love. But could she afford to be the romantic young woman she was before Will was born? Thomas had been right about a few things, things she couldn't ignore. Her son needed a father, and Thomas did have a strong, solid business. He could give Will things she couldn't. While she'd had Yankee friends in Middlefield who were raised by single parents, Deborah believed in the Amish way of raising children with both parents.

And although she found Thomas humorless and prideful, she couldn't reject him outright, not without praying about it. Maybe once they got to know each other, his better qualities would reveal themselves. "*Danki*, Thomas. I will think and pray about it."

He took a step closer to her, a slight frown on his lips. Was he insulted she hadn't said yes to his proposal right away? "One other thing I want you to think about, Deborah. Not many Amish men would be willing to take in a *sohn* born outside of marriage. Especially a Yankee *mann's sohn*. But I am." He turned and walked out the gate.

Deborah sighed and watched him get inside his buggy, her thoughts a confused mess. When she walked into the living room she saw Sadie seated on the couch, reading her magazine. Deborah crossed her arms over her chest. "Were you watching us through the window?"

Sadie lowered the *Enquirer* and peered at Deborah over the top. "*Moi*? I've been reading my magazine the entire time. I'm surprised you would think I'd stoop to watching out of windows like a little old lady."

"Your magazine is upside-down."

Her aunt flipped it right-side up, then tossed it on the coffee table in front of her. "Okay, guilty as charged. But just for the record, I'm a *young-*

ish old lady peeking out of windows." She looked at Deborah. "So who is your gentleman caller?"

Deborah plopped on the couch beside her. "Thomas Smucker. Owner of Smucker's Hardwoods."

Sadie nodded. "I've heard of that company. Pretty successful, I think."

"He wants to marry me."

"What?" Sadie sat up from the couch, brown eyes wide. "Do tell." But as Deborah explained Thomas's proposal, her aunt's expression turned from surprise to disapproval.

"I don't like him already." Sadie pointed at Deborah. "You deserve better than that."

"But he's being practical. And I should too. I don't have many options, and I want the best for Will. It's possible that I could grow to love him, in time."

Her aunt shook her head. "I can't believe I'm hearing this. You would give up on love that easily?"

"I'm an unmarried Amish woman with a *sohn* whose father is a Yankee and has never wanted anything to do with him. That definitely limits my options."

"Well, I think he's a king-size jerk." Sadie stood up from the couch. "You're a grown woman and I can't tell you what to do, but I can give you some advice. Don't marry someone just for Will's sake. I know you love your baby, but you have to be happy too."

"Will's happiness is the only thing that matters to me."

Sadie's features softened. "That's wonderful, Deborah. It really is. But Will won't be happy if you're miserable. Think about that before you agree to marry the first man who offers." She took her cell phone out of the pocket of her blinding shorts. "Now, I don't know about you, but I'm hungry."

"I can make something—"

"Nonsense." Sadie flipped open her phone. "The good Lord wouldn't have provided takeout if He hadn't intended us to use it. What are you in the mood for? Pizza or Chinese?"

The night after the accident, Zach sat in the kitchen of his house, drumming his fingers on the edge of the table. He leaned back in the oaken chair, his ankle propped up on the opposite knee. He knew he appeared nonchalant, emotionless, but inside, his stomach churned like an old gas motor.

His father stood in front of him, his thick arms crossed over his chest and resting on his slightly protruding belly. His gaze continued to bore into Zach. *The look.* Zach had been on the receiving end of *the look* for years now, ever since he was eight years old and *Fraulein* Gruber had paid his parents a visit after school. Zach had glued her math book to her desk while she was outside supervising students for recess. At the time he'd considered it necessary revenge for making him stay inside to finish his morning schoolwork. Now he saw it for the *dumm* stunt it was. But he'd been making similar stupid mistakes ever since.

Still, damaging the schoolhouse hadn't been a thoughtless attempt to churn up a little excitement, as he tended to do when things got boring. For once his intentions had been innocent. He'd tried not to hit the deer, for Pete's sake. That should have gotten him a little mercy. But from the piercing intensity of *the look*, it hadn't.

"The school board members examined the damage this evening." His father shifted his gaze to Zach's drumming fingers. Zach stilled his hand. "The entire back half of the *schulhaus* will have to be rebuilt."

I could have saved you the trip and told you that.

"Some of the men agreed to get together this Saturday and put up a wall. They'll have to do it when they get off work, which means there won't be much time to do anything else." Uncrossing his arms, his father stroked his collar-length beard, which was almost completely gray.

Only a few strands of dark red remained. "The rest will be up to you."

"The rest?"

"The cleanup, the flooring, the painting. You'll be expected to pay for materials and any labor. You'll have to pay to replace the desks you destroyed. Byler and Sons agreed to make new ones as soon as possible, and they should have them done in a week or so."

Zach gulped. He already owed Rick money for repairs on his truck, plus he'd spent his last few bucks paying for the tow. At least Rick hadn't ended their friendship over it. Rick had been angry, but he was a good guy. Zach considered himself lucky.

But as the dollars added up in his mind, he saw his luck slipping away. How was he going to pay for everything? He didn't even have a job. Not that he hadn't tried. Since he'd finished school, he'd held a few short-term jobs, mostly helping out some of the Amish with their businesses. But he hadn't worked in over three months. And he wasn't the only one struggling to find work.

"This week you'll have to clean up the *schulhaus*," his *daed* continued. "Get it ready for the men to work."

He nodded. "Whatever I need to do." He dropped his cool façade and looked up at his *daed*. "I know I made a huge mistake. I'm really sorry."

"You're always sorry." *Daed's* look intensified. "You say the same thing every time you're in trouble. Then you turn around and do something else *dumm*."

If he had a dollar for every time his father called him stupid, he'd be able to pay for the schoolhouse repairs and have some left over. Over the years he'd let the comments roll off him, but he couldn't tonight. "It was an accident! An honest mistake. Would it have been better if I'd flattened the deer?"

"You should never have been in the truck!" His father scrubbed his hand over his face, then lowered his voice, bending over slightly. His green eyes, so similar in shade to Zach's, drilled into him. "You may not have joined the church, but you're expected to follow the rules as long as you live under my roof."

Zach could repeat this speech from heart.

"You embarrassed me tonight. I had to sit at that board meeting while everyone talked about fixing the damage my *sohn* caused because of his recklessness." He straightened and started to pace. "And all you have to say for yourself is that you're sorry. That's not *gut* enough. Not this time. This is your last chance." His voice shook. "You're eighteen years old. Time to grow up and be a *mann*. Take responsibility for your life."

"I am taking responsibility—"

"I had to bail you out again and smooth things over with the school board members."

"I offered to go with you."

His father shook his head. "You would have made everything worse. You always do."

Zach withered. He'd been hearing these things all his life, but this time it was different. It wasn't the warning that his father had given him. He'd heard that before too. This time something else spoke to him, something deep inside his soul.

He collected himself and straightened his shoulders. "I'll take care of it." Zach meant every word, more than he ever had in his life. "Everything will be ready by Saturday. And I'll do the rest of the repairs myself and pay everyone back."

"You better. Because I'm serious, Zach. You're a grown *mann* now. The time for being a *kinn* is gone. Stop embarrassing yourself and our *familye*." With those words, his father left the kitchen and headed for the front door. It slammed shut behind him, making Zach flinch.

Zach dropped back in the chair. He knew it was going to be bad, but not this bad. Every word his father said cut him deep inside, adding to the slashes his behavior had brought over the years. But until today he'd never been truly inspired to change. His father was right. He was always doing stupid things, getting into trouble. Forgetting promises, getting distracted. Now his mistake was costing both him and the community time and money. Not to mention he'd disappointed his father again. He wanted to change, to stop humiliating his parents and siblings. But he wasn't sure how.

His mother came into the kitchen, giving him her usual sympathetic glance, but not saying a word. He was the youngest in his family, with three older brothers who had already left home. Two were married and one had moved to Indiana. He'd never experienced any compassion from them. They had always thought he was a problem child too.

Mami filled a metal teakettle with water from the tap, then set it on top of the gas stove and turned on the burner. She gazed at the flame, the white strings of her prayer *kapp* trailing down the back of her light-green dress. Unlike his father, she only had a few strands of gray, and although she was in her late forties, she looked ten years younger. She turned and looked at him. When he saw the lines of worry and fatigue around her eyes, his heart lurched. "I'm sorry, *Mami*."

"I know you are." She turned back to stare at the flame, her hands folded in front of her and resting against her white apron. "But I wish you understood how you're hurting your father."

Zach knew he was hurting her too. He could see the pain on her face. It was the same agonized expression she always had when he'd done something wrong. "I don't mean to."

"You never do." She sighed, wiping her finger underneath her eye. Finally she turned to him, her eyes red, and he could tell she'd been crying. His heart ached like a knife had twisted inside. "I support your *daed*, Zach. You can't keep doing irresponsible things. I've been on your side all these years, but I can't be anymore."

He stood and went over to her. "*Mami*, you have to believe me. I want to be a better *mann*. Like *Daed*. And my *bruders*." He never admitted that he'd looked up to them before. Maybe because until this moment, he'd never known he had. But his father and brothers had everything he wanted in life. Steady jobs, and in his father's case, his own small engine repair shop. Families. Respect from the community. "I know I have a long way to *geh*."

His mother reached up and touched his cheek. "Just remember, you can't do this on your own, Zach. I think that's part of your problem. If you'd rely on God to help you, you'd understand you're not alone."

"I wish it were that simple." He believed in God, but over the years, he had questioned Him. He'd grown up hearing over and over that God had a plan, that everything that happened in life was God's will. But if God had a plan for him, why did Zach fail at almost everything? School had been a complete disaster, and now he couldn't find—much less keep—a job. He was going nowhere, and even if he wanted to get married, he had nothing to offer his future wife. At that moment the only thing he was sure of was that things had to change. *He* had to change, unless he wanted to spend the rest of his life fighting his demons.

"I know you've had to struggle, Zach. Your father doesn't understand, but I do. Just don't think that God has given up on you. He hasn't. He never will. And since He believes in you, all you have to do is believe in yourself."

Zach turned away. Cracking walnuts with his bare hands sounded easier. But what other choice did he have? "I'll try harder. I promise."

"I know that you will, Zachariah, because I believe in you too. And every day I'll be praying for you, just as I have since the day you were born."

Chapter Four

"Mail call!" Aunt Sadie sailed into the living room, a plastic bag of groceries hanging over one jiggly arm and holding a handful of mail, her thick, bright-red lips stretched into a smile.

Deborah glanced up from her knitting. She figured her aunt must spend more on a month's supply of her trademark lipstick than she did on food.

Sadie set down the bag on the coffee table in front of the yellow-and-pink-flowered couch and thumbed through the mail. "Bill. Yuck. Another bill. Double yuck." She sighed. "This is what I get for not going to the post office for a few days. And here's one from the electric company. I wonder how much they're gouging me for this month."

"You could always turn the power off." Deborah settled back in her aunt's soft-cushioned recliner and went back to knitting. She had been working on her son's small, dark blue mittens for a week now, but it was slow going and she couldn't get the thumb right. Maybe she should just give up and buy Will a pair at the discount store where she worked a couple of days a week. But she was determined to complete this project. Even though it was the end of August, her son would have warm mittens and a scarf by fall.

Chuckling, Sadie tossed the bill on the table. The plastic bag rustled from the movement. "My dear, you could live just fine without electricity, seeing as you've only lived here two years. It's been twenty-five years since I left the Amish. I don't think I could survive without my *Desperate Housewives*." She continued going through the letters, then came to the last one. Her penciled-in eyebrow lifted and she looked at Deborah, handing her the small envelope. "It's from your sister."

Surprised, Deborah set her knitting in her lap and took the letter. Her aunt was right. She'd recognize Naomi's precise print anywhere. A sense of dread gripped her. Her sister hadn't written or visited since she'd left Middlefield. Shortly after Will's birth, her parents had come for a visit to meet their new grandson. But Naomi had stayed behind, saying she didn't have time to travel so far, even to meet her nephew. But Deborah knew the truth. Although her father and mother had accepted Will and the circumstances surrounding his conception, her sister never had.

Maybe now she was planning to visit. That had to be the reason for her letter. Relaxing a bit, she slipped her finger underneath the seal and opened the envelope. She hoped her parents would be able to come too. Her mother would be surprised to see how much Will had grown. He'd been walking since he'd turned one and was getting into everything. He was a normal, healthy child. That's all she had prayed for before he was born, and despite her mistakes, God had seen fit to bless her with one.

If her mother visited, she could also talk to her about Thomas. Since he'd asked her to marry him yesterday, she'd been trying to figure out what to do. She needed her mother's wisdom, something she'd rejected up until she'd gotten pregnant with Will. As a teenager, Deborah thought she knew everything and that her parents didn't understand her. Now she realized she knew almost nothing, especially when it came to men. Her mistake with Chase proved that.

Sadie sat down on the couch and reached for a *Star* magazine from the table. "Heavens, it's a hot day," she said, fanning herself, despite wearing a black tank top that was too tight and more than a little inappropriate for her age. Her knobby knees peeked out from beneath the hem of her neon pink shorts. "So what does your sister have to say for herself? It's a travesty that she hasn't written to you before now, if you ask me."

Deborah opened the letter and frowned. There were only a few words on the page. She read them, then clenched the letter in her hand.

Sadie pitched forward to the edge of the couch, the magazine dangling between her legs. Her round belly pressed against the pink shorts. "Honey, what's wrong?"

Tears formed in her eyes, and she looked at her aunt. "*Mami's* gone."

"Gone? What do you mean, gone?"

"She died." Deborah could barely get out the words. "A couple days ago."

Sucking in a breath, Sadie jumped up and went to Deborah. She sat on the end of the coffee table and took Deborah's hands in hers. "Heavens, *kinn*. I'm so sorry."

Deborah had never heard her aunt speak in *Dietch*, and at that moment she barely noticed. Sorrow enveloped her in a cold wave. She hung her head, the white ribbons of her *kapp* dangling by her cheeks.

Sadie lifted Deborah's chin. "Did Naomi say how?"

She shook her head. "She didn't say anything. Only that the funeral is Wednesday. *Aenti*, why didn't she or *Daed* call and let me know? Why tell me in a letter?"

"I'm not surprised you didn't hear from Naomi." Sadie's red-painted lips pressed into a line. The relationship between her and Deborah's older sister had been strained for years. "But your father? It's unforgivable, him not telling you himself."

"Nothing's unforgivable, *Aenti*. I'm proof of that. So is Will."

Sadie's expression softened. She blew out a breath, and the scent of cinnamon gum hovered between them. "I'll drive you to Middlefield. Don't worry, Deborah. You will be there in time for the funeral."

Deborah wiped the tears from her cheek. "You don't have to do that. Will and I can ride the bus."

"My grandnephew will not ride a bus, not when he can be perfectly comfortable in my car." Sadie gave her a half-smile, her eyes misty. "Martha was my sister-in-law and a wonderful woman. This is the least I can do."

"The least?" Deborah sniffed, and reached for a tissue from the box on the end table by the chair. "*Aenti*, you've done so much for me." She felt a sudden rush of gratitude for her eccentric aunt. "You took me in when I was pregnant and alone. You never judged me or treated my son differently."

"Why on earth would I do that? People make mistakes, Deborah. We're not perfect. I may not be Amish anymore but I still believe in God's mercy. That boy upstairs is precious in the Lord's sight. No reason he would be less precious in mine." She patted Deborah's hand and then stood up. "We'll leave right now."

"Now?"

"All right, maybe in a couple hours. We'll be in Ohio by late tonight."

Deborah nodded. She put her knitting in the basket on the floor by the chair and stood. "I'll go upstairs and pack." But first, she read the letter again, unable to help herself.

Mami died. The funeral is Wednesday. Naomi

Her throat constricted as she folded the letter. Her mother's image filled her mind, along with flashes of memories, so many they all ran together. Good memories, like helping *Mami* make supper in the kitchen. Working with her in the garden. Fighting with her sister, then *Mami* coming to her to comfort her, saying she understood because she was also the baby in her family.

Then the bad memories came. The distance that had grown between them when Deborah turned sixteen and started to rebel. She'd longed for the attention she'd gotten when she was younger, but her behavior had the opposite effect of pushing her parents away. She relived the disappointment in her mother's eyes when she told her she was pregnant with a Yankee's baby. The pain of telling her goodbye when she left to have her baby in Paradise, too ashamed to face the community.

She reached the top step, sobbing as the last memory came into view. Her mother's joy at seeing Will after he was born. The total acceptance of her grandson. *Mami's* last words before getting on the bus to go back to Middlefield.

When you're ready to come home, we'll be waiting.

Deborah wiped her eyes with the soaked tissue and took a deep breath before she went into the bedroom she shared with Will. The last thing she wanted him to see when he woke from his nap were her tears. Once she composed herself, she walked into the room.

His crib was in the far corner of the room, away from the window. She had pulled down the shade earlier when she'd set him down for his nap, but the bright summer sunlight peeked through the sides and bottom of the shade, casting thin beams of light throughout the room. Tiptoeing to his crib, she looked at her son. Dark brown hair, the same color as her own, covered his head. His black eyelashes rested against his rosy cheeks. The room was warm, and he wore a small, white, short-sleeved one-piece, his chubby legs spread apart as he slept.

She closed her eyes against a new onslaught of sadness at all the milestones her mother would miss. Regrets kept slamming into her, reminding her that she should have done things differently. It wasn't the first time such thoughts had assaulted her. She looked at Will and knew there was one thing she didn't have a single doubt about. Having her son. He was her life, her hope, her dreams, all rolled into one. No matter the circumstances of his birth, he was meant to be here. And she would never, ever regret that.

True to her word, Sadie had them on the road less than two hours later. As they passed through Lancaster County, Deborah remembered Thomas's proposal. In the wake of the news and rushing around to pack, she'd forgotten all about it.

Sadie glanced at her, wearing a huge pair of tortoiseshell-rimmed sunglasses that covered nearly half her face. "Did you forget something?"

She glanced over her shoulder at Will, who was playing with a rubber duck in his car seat. Love swelled inside her as she watched her contented son. "It's nothing that can't wait."

"Yoo hoo! Moses, we're home!" Sadie yodeled as she entered the house.

Deborah followed closely behind, clinging to

Will, who wanted to get down. She put her mouth close to his little ear. "Not yet." She didn't want Will running wild all over the house or making a bad impression on her father. Especially now. It was late, after ten, and her father and sister were probably asleep.

"Moses!" Sadie yelled one more time. "Where is that man? I honked the horn twice; surely he heard it. At least he could come down here and help us with the bags." She turned to Deborah and removed the diaper bag from her shoulder. "Here sweetie, let me take yours. I thought Naomi would be here too. Not that she would welcome me with anything but the cold shoulder, but still. Manners are manners."

Will kept clawing at Deborah. She couldn't blame her son for wanting to be free. He'd been stuck in a car seat for hours, something he wasn't used to. "Will, settle down!"

He stopped squirming, but only for the moment. Deborah carried him further into the living room before setting him down on the couch in front of the picture window. She tucked the tail of his light blue shirt into his small, gray, broadfall pants. Someone had turned the light on in the living room, so she knew her father and sister had gotten the message from their Yankee neighbor about their arrival. Otherwise the house would be completely dark.

She took her bag from Aunt Sadie and pulled out a little rubber and plastic car for Will to play with. As soon as she handed him the toy, he grinned, displaying his tiny, two top teeth, the only ones he had so far. He took the car and started rolling it across the couch cushions, happy for the moment.

Deborah plopped on the couch and leaned her head back. She didn't know how her aunt could be so perky after the long car ride. Deborah was exhausted. She hadn't realized traveling could be so tiring, especially with a toddler who had a voracious appetite and off-schedule sleeping patterns.

Sadie planted her hands on her ample hips. "Wait until your grandfather sees you, Mr. Adorable! He'll eat you right up!" Sadie bent over and tweaked the child's nose. Will giggled, as he always did when she fussed over him.

Deborah smiled. A few minutes passed, but her father and Naomi still didn't appear. Where were they? Her aunt was right; one of them should have at least greeted them by now.

Her gaze landed on an old hickory chair her great-grandfather had built eighty years ago. A colorful, worn quilt was folded over the back. Her mother always laid that quilt on her lap in the wintertime when she was sitting in the living room, often reading a book or working on a cross-stitch project. A lump formed in her throat. She swallowed it down, still not completely accepting that she was back home to say goodbye, instead of hello, to her mother.

Aunt Sadie sat down next to Deborah, putting an arm around her shoulders. Her black-and-purple-striped tank top and lemon-yellow shorts stood out in the austere room like a zebra at a horse auction. "It'll be all right, sweetie. It hurts more than anything right now, but your *mami* is at peace."

"I know." Deborah wiped her nose with the top of her index finger. "I keep reminding myself of that. But sometimes it's cold comfort."

Sadie nodded. "When my Rodney died, I thought I wouldn't make it. It's hard on the ones left behind. So very, very hard." Sadie kissed her on the cheek and stood up. "You keep an eye on that pipsqueak while I go look for my brother." She walked out of the room, calling out, "Moses! Show yourself! Your buggy's in the driveway, so I know you're here. Now give us a proper greeting!"

Deborah looked around the small living room. Two years wasn't that long of a time, but it seemed like forever since she had last sat in this room, telling her parents that she was pregnant. She had expected them not to care, to ignore her as they had when she turned sixteen. But her mother had burst into tears and her father had stared at the floor for a long, long time, not saying a word. She had hurt them; she knew that now. Her sister wouldn't even speak to her, other than to say she was embarrassed that they were related. In her quest for the attention she craved, she had made a mistake that had affected not only her, but her entire family.

It had been hard to leave Middlefield, and especially difficult to leave Elisabeth Byler, her best friend who had stood by her during that terrifying time when she had no idea what to do. Elisabeth had visited her only once before Will was born, but she had written several letters. They had been her only tangible connection to Middlefield.

Will started to climb down off the couch. He steadied himself on anything he could grab hold of, no matter how off balance it was. Deborah snatched him up and pulled him toward her, then lifted up his blue short-sleeved shirt and tickled his belly. He giggled, his gunmetal-gray eyes growing wide. She could see more and more of his father in him with each passing day, especially in his smile. But since Chase rejected his son before he was even born, Deborah had considered Will 100 percent hers.

He struggled once again to get down, using his chubby arms as leverage. Instead of letting him go, she gathered him up in her arms and stood, resting him on her left hip as she left the room in search of her father and Sadie. Her aunt should have found him by now. The house wasn't that big, only three bedrooms upstairs, a dining room that her family had only used for company downstairs, along with a serviceable kitchen and the tiny parlor, and of course, the unfinished basement where they had held church over the years.

As she and Will neared the kitchen at the back of the house, she could hear a faint rattling sound, as if someone was clanging two dishes together. Low light came from the room. Naomi had to be in there. Her stomach twisted into a pretzel. Would her sister say anything to her? Or would she just ignore her, like she had most of their lives? Her elder by ten years, Naomi had never had anything but a volatile relationship with Deborah. And what would she say about Will? Would she continue to pretend that he didn't exist? The thought pained her more than the memories of her sister's constant dismissal.

Deborah willed her nerves to steady as she entered the kitchen. "Naomi?"

Naomi didn't turn around right away. She finished drying a plain white dish, then put it in the cabinet to the right of the sink.

Some things never change.

Finally Naomi turned toward them. Her sister

looked a little older than the last time she had seen her. Deborah noticed a couple of silver strands threading through her dark brown hair, which was parted neatly in the middle and covered with a white handkerchief instead of a *kapp*. Naomi had always been thin and willowy with sharp features. Deborah had never been as slender as Naomi, but she'd packed on the pounds since Will's birth and still had several stubborn ones to lose.

Naomi folded the damp dishrag into a small square and laid it on the edge of the sink. Her steely eyes narrowed a bit, but her gaze never went to Will, even when he started protesting about being held again.

Deborah shifted him in her arms, but that didn't stop him from trying to get out of her embrace. "Enough!" Deborah's command settled Will, and he leaned his head against her shoulder. He probably sensed the tension in the room. It was thick enough to slice with a hacksaw.

Naomi still didn't react. "It's late."

"I know. We didn't have much of a choice. I wanted to be here for the funeral." Her chest constricted. "Why didn't anyone call me when she died? I would have been here sooner."

Will whimpered. Deborah hadn't realized how tightly she'd been holding on to him. She released her grip and set him down on one of the kitchen chairs. "Stay there, *lieb*." She held up her hand, palm facing out, the signal for him to stay put. She smiled when he complied. "Why didn't you let me know about *Mami*?"

"I wrote you right after she died. It's not my fault the mail is slow."

"You should have called."

Naomi crossed her arms, her foot tapping against the floor. "You shouldn't have left. If you wanted to be a part of this *familye*, you would have stayed."

"You know why I left."

"Then you have no one to blame but yourself."

Aunt Sadie suddenly burst into the room. "I can't imagine where your father is, Deborah. I've looked everywhere—" Her gaze landed on Naomi. In an instant an uncharacteristic frown tugged on her mouth. "Naomi."

Naomi didn't say anything. She adjusted her kerchief and walked out of the room, her chin lifted. Her gaze remained straight ahead.

Sadie pressed her red lips together. "That woman is enough to try the patience of St. Peter himself. Can you believe she is the only member of this family who shuns me? Even your father didn't do that when I decided not to join the church, before that self-righteous whippet was even born!"

"*Aenti*, please." Deborah went to her and put

her arm on Sadie's shoulder. "You shouldn't let her upset you."

Sadie's expression relaxed. She cupped Deborah's chin. "And you should take your own advice. I can see she's lit a fire under you already."

Deborah grimaced. "She's always known how to rile me up."

Letting go of Deborah's chin, Sadie clucked her tongue. "You two are like sugar and vinegar, you know that? I used to think it was because there's such an age gap between you, but now I see it has more to do with personality than anything else. She needs to loosen up."

Will climbed down from his chair and held up his arms to Deborah. She started to pick him up, but Sadie slid over and grabbed him around the middle. "Let me get this doodlebug something to eat. Deborah, go see if you can find your father. I checked the upstairs and the basement."

"He might be out in the barn."

"Why would he be out there this late at night?"

"Sometimes he'd *geh* out there just to think."

"I can name a dozen less smelly places to think, but to each his own." Sadie carried Will to the pantry. She brought her red mouth close to his ear. "I doubt we'll find any Twinkies here, but I'm sure we can conjure up something decent."

Deborah walked out of the kitchen and into

the small mudroom by the back door. A lantern hung on a long peg attached to the wall. She took it and lit it with a match from the cast-iron match holder affixed next to the peg. A glow filled the darkened room and she walked outside.

The scent of cow dung instantly hit her. Her father raised Angus cows, selling off part of the herd each year. She held up the lantern. To the right of the backyard was a split-rail fence, boxing in the several-acre pasture where they grazed. As she moved forward, the light illuminated the pasture, and she was surprised to see the grass had grown several inches high. Usually the cows kept it shorn close to the ground.

Turning to her left, she saw the barn. Her father had always run the farm by himself. She and Naomi, along with their mother, had helped out with some of the chores—feeding the cows, weeding the garden and the fields, and helping with the harvest. But her father had gladly shouldered the bulk of the work. She knew he had slowed down in the couple of years before she'd moved to Paradise. But had he slowed down that much? Maybe she hadn't really noticed how much he'd aged until now. How could she, when she'd been so focused on herself and Will?

As she neared the barn, she spied the chicken coop, and a few yards behind it, the goat pen. The goats had been asleep, but a few of them rose when they heard her, pressing their noses against the chicken-wire fence. She ignored them, knowing they would settle back down once she disappeared. A few flies hovered inside the doorway of the barn. She brushed them away as she walked inside, raising her lantern higher.

Her father had always kept a modest herd, no more than thirty at a time. A few cows huddled around a bent metal feeding ring, munching on the remnants of a round bale of hay. The barn was partially open air, with two large windows cut into the north and west walls for ventilation. Still, from the overwhelming smell, she could tell the barn hadn't been cleaned for several days. She searched the rest of the barn, but her father wasn't there.

Her concern growing, she left the barn and glanced at the field. "*Daed*?" she yelled, walking behind the barn toward the small pond a few yards away. Like the pasture itself, the grass and cattails surrounding the murky water were overgrown.

None of this made sense. Her father always took better care of their property than this. "Take care of the land and it will take care of you," he'd always said. She would have never thought he'd ignore those words.

She walked past the pond and several yards into a pasture that ended at a line of thin woods.

The clouds that had cloaked the black sky drifted apart, and the silvery light from the moon shone down. It illuminated a large pile of brush, rotted logs, and twigs at the far end of the pasture, beside the split-rail fence that marked their property. Near the brush pile, she caught a flash of movement. She hurried toward it.

The pile had always been there, with her father adding to it over the years. He always planned to burn it, but never did. As she walked closer, she could see it had grown taller than she was. The scent of rotting wood and sweet grass filled her nostrils. She circled to the back of the pile and let out a relieved breath. Her father stood beside the fence, his hands in his pockets, staring straight ahead. She rushed to him. *"Daed!"*

When he slowly turned to look at her, she frowned. Glassy brown eyes stared back from his sun-weathered face. He seemed to gaze right through her. Crumbs of food blended in with his long, matted beard. He'd always worn it longer than most Amish men, but he had been particular about its appearance, combing it out and shaping it into a dull point so it didn't completely take over his face. Sweat stains darkened his light blue shirt. Wrinkles creased his trousers. He looked as if he'd slept in his clothes for days.

"Daed?" She repeated his name, softer this time. "Are you all right?"

He stared at her, then blinked. "Deborah?"

"*Ya, Daed.* I'm here."

He looked at her for a moment before facing the brush pile. "Your *Mami's* gone." His voice was flat.

"I know. Naomi told me." She wanted to ask why he didn't call her, but his behavior unnerved her enough to keep that question to herself.

Hatless, he rubbed his damp forehead, a strip of white compared to the rest of his tanned face. "She said you couldn't come."

Deborah froze. "She did?"

He nodded, still not looking at her.

Why had her sister told him she couldn't come? Naomi hadn't even asked Deborah if she could come, and Naomi's letter barely made it in time… But her father wasn't in the frame of mind to give her answers.

"How did you get here?" he asked.

"*Aenti* Sadie drove. I got Naomi's letter today, and we left right afterward. She brought both me and Will."

Deborah waited for him to ask about his grandson. When he didn't, she shoved down her disappointment. "They're both in the house, waiting for you." She paused again. Her father stood so still, she wasn't sure he was listening. "*Daed,* did you hear me?"

"*Ya.*"

But she wondered if he truly did. A couple of the cows lowed in the distance. "When was the last time you let the cows out?"

He looked at her. "What?"

"The cows. I was in the barn a minute ago. They need to go out, *Daed*."

His eyes narrowed. "You're telling me how to take care of my cows?"

"*Nee*. I'm just surprised that you've kept them in the barn for so long. Usually they roam the pasture—"

"You have a lot of nerve. You don't have a right to question anything here."

His glare was the first hint of emotion he'd shown, and it scared her. "*Daed*, I didn't mean—"

"*Geh*. Now! Leave me be! *Geh* back to Pennsylvania. We don't need you or your *kinn* here."

Her eyes burned with tears. She turned and ran back to the house so fast she nearly fell down a couple of times. When she dashed into the kitchen, she scooped up Will, who had been sitting at the table eating peanut butter and crackers. Her father had never yelled at her like that before. He'd always been a staid, but kind, man. Brushing a trembling kiss against her son's cheek, she fought for control.

"Deborah?" Aunt Sadie put down the remnants of a sandwich and got up from the chair at the end of the table. "Child, what's wrong? Did you find your father?"

"Ya." Her voice quaked and she swallowed, trying to catch her breath.

"Where is he?"

"Out in the field." She set Will back down in his chair. He picked up a saltine peanut butter sandwich and bit into it, smearing the creamy peanut butter on his chin. Deborah snatched a paper towel from the roll near the sink and dampened it with water, then wiped his chin.

"Mmmmf!" he protested, turning his head away from her.

Sadie stood next to her. "You might as well wait until he's done, or you'll be wiping after every bite."

Will looked up at her, shoving another cracker in his mouth, his stubby fingers covered in peanut butter.

Sadie touched Deborah's arm. "For heaven's sake, you're shaking, and your face is stark white. Sit down and tell me what happened." She guided Deborah to a chair.

Deborah sat. While she had expected her sister to reject her, her father's vehemence caught her completely off guard. Even when she had told him she was pregnant, he hadn't reacted so harshly. The man she saw in the pasture was a stranger to her.

"What did your father say to you?" Sadie sat down next to her.

"He doesn't want us here. No one does. You saw how Naomi reacted."

"Forget about her for a minute. Your father would never reject you, Deborah."

"You didn't hear what he said. There's something wrong with him, *Aenti*." She tried to describe what he looked like and what he'd said in the field.

Sadie tapped her chin, her bloodred fingernails matching her lipstick. "Moses and I haven't always gotten along, and we haven't talked much over the years. But he's a good man. This isn't like him." Her penciled-in brows furrowed and she stood up. "Where did you say he was?"

"Far end of the pasture. Behind the barn. Why?"

"Let me talk to him. My *bruder* and I are long overdue for a conversation." She hurried out of the kitchen, a blur of purple, black, and yellow.

Will picked up his light blue sippy cup and took a drink. He pulled the spout out of his mouth and held it up to Deborah. "Ma?"

"You want more?" Deborah took the cup from him. She lifted the half gallon from the table and poured more milk into his cup. She handed it to him, and he took a long drink, his slurping cutting through the silence in the kitchen.

Her father's and sister's reactions made her think about what Thomas said right before she left. At least he wanted her, or what she could give to him, enough to marry her. But her own family didn't seem to want her here. Tears filled her eyes, but she refused to let them fall in front of Will. After the funeral they would return to Paradise. And while a part of her had always remained in Middlefield, it was now clear to her that this was no longer her home.

Will finished his snack and Deborah cleaned the kitchen, leaving everything spotless. Knowing her sister's fastidious tendencies, she didn't dare give Naomi cause to complain. She went into the living room with Will to wait for her aunt to return. He walked around the room, inspecting everything, then started playing with his car again. Within a few seconds, he started yawning. Deborah took him in her arms and snuggled him close. As he laid his head against her shoulder, she leaned back in the chair and closed her eyes, wondering about her aunt and father, saying a silent prayer that Sadie would be able to reach him.

Footsteps sounded in the hall and Sadie appeared. Her father followed, his head dipped. Sadie sat down on the couch and motioned for Moses to join her. Her father sat and looked at Deborah, his eyes red as if he'd been crying.

A chill swept over Deborah. Never had she seen her father cry or show a moment of weakness. He hadn't been very demonstrative, especially during her teenage years. To see him so vulnerable unnerved her.

"Moses has something to say to you." Sadie's usual boisterous tone was subdued. She looked at Moses, who glanced at her for a split second before focusing on Deborah.

"I'm sorry, *dochder.* I shouldn't have said what I did. I don't even know why those words came out of my mouth." He glanced at Sadie. "*Mei schwester's* right, I can't push away my *familye.*"

Sadie put her hand on her brother's shoulder, nodding.

He leaned forward. "I want you to stay."

She wanted to believe him, but his stinging words still echoed in her mind. "What about Will?" She gripped him. He shifted in her embrace but didn't wake up.

Her father looked at Will, and his eyes turned glassy. "Of course. My *grosssohn* is always welcome. I'm sorry I made you think otherwise." He kept his eyes on Will. "Martha…" His voice broke as he said his late wife's name. He swallowed. "Your *mami* would have been so happy to see him. She missed him. We both did." He looked at Deborah again. "We missed you too."

"Oh, *Daed.*" This time she couldn't stop the

tears from slipping down her cheeks. "I'm so sorry I wasn't here for you."

"It's all right. We both understood why you left. And we always knew you'd come back here, when you were ready." His head drooped. "I just wish…"

"I know." She sniffed, wishing she could hug her father, but not wanting her movements to disturb Will.

Sadie made a loud honking noise as she blew her nose, and Deborah noticed her aunt had thick, black streaks of mascara running down her cheeks.

"Are you okay?"

"I'll be fine." She wiped her face with the soggy tissue then grabbed another before patting Moses on the knee. "Now go upstairs and get a bath. Change clothes too." She blew her nose again. "You stink."

Her father didn't say anything, just got up and left the room. As he moved past Deborah, he touched her shoulder for a brief instant, then walked away.

Deborah wiped her own cheeks with the back of her hand. "What did you say to him?"

Sadie dabbed at the corners of her eyes. "Not much. I've never seen Moses like this before, even when our parents passed. He's grievin' hard, Deborah, and he needs you." She looked at Will's sleeping form. "He needs that little ray of sunshine too. This place could use some cheering up, pronto."

"But Naomi's here. Hasn't she noticed how *Daed's* been acting?"

"Who knows? Your sister has always been caught up in herself. I doubt she's noticed much of anything around here, except maybe some stray dust that must be attacked immediately or the world will end."

Deborah glanced down at Will, then looked back at her aunt. "I don't want to be too hard on her either. She's lost *Mami* too." She didn't tell her aunt what Naomi had told their father. She wanted to give her sister the benefit of the doubt. Maybe Naomi truly thought Deborah couldn't come home, but Deborah couldn't understand that reasoning. Still, she didn't see the need to widen the divide between her aunt and sister.

"You're right." She stood up and walked over to her suitcase. "Moses said I could have Naomi's room upstairs, but he's not thinking straight. I don't want to upset her applecart any more than I already have. I'll just stay in a motel tonight."

Deborah's brows shot up. "*Nee, Aenti.* You don't have to do that. You can stay in my room."

"And displace you and Will? I don't think so. A motel will suit me fine. I need my little luxuries anyway. Air-conditioning and cable TV for starters." Her red mouth split into a grin. "After breakfast tomorrow I'll take you and Will to Walmart so you can get a bed for him."

"Are you sure?"

She nodded. "Yep. I'll stay on a couple of days, but then I have to head back home. I only took a couple days off. My boss will have my hide if I'm gone any longer than that."

"I appreciate you bringing me. And talking to *Daed*." If Will wasn't fast asleep in her lap, she would have jumped up and hugged her. She had to settle for hugging her son instead.

Chapter Five

Early Tuesday morning, soon after dawn, Ruth steered her buggy down the gravel drive that led to the schoolhouse. The twitter of birds chirping filled the air as they flapped their wings between the large oak trees. Her horse, Casey, whinnied, shaking his chestnut-colored tail. With the exception of the gaping hole in the plain white schoolhouse, life seemed completely normal. She sighed. Yesterday she was supposed to start teaching. Today, she would be picking up the pieces. Literally.

Gabriel had stopped by her house after the board meeting last night and told her the plan they had devised to get the schoolhouse up and running. Since most of that plan depended on Zachariah Bender to come through, she knew she had to do her part to get things back in order.

From what she knew about Zachariah, he couldn't be relied on to do anything.

She guided the buggy to the hitching post on the west side of the schoolhouse. Once she got out and secured Casey in a shady spot, she reached inside the backseat of the buggy and pulled out a large pail filled with cleaning supplies and old rags. Construction would begin on Saturday, so she wanted to clean up some of the mess inside before then. Armed with her equipment, she went inside the schoolhouse, feeling a bit better already. She couldn't sit at home marking time, waiting for things to get done.

The hole faced the driveway, so she didn't bother going around to the front door. She walked to the opening and peered inside. The frustration she had fought so hard to keep at bay started to return. Now that the truck was gone, she could see the extent of the damage. Boards dangled overhead. The wood-planked floor, which hadn't been fancy in the first place, was ripped up in places. Half of the student desks were destroyed. The bookshelf against the wall where she kept her textbooks, teacher's guides, and educational magazines lay facedown on the floor. Her shoulders drooped. It would take forever to clean this up.

She took a deep breath, determined not to be discouraged. She'd accomplish nothing by gawking at the disaster. She eyed the floor and decided it was stable. As she made her way through the debris to the front of the room, she noticed how untouched her desk looked, except for the dust that had settled on it. Reaching inside her bucket of supplies, she retrieved her polished apple and put it on her desk. She smiled, feeling a bit hopeful after all.

"What are you doing here?"

She turned around at the sound of the male voice, her brows lifting as she saw Zachariah standing in the middle of the hole, his hands on his narrow hips, a tool belt slung over his shoulder. He'd shown up, and early at that. "I'm here to work."

He stepped through the opening and navigated his way over to her. His face was ruddy from the morning heat. "I appreciate the thought, but I can handle this. It's my mess to tackle." He met her gaze. "You don't have to stay."

She regarded him for a moment. He had pushed the brim of his straw hat back so that she could see a bruise almost identical to her own. He had the traditional Amish haircut, his reddish brown hair curled over his ears and cut blunt in the back. Pale brown freckles covered his face, making him look boyish, in a handsome and unconventional way, but she didn't find him appealing. The only thing that appealed to her was getting the schoolhouse in working order. "There's lots of work to be done, Zachariah. And four hands are better than two. We should stop the idle chitchat and get busy."

His lips curved into a crooked grin. "Idle chitchat, huh? Now there's a phrase you don't hear very often."

She frowned. "Are you making fun of me?"

His grin faded. "*Nee*, not at all. Just making a comment."

"I think we should do less conversing and more working, don't you?"

He gave her a small salute, then turned and walked away.

Now she didn't know what to think. He probably was making fun of her. He wouldn't be the first boy to do that. She'd been teased plenty in school for being a know-it-all and a teacher's pet. But the worst had been when she was accused several times of being a snob, of using big words to impress adults. She couldn't help that she had a strong vocabulary. If she knew a variety of words, why not use them? Her aptitude for learning had separated her from her classmates at times. But whenever she felt ostracized, she just dug deeper into her studies. That had satisfied her, for the most part.

Yet there had been times, especially at recess, when she sat off to the side of the playground, pretending to be involved in the book she held in her hand. No one knew how she'd watched the other students running around, playing games, and generally having fun with each other, and wished she could join in. Every once in a while she would see a couple of girls standing on the fringes, talking and laughing, and she'd try to be a part of their conversation. But most of the time they wanted to talk about boys, a topic she had no interest in. If she remembered correctly, more than a few of them had crushes on Zachariah.

Her mind snapped back to the present. She noticed Zachariah had already started to work and now she was the one lollygagging around. She started moving the undamaged student desks to the side. They were nicked and scuffed from years of use, but still serviceable. They were also easy to move, and within a short time, ten of them were against the wall, underneath a double-paned window across the room from the white, wooden door at the front. Once she had cleared a decent amount of space, she took the broom from the small closet by the blackboard and started sweeping.

Zachariah was working at the opposite end of the schoolhouse. He picked large pieces of wood and boards off the floor and tossed them into a pile outside the building. Ruth occasionally glanced up from her sweeping, noticing that he worked quickly and efficiently, often lifting and throwing heavy-looking pieces of debris as if they weighed next to nothing.

"Hey, Ruth."

Her head jerked up and she stilled the broom. Dust flew up her nose, making her cough. "What?" She waved the dust cloud away with her hand.

"Glad to see your forehead is looking better."

She blinked, surprised that he would bring it up so spontaneously. She peered at him from across the room. "Yours looks better too."

"Skin's starting to turn purple, so I guess that means it's healing." He picked up another large chunk of the wall and flung it outside. "I know I told you this before, but I'm sorry. I never meant for this to happen."

She swung the broom back and forth as she moved closer to him. Dust puffed up in the air again. "It's all right." But it wasn't all right, and they both knew it.

"I promise this will be fixed up soon."

"I hope so."

He tossed another chunk of wood and looked at her. "You don't sound convinced."

She didn't reply, since he was right. Knowing that she'd had no input in the situation made it worse. "Do you have any idea when you'll be finished with the repairs?"

He shrugged. "Maybe a week. Or two or three. Hard to tell."

She moved her broom faster, turning her back on him.

After a lengthy pause, he resumed working.

A few minutes later she spotted him over her shoulder and saw that he had picked up the pace, gathering up the rubble and throwing it out of the schoolhouse with more force than before, his jaw-line stretched taut.

They kept to their separate sides of the school-house, working for the next couple of hours but not speaking to each other. When it was lunch-time, Ruth was surprised to see how much they had accomplished. Almost all the big chunks of debris had been removed, piled up just outside the hole. The next task would be to collect and remove all the smaller pieces.

Sweat streaked the back of Zachariah's light blue shirt. He removed his hat and swiped his forehead with the back of his hand. "It's too *hees* in here. I'm breaking for lunch."

A bead of perspiration dripped down the side of Ruth's cheek. They had both worked hard this morning, and she had to agree it was time for a break. Since she'd left her lunch in the buggy, she followed him through the hole and outside. She went to the water pump first, which was situated a few yards behind the schoolhouse next to a small storage shed, and pumped the handle to rinse off her dusty hands.

As she walked toward her buggy, she passed by Zachariah leading his horse to the pump. When she reached her own horse, she turned and saw that Zachariah had moved the large silver tub from beside the shed and placed it under the pump where his horse was drinking water from it. He now stood beside his horse, petting its chestnut flanks and waving away pesky horse-flies as he spoke, his voice so low she couldn't make out the words. Ruth moved to her horse's head and petted Casey's nose as she watched Zachariah lead his horse back to the hitching post, take a feed bag out of his buggy, and attach it to the horse's muzzle.

"Want me to water your horse?" Zachariah leaned against his buggy, his arms folded across his stomach.

"I can do it."

"I'm sure you can. I'm just offering to do it for you."

Ruth didn't say anything for a moment. She struggled to reconcile the polite man in front of her with the irritating pest she remembered from school. His green eyes shined as he looked at her, the trace of a smile on his lips. Now she understood why the girls in school had found him attractive. But he definitely wasn't her type.

"I'd rather take care of Casey myself." Once she untied the gelding, she led him past Zachariah's buggy to the pump and gave him a long drink, then brought him back to the hitching post and gave him his feed bag.

"Care to join me?"

Ruth peered around Casey's head and saw Zachariah sitting in the shade of the oak tree. He brought a sandwich to his mouth and took a bite. Giving her a closed-mouth grin, he patted the empty spot next to him.

For a moment his offer seemed tempting. Not because she wanted to sit next to him, but because it felt good to be out of the schoolhouse for a while. But she couldn't lounge outside, not when she should be working at her desk. "I have to put together an order for more school supplies. Many of them were ruined in the accident."

His grin faded, taking the sparkle that had been in his eyes with it. Shrugging, he said, "Suit yourself."

She turned and went back inside the schoolhouse. Her eyes took a few minutes to adjust after being in the bright sunlight. She sat down and set her lunch on her desk. Bowing her head, she prayed in silence before pulling a banana out of her lunch bag and peeling it open. She took a bite out of it, then slipped on her reading glasses and thumbed through a school supply catalog, trying to ignore the mess around her.

* * *

Zach took another bite of the peanut butter and jelly sandwich he'd thrown together and tossed in his lunch cooler that morning. He'd gotten up extra early, remembering the talk with his mother and how he promised he'd change. He meant it too. Managing to be at the schoolhouse a little past dawn wouldn't change his life, but it was a step in the right direction, one of many he hoped to make.

He propped his forearm on his bent knee, then pressed his back against the trunk of the tree. He took another bite of sandwich and thought about Ruth. On impulse he'd invited her to sit next to him, and as soon as he had, he regretted it, knowing she would refuse. He hadn't seen her smile once, although he had to admit there wasn't much to smile about right now. Still, it wouldn't hurt for her to relax a bit. Even as she swept, she'd had a white-knuckle grip on the broom. And he was puzzled by her reaction to him offering to water her horse. It was like she thought he doubted she could do it, and that wasn't the case at all. Then earlier she'd asked if he was making fun of her. His mind wandered back to when they were in school. Had she always been this defensive? He didn't know; his memories of school were pretty fuzzy. Probably because he'd spent as little time there as possible—physically or mentally. Well, he wasn't about to extend any more offers to her. He wouldn't set himself up for failure.

Zach finished the last of his sandwich and headed for the water pump again. The midday sun enveloped him in an oppressive, humid cocoon. August and still broiling hot. He'd be glad when October rolled around and cooled things off for a long while.

When he reached the pump, he took off his hat and dropped it on the ground, then started pressing up and down on the handle. Water gushed out and he stuck his head underneath the flow, wetting his neck and his hair, a thin stream of cold water trailing down his back. His shirt and pants were getting wet, but he didn't care, it felt so good. Cooled off, he shut off the pump and threw his head back, shaking the excess water out of his hair.

"Oh!"

He spun around and saw Ruth standing behind him, her hands up as if she were warding off something dangerous. Drops of water covered her face and the front of her dress.

"Whoops."

Chapter Six

Ruth stood beside Zachariah, her mouth wide-open and her face wet with water. When she had come out to the pump to get a drink of water, she had seen him dip his head underneath the flow, but she hadn't expected him to shake his long, thick hair out like a dog. When she recovered from the shock of the unexpected shower, she closed her mouth and removed her water-spattered glasses.

"Sorry." Zachariah slicked back his wet hair with his hand. "Didn't see you back there."

"Obviously." She tried to dry the lenses of her glasses on her dress, but the polyester blend wasn't absorbing the moisture; it just smeared it around.

"Here." He held out his hand.

"What?"

"Let me have your glasses."

"Why would I do that?"

"Just give them to me. I promise I won't break them."

She hesitated. "Your past deeds say otherwise." The snippy words slipped out, revealing her frustration. When she saw his lips press together, she knew she'd irritated him. "*Ya*, but I'm hoping someday folks will stop holding my past against me." He tilted his head, beads of water sliding down his cheeks, exasperation in his tone. "Look, I just wanted to clean your glasses for you. I didn't think you'd make such a big deal about it."

"I have a napkin inside." But before she could say anything else, he took the glasses from her. "Hey!"

He pulled his shirttail out and wiped the lenses with it, then held them up before handing them back. "See? No harm done."

She put the glasses back on, the lenses perfectly clear, and actually cleaner than they'd been before he'd splashed water on them. "I wish you wouldn't have done that."

"Why?" He tucked his shirt back in.

"Because they're *my* glasses. I can clean them myself."

"Do you always do this?"

"Do what?"

"Make things difficult? I'm trying to be nice here. Although it beats me why I even bother."

His words gave her pause. He was right. He *was* being a gentleman, albeit a gentleman out of guilt. Still, she didn't need to be rude. "*Danki,*" she said. "I appreciate you cleaning my glasses."

"That's better."

There was the crooked smile again. She ignored it and stepped past him to the pump, holding the cup she'd brought underneath the stream of water. When she turned around, he was gone.

She headed back to the schoolhouse and walked inside. Zachariah was already there, munching on a candy bar as he picked up what looked like part of a student desk. She looked at the candy, causing him to glance at it, then back at her. "What?"

"That's not very healthy."

His eyes widened, his right cheek protruding with food. "You got something against candy bars?"

She shook her head. "They're full of sugar and preservatives. You're better off eating homemade cookies."

"Are you offering to make me some?"

She froze for a moment, surprised.

"I'll take that as a *nee.*" He grinned and licked a small bit of chocolate off his top lip, then threw the empty wrapper on a small pile of trash.

She wished he'd quit smiling at her. "I'm not a very *gut* baker."

"That's too bad. Because you're right, a homemade cookie beats a candy bar hands down." He gave her another sly look, then turned around and started working again.

Ruth frowned. Why had he looked at her that way, like he was sharing some sort of private joke with her? Her face became hot, and the temperature in the schoolhouse felt stifling. She picked up the catalog off her desk and started to fan her face.

The afternoon passed by quickly, and by four o'clock, they'd moved all the debris out of the schoolhouse. The unharmed desks and furniture were pushed up in front of the chalkboard. Zachariah picked up his tool belt and walked to the hole in the wall. "I'm gonna have to call it a day."

She placed a tattered map of the world on her desk. "All right. I just have a few things to finish up here and I'll be leaving too."

He stood in the middle of the open hole, much like he had when he first arrived, including carrying his tool belt on his shoulder. He shook his head. "You should go home. I'm not sure how safe that partial wall is. It wouldn't be *gut* if it came crashing down while you were here alone."

"I'm sure the wall is perfectly safe."

"Ruth, don't argue with me on this. Get your stuff and get in the buggy."

Her shoulders tensed. "You're ordering me?"

"I'm strongly requesting."

"I won't stay very long. You don't have to worry about me, all right?"

He strolled toward her. "I'm not worried about you, Ruth. You've made it plain to me that you can take care of yourself."

She lifted her chin. "*Gut.* I'm glad you realize that."

"But it would be irresponsible of me to leave you or anyone else here when I'm not sure about that wall, or the rest of the structure. And even though you're telling me you'll only stay for a short time, I know how much you want to get this *schulhaus* up and running. You think you'll be here for a little while and the next thing you know it will be sundown."

She looked away. That sounded like something she'd do. And she couldn't argue his point, even though it surprised her that he was being so conscientious. He'd been full of surprises all day long. "I'll grab my things."

They both walked to their buggies, and she put her supplies in her vehicle. But when she went to untie her horse, she found Zachariah standing there, handing her the reins. She thought to say something but let it drop. He wouldn't listen anyway. When she got inside the buggy, she took the reins and looked at Zachariah.

He brushed away a horsefly and met her gaze. "Now don't get any bright ideas about coming out here alone tomorrow morning."

"But—"

"Are you always this stubborn?"

"*Ya.* I am."

He smirked as he walked away. "Thought so."

"Being stubborn isn't always a bad thing," she called out to him.

"Never said it was." He jumped into the buggy and gestured for her to lead the way.

She frowned as she pulled out of the driveway of the schoolhouse, still unsure what to make of him. Today he seemed nothing like the boy she remembered. Everything he said and did went against her impression of him. She might be stubborn, but at least she wasn't confusing.

Why are women so confusing?

Zach shook his head as he made his way down Burton-Windsor Road. Several cars whizzed by him on the two-lane road, but he barely noticed them. Instead his mind was still on Ruth Byler. Why, he had no idea. She was the most unusual girl he'd ever met. Even a little *seltsam.* And yet he couldn't stop thinking about her. Had she always been that uptight in school? He remembered her being smart, getting good grades all the time, and having all the answers. Teacher's pet, he and some of the kids had called her. From what he could tell, she never seemed to mind. But then again, he hadn't paid that much attention to her.

A hot breeze hit him square in the face. He urged his horse down the road, flanked by two huge green fields on his left and right. Several black cows grazed on one of them, and the scent of manure was heavy in the air.

He was glad she'd given in and left when he did. He wouldn't have left her in the building alone, even if he risked being late for supper, something his father was a stickler about. Fortunately, though, he'd be home in plenty of time. That should make his *daed* happy.

As he turned left onto Hayes, he passed by Kline's Buggy Shop. The Klines had just moved into the area, and the shop was only a couple of months old. Zach had stopped there once with a friend to order a new wheel. An idea came to him and he turned in the driveway. He pulled his horse to a stop, jumped out, and went inside.

A man about his father's age stood behind a short counter. He wiped black grease from his hands on a dingy rag and set it next to the plastic cup of pens on the counter. "Just gettin' ready to close up. Is there somethin' I can help you with?"

Zach took a quick glance around the shop. It was small, but every bit of space was filled. To the left were two buggies, both almost framed. The chemical scent of paint seemed to permeate everything. The two large tanks of compressed air next to a pneumatic paint sprayer explained why. He noticed buggy parts hanging on the wall—rearview mirrors, red hazard triangles that were displayed on the backs of all Ohio buggies, packages of gold reflective tape.

"Are you *Herr* Kline?"

"Ya?" The man looked a little wary.

"I'm Zach Bender. I live down the road, a few houses away. I wanted to see if you needed another worker in your shop."

The man curled his lips inward, his shaggy beard lifting a little with the motion. He sized Zach up. "I don't think I do. I've got two *buwe* here to help me out."

Zach hid his disappointment. It had been worth a shot. *"Danki.* Thought I'd try anyway. You've got a nice shop here. *Gut* luck with the business." He turned to walk away.

"Wait."

Turning, Zach faced him. The man came out from behind the counter and stopped a few feet in front of Zach. "I might be able to use you part-time. Business is picking up and sometimes I've got my *frau* and *dochders* out here working at night to help keep up. And my two *sohns* help out, but I can only count on one of them. The other one…" He shook his head. "Anyway, I know *mei frau* would appreciate not having an extra job to do. I can't use you much, just a couple half days a week and probably a few Saturdays. But if business keeps up, it might turn into more."

Zach grinned so wide his face started to hurt. "*Danki, Herr* Kline. I'll take whatever you've got."

The man smiled back. "I know how it is trying to find work. That's part of the reason I opened up my own shop. And so far God's seen fit to bless it."

They discussed a few more details, then Zach jumped back into his buggy to hurry the rest of the way home. Kline's words about God blessing his shop, and his mother's reassurance that God always had a plan, gave Zach a jolt of hope. Maybe God did have something good in mind for him after all.

He arrived in time for supper, and after hanging his hat on a peg in the mudroom, he opened the door to the kitchen. His mother was putting a large plate of gravy-smothered pork chops in the center of the table next to a large bowl of steaming mashed potatoes and a smaller dish of green beans seasoned with chunks of bacon. His mouth watered as his stomach rumbled. Next time he needed to pack more than a peanut butter sandwich and a candy bar. But as eager as he was to eat, he couldn't wait to let his parents know about the job.

His mother greeted him with a smile when he sat down, but his father bowed his head without saying anything. Zach followed suit, silently giving God thanks for providing the job. When the prayer was over, he passed the pork chops to his father. "I've got some news—"

"Did you *geh* to the *schulhaus*?" His father stabbed at a large chop with his fork, not looking at Zach.

"*Ya.* I was there by six. We got a lot done today."

Daed finally looked at him. "We?"

"Ruth Byler was there. I tried to get her to *geh* home, but she refused. In a way I don't blame her. She is the teacher—"

"Is it ready for Saturday?"

"Not quite." Zach slid a pork chop onto his plate, then passed the dish to his mother. "I have to haul off all the wood and other broken stuff, and there's some more cleaning up to do. But trust me, it will be ready by Saturday."

His father served himself a healthy scoopful of mashed potatoes. "It better be."

Zach wasn't going to let his father's foul mood ruin his good one. "As I was saying, I have some other news too." He glanced at his mother, glad to see her expression relaxed for once. "I got a job."

"That's wonderful." His mother clapped her hands together. "Isn't that *wunderbaar*, Gideon?"

"Doing what?" his father asked.

"Working part-time at Kline's Buggy Shop. The new one down the road. He said he couldn't give me a lot of hours, but that the business is doing well and hopefully it would become full-time."

Daed took a bite of pork chop and chewed, not saying anything. Then he turned to Zach. "What do you know about making buggies?"

"Not much, but I'm willing to learn."

"Let's hope you don't burn down his shop." His father turned his attention back on his food.

"*Daed*, I was twelve when I lit those newspapers. And I didn't burn down the shop."

"You nearly killed my business with your reckless behavior, that's what you did. Speaking of business." *Daed* wiped several drops of gravy from his chin with a white napkin. "I've got a new employee starting tomorrow morning."

Zach dropped his fork. It hit the dish with a clatter. "What?"

"His name's Johnny Mullet. Finished school last year. He spent the whole summer looking for a job, but couldn't find one. I told his *daed* he could work for me."

"I don't believe this." Zach clenched his fists. "You had a job and you hired someone else instead of me?"

"I need someone responsible."

"And you think Johnny's more responsible than me."

"I never said that."

"But you meant it." Silence enveloped the kitchen. Zach bit his tongue to keep from lashing out, almost drawing blood. He looked at his mother, who kept her head down, but she hadn't touched a bite of her food. She would never defy her husband. And until now, Zach had never wanted her to. But he desperately needed someone on his side. When she didn't look up, he knew she wouldn't say a word.

His father added a sprinkle of salt to his meal. The room suddenly seemed ten times too small. He had to get out of there. His appetite gone, he stood. "Have to *geh* check on Maggie."

Zach kept his composure as he left the house, but once outside, he lost it. He stormed to the barn a few feet behind the house. He'd already fed his horse before coming in for supper, but he grabbed a pitchfork and started throwing clumps of hay into her stall anyway. After a few minutes, he slammed the pitchfork on the ground.

How could his father do this to him? *Daed* knew Zach needed money to repair the schoolhouse, but he hadn't said a word about having a job available or hiring anyone. Not until now. Zach barely knew this Mullet kid, and he was sure his father didn't know him that well either. Yet he trusted him enough to work with him in the shop? Trusted a near stranger more than his own son.

Zach sat down on a hay bale and ran his hand over his dripping face, taking in a deep breath. The barn smelled of horse sweat, old hay, and manure. He had half a mind to forget about being responsible and prove his father right, along with everyone else. Even Ruth didn't trust him, and she barely knew him. Which didn't make sense. He'd shown up at the schoolhouse and worked hard, as he'd promised. What did he get in return? Just a snobby attitude. She was even too good to eat lunch with him. Then he got himself a job, like he said he would. And how did his father act? Like he couldn't care less. Not a pat on the back or a word of encouragement. Just his past failure rubbed in his face over and over again.

Great plan, God.

Chapter Seven

❧

Deborah woke to the sight of Will standing by the edge of her bed, his face only inches from hers. Not realizing who he was at first, she sat straight up, her heart pounding. Then her son's face came into focus. "William Moses Coblentz, don't do that again. You almost scared me to death."

Will's eyes widened and his lower lip started to tremble. "Ma."

His mewling of her name brought her fully awake, and she picked him up. "It's okay, *sohn*." She hugged him close. Her mother was being buried today. Kissing his cheek, she fought the tears, keeping them from Will. Her heart felt like a rock in her chest. How was she supposed to get through this? *Lord, be with me today.*

She dressed Will, then sat him on the braided rug in the center of the floor with a toy drum that played music. While she put on her black dress, white *kapp*, and black stockings, she thought of what Naomi's reaction to the fancy toy would be. But right now Deborah didn't care. It was one of Will's favorite toys, and she wasn't about to take it away from him. She scooped him off the floor and carried him downstairs and into the kitchen. Naomi was there, setting out a platter of coffee cake on the table.

"I don't have time to cook breakfast." Naomi picked up a carton of orange juice and placed it next to the cake. Also dressed in black, her white apron was cinched tightly around her tiny waist. She looked at Deborah. "I suppose you'll have to take him to the funeral."

"There's no one to watch him."

"I can watch him." Sadie came into the kitchen. She took Will from Deborah's arms and planted a big kiss on his cheek. He giggled. "He'll be fine with me."

Deborah looked at her aunt. "Aren't you going to the funeral?"

Sadie shook her head. "I thought about it, but I should stay here. I can be more useful watching Will and getting things ready here. I'm sure you'll have lots of company before the service is over." She glanced at Naomi. "That's if I'm allowed."

Naomi didn't say anything for a long moment. Finally, she nodded and left.

With a sigh, Sadie sat Will in the chair. "I'll never understand her. Hard to believe you came from the same parents." Her head shot up. "Oh, sweetie. I'm sorry."

Deborah swallowed. "It's all right." She understood that Sadie hadn't meant to be insensitive. She also understood how Naomi was feeling. They were the only two who could share the pain of losing their mother. Well, they could if Naomi was willing to. But Deborah didn't have the will to try and forge a truce, since she knew it wouldn't work anyway. Today, though, she didn't want to fight with her sister.

On the way home from the cemetery, Naomi sat in the front of the buggy with their father while Deborah sat in the back. Naomi hadn't said a word during the service, or when their mother was laid to rest. She also hadn't shed a tear. But Deborah had cried enough for both of them.

Their *daed* turned the buggy down their drive, and Deborah noticed several buggies already outside their house. As soon as they parked in the barn, Naomi got out and hurried to the house.

Deborah expected her father to get out too, but he remained, staring down at his lap. Alarmed, she moved to sit beside him, placing her hand on his arm. *"Daed?"*

His black hat was pulled low on his head, enough so that she could only see half his face. "I'm all right, Deborah. I just need a few moments alone. *Geh* check on Will. I'll be along shortly."

She hesitated, unsure what to do. Then her father looked at her, his eyes clear but still filled with grief. "All right. I'll see you inside."

Deborah started for the house but stopped just short of the front porch. A sudden attack of nerves hit her. The same people inside the house had been at the funeral, but she was so focused on her father and consumed with grief at the sight of her mother being buried that she hadn't paid much attention to them. But now she had to face everyone, something she hadn't done since she'd gotten pregnant and left Middlefield. The Amish weren't a judgmental people, but knowing that didn't make her less nervous. She wasn't worried for herself as much as she was for Will. She couldn't take it if anyone rejected her child, no matter the circumstances of his birth.

"Deborah!"

She looked up to see a young, blonde-haired woman dash out the front door. Her nerves quieted and she grinned. "Elisabeth!"

Elisabeth Detweiler held out her arms and ran

to her, enveloping her in a big hug. "I didn't get a chance to greet you properly at the funeral." She took a step back, her arms still around Deborah's shoulders. "I'm so sorry about your *mudder.*"

Deborah's grin faded. "*Danki.* Oh, Elisabeth, I'm so glad you're here." Tears burned in her eyes.

Elisabeth nodded. "I've missed you, *mei freind.*"

"Me too." Deborah didn't realize how much until now. Elisabeth was the best friend she'd ever had. She remembered the time she had invited her to a party at the Yoders' barn. Elisabeth hadn't wanted to go, but Deborah had badgered her into it. At the time she had thought she was cool. She had been running around with some wild Yankee kids, and several Amish kids who were into partying. At the party, she had gotten drunk and had no idea how Elisabeth got home. During those months, she'd been a terrible friend to Elisabeth, even refusing to speak to her for a while.

Then when she became pregnant with Will, the only person she could turn to was Elisabeth, and Elisabeth had been a supportive and faithful friend. They had been close ever since.

"I saw your Will inside." Elisabeth smiled. "He's adorable. Looks just like his *mami.*" She winked.

Deborah had always thought he looked more

like Chase, but she liked hearing the compliment. "Was he still with *Aenti* Sadie?"

"*Ya*. She's holding on to him tight." Elisabeth linked her arm through Deborah's. "Let's *geh* inside. *Mami* and Moriah are helping Naomi in the kitchen."

They went inside. People were milling throughout the house, talking and eating. There were even a few bursts of quiet laughter, and for that, Deborah was grateful. Her mother would have wanted her family and friends to celebrate her memory.

Elisabeth released her arm. "Do you want something to eat or drink? I'll be happy to get it for you."

Deborah shook her head. "That's all right. I should *geh* help Naomi."

"Don't worry about that. *Mami* and Moriah have everything running smoothly. They tried to get your sister out of the kitchen so she could visit with everyone, but she refused." Elisabeth paused. "Have you had anything to eat today?"

"I'm really not hungry—"

"Deborah, you have to eat something. It's late afternoon. You don't want to get sick." When Deborah started to protest, she held up her hand. "I'll be right back. You can at least eat a cookie. And don't worry. I didn't make them; *Mami* did." Elisabeth took off before Deborah could say anything else.

Still standing near the front door, she searched the living room for her aunt and Will. She saw both of them across the room, Will sitting in Sadie's lap, his finger in his mouth and an expression of wonder on his small face as he stared at all the strangers. She walked toward them, only to bump into a tall Amish man.

"Sorry." He looked down at her. "I should have watched where I was going."

"*Nee*, it was my fault." She stared up at him in sudden recognition. "Hello, Stephen." She didn't know Elisabeth's younger brother very well, only from passing conversations when visiting the Byler house a few times over the years. He was two years younger than she and Elisabeth, and she'd never paid too much attention to him. It was hard not to pay attention to him now. He seemed to have grown six inches since the last time she'd seen him. She'd never been good at estimating things, but she figured he had to be at least a foot taller than she was, with broad shoulders and a lean frame. Deborah shifted her gaze to his face. His eyes were a similar blue color to Elisabeth's. But that's where their similarities seemed to end. His hair was a darker blond, nearly light brown, which matched his thick brows. He had a long face, but it suited his large frame.

"I'm sorry about your mother."

He had the deepest voice she'd ever heard, a rich, strong tone. "*Danki*. And *danki* for stopping by."

Elisabeth showed up, holding Will in her arms. "I didn't get a chance to get the cookies, but I thought you'd like this better."

Will held out his arms to her. Deborah took him and kissed his cheek.

"If you'll excuse me." Stephen stepped to the side. "It's getting a little crowded in here. Think I'll step outside for a minute."

Deborah watched him go, still amazed by his size. "It was nice of him to stop by after the funeral."

"I know he wanted to pay his respects," Elisabeth said. "And he's right; it is too crowded in here. We should *geh* on the porch. It'll be easier to talk there."

As they threaded their way through the crowd, Deborah paused to accept everyone's condolences. When they made their way out to the porch, they sat down on the chairs, and Deborah settled Will on her lap. She looked at her friend. "So tell me about married life." When Elisabeth didn't answer right away, she added, "It's okay. I'm happy for you and Aaron. I'm glad you found each other. I wish I would have been able to come to the wedding. It was too close to my due date."

"I understand." Elisabeth smiled, her lovely

blue eyes twinkling with happiness. "Married life is wonderful. I've never been so content. And Aaron has the patience of Job himself. He eats the terrible suppers I make without complaint. All he says is 'You're improving.'"

Deborah laughed. "And are you?"

"*Nee*. Not at all. But he's sweet to want me to think that."

Deborah smiled. Talking to Elisabeth helped her forget about her grief for a moment. "Maybe you need some cooking lessons."

"*Mami's* tried." Elisabeth let out a dramatic sigh. "Unlike Aaron, she doesn't have infinite patience. Oh well, he isn't going hungry. That's all that matters."

Elisabeth's words made her think about Thomas. He had to have some patience, too, considering he'd waited so long to get married. But she didn't know the reasons he had waited, except that he wasn't concerned about marrying someone he loved.

Maybe her aunt was right. She should forget about Thomas and wait on love. She saw the way Elisabeth's eyes shone with love as she talked about Aaron, and deep down she wanted that kind of devotion for herself. But one thing made her hang on to the idea of marrying Thomas. He had already accepted Will and would be a father to him. She couldn't be sure anyone else would be willing to do that.

Elisabeth reached out and touched Deborah's hand. "We shouldn't be talking about me. How are you doing? This has to be so hard on you."

Deborah nodded. "I miss her very much." She touched Will's head, running her fingers over his baby-fine, dark brown locks, which had started to curl at the ends. "I regret she didn't spend much time with Will. I should have come back as soon as he was born."

"Why didn't you?" Elisabeth's eyes widened. "Is that terribly nosy of me?"

"*Nee*, it's okay."

"It's just that I always wondered. I knew why you left, especially after how Chase reacted. He was awful."

"I didn't leave just because of Chase. I left because I was scared. And embarrassed. After Will was born, it was just easier to stay in Paradise. I didn't have to worry about anyone judging me or my *sohn*." She swallowed the lump in her throat. "But my selfish fear kept my *mami* from knowing her first *grosskinn*."

"You didn't know this would happen. You did what you had to do."

Deborah shifted Will in her arms, noticing he had fallen asleep. She hadn't been able to get him on a schedule yet. He would probably be up late tonight, but she didn't want to disturb him. "I keep telling myself that, but it doesn't make me feel any better. I wish they would have told me she was sick."

"I can't believe Naomi didn't tell you," Elisabeth said. "If I had known, I would have written you right away. I just assumed she or your *daed* had let you know."

She looked at Elisabeth, shaking her head. "*Nee.* They didn't. Although I can understand why *Daed* didn't; he's not much for writing letters. But Naomi…." Deborah touched her bottom lip, fighting to contain her sorrow. "*Mami* had cancer for months, Elisabeth. I could have come back here and helped take care of her." She sighed. "I've made so many mistakes."

"We all make mistakes, Deborah."

"But not like this."

Elisabeth's eyes widened even more. "You regret having Will?"

"*Nee.* He's my life."

"I can see that." Elisabeth's tone softened. "I can also see you're a good *mudder.*"

"I'm trying to be. I can't imagine being without him. I don't want to imagine it. But I wish the circumstances were different. He'll grow up without knowing his *daed.* I don't think that's right."

Elisabeth frowned. "But that's not your fault.

You went to Chase and told him about the *boppli*. He chose not to be part of Will's life, and to be honest, I think you're both better for it. He's not a *gut* person, Deborah."

She looked up. "Have you seen him since I left?"

"Don't tell me you want to see him again."

"*Nee*. I don't. At least not for my sake. But if he met Will and saw how wonderful he is, maybe things would be different."

"But would they be better? He's not Amish and won't be. Even if you were to get together, you'd have to leave the Amish to do so. Would it be worth it?"

She hesitated, then shook her head. "At one time I thought it would. But I'm happy being Amish. I want to raise my *sohn* Amish, with a family that cares for him. I would have never married Chase."

"I'm glad to hear you say that. And to answer your question, I haven't seen him since the last day you spoke to him, right before you left. I don't even think he's working at Mary Yoder's anymore. He could have left Middlefield as far as I know."

"Then there's no reason to think about him again." She said the words, but she knew how difficult it was to try to forget about him. A light summer breeze kicked up, caressing the back of her neck as she stared at the top of Will's head.

"I see Stephen has found your *daed*," Elisabeth said.

Deborah looked up to see Stephen and her father outside. Her father had gotten out of the buggy, but still hadn't gone in the house and instead lingered near the barn as Stephen approached him. Obviously *Daed* was avoiding facing everyone, but he didn't seem to mind Stephen's company. "Stephen has really changed while I was gone. I don't remember him being that tall."

"He probably wasn't that tall last time you saw him. He had a huge growth spurt last year, right before he turned nineteen. He even towers over Tobias, and Tobias is taller than all of us. Tobias isn't real happy about that, let me tell you. He doesn't like looking up to his little *bruder*."

For the first time that day Deborah smiled. "Is Stephen a carpenter too?"

"*Ya*. All my *bruders* are in the family business. And Aaron's still working at Gabriel's blacksmith shop. He really enjoys smithing, although he likes shoeing the horses best." Elisabeth tapped her finger against her chin, her blue eyes widening. "Oh, and I guess you didn't know, but I have a new nephew."

"Really? Which one of your siblings had a *boppli*?"

"None of them." A cheeky grin appeared.

"No one had a *boppli*, but you have a nephew?"

"Uh huh. Lukas and Anna adopted a *bu* about a year and a half ago. He's sixteen now. His name is Sawyer. He's a Yankee too. Well, not anymore."

"He's Amish now?"

"He hasn't joined the church, but he's really taken to the Amish ways. Do you know Daniel Mullet and his family?" When Deborah shook her head, Elisabeth said, "They live near an abandoned barn that was destroyed in a fire a while back. But the barn was still standing, and Sawyer was living in it."

"He was living in an Amish barn? Why?"

"He ran away from his foster family. It's a long story, but Mary Beth Mullet and her brother Johnny found him and hid him for a while. Eventually he had to *geh* back to the group home, but then Lukas and Anna decided to foster him for a while. After a few months they ended up adopting him. It's like he's been a part of the family all along. Hopefully you'll get to meet him soon. Lukas will be hosting church in a few weeks. I'd love if you and your family would stay for lunch afterward."

"I'd like that." Her emotions began to overwhelm her. "Elisabeth," she said, trying to keep her voice from catching. It didn't work. "You're such a *gut freind*, more than I deserve. You've always been there for me. Even when I was awful to you."

Elisabeth looked surprised. "You were never awful to me."

"I was at the Yoder's party. I should have never talked you into going…I shouldn't have gone either."

"Deborah, that's all in the past."

"Sometimes the past won't leave us alone."

Elisabeth reached for Deborah's hand. "And sometimes, *mei freind*, we have to stop paying so much attention to it."

"Nice pasture." Stephen looked out at the huge field before him, breathing in the scent of sweet timothy grass mixed with hay from the bales stacked nearby. Several yards away, brown and black cows, with noses to the ground, ate their fill. He turned to Moses, who stood beside him. "How many head of cattle do you have here?"

"About thirty. We're down in numbers right now. It's been a rough year." The old man's face sobered. "I didn't get a chance to tell you before, but *danki* for helping with Martha's grave."

"It was my honor." Stephen's father had asked him to help dig the grave this morning. It was a sobering task, one he didn't enjoy at all. But he could shovel faster and remove more dirt than most of the other men who had assisted. He saw the sorrow in Moses's eyes. He imagined the pain of losing a spouse had to be unbearable, and he didn't know what to say. Instead he stared out at the pasture again, shoving his hands in the pockets of his black pants.

Finally Moses spoke. "It's been getting too much lately." He looked up at Stephen, his head tilted far back. "The farm, I mean. Over the years I've had a few *freinds* help me when they could, and of course, *mei dochders* and Martha…" He gulped and looked away. "They did their share. Then Deborah left and Martha got sick. I just kind of let things *geh* after that. I've had to rely on Naomi for a lot of things," Moses said. "But I can see it's getting to her too."

Stephen didn't know Deborah very well, only through her friendship with Elisabeth. Even so, he, like everyone else in the community, knew why she had left Middlefield. He had to say that her son was a good-looking boy. Stephen had always had a soft spot for kids, and he enjoyed spending time with his nieces and nephews. More than once he'd been called on to babysit and had agreed without hesitation, even though some of his friends thought watching children was women's work. Not that it mattered to him what they thought. He was never one to let other people's opinions bother him.

"How many animals do you have besides the cows?" Stephen asked.

"A few chickens, couple goats, three pigs. Nothing like I had a couple years ago. It's impossible to keep up with it all."

Stephen frowned. Moses owned a great piece of land, and it was plain to him that his farm had been successful at one time. But now everything seemed to be in need of repair or refurbishing, from the barn to the chicken coop. The crops were almost taken over by weeds, and the corn in the field was shorter than it should be by this time. The farm mirrored its owner's sorrow. The only thing that seemed to be in good shape was the vegetable garden in the backyard.

The sound of cows lowing filtered through the air. "I should probably check on their feed," Moses said. "They eat pretty *gut* during the day, but when they come in tonight they'll want some grain."

"Mind if I come with you?"

"Suit yourself." Moses lumbered to the barn.

Stephen followed. He suspected the cows had plenty of feed. Moses was probably using this as an excuse to get out of going inside. Not that Stephen could blame him. The modest-size farmhouse was teeming with people. He'd rather be out here too.

When they entered the barn, he saw that the cows' feed ring was full. The few cows who had stayed inside to avoid the heat stood up and walked over, stopping at the metal fence that kept them penned up in the majority of the barn, their tails slapping at the flies buzzing around them. Slowly they chewed their cud.

Moses looked the cows over and nodded. He held out his hand to one of the larger brown ones. Her tongue flicked out and licked his palm. "My *schwester* says I should hire someone to help out part-time, but I don't know."

Stephen reached out and touched the top of another cow's nose. She jumped back, then tentatively sniffed his fingers. "Hope you don't mind me saying, but that might be a *gut* idea." He glanced at Moses. "That way all the work won't be on you."

Moses rubbed the back of his neck. "Problem is, I can't afford to pay much. Next to nothing at all. I'm not sure where I'd find someone who'd be willing to work here for practically nothing."

Stephen nodded. That was a problem. Then a slow grin suddenly spread on his face. He faced Moses. "I think I know someone."

The old man looked up. "Who?"

"Me."

Moses scoffed. "You have a job already. Why would you want to work here?"

"Why not? I can help you out temporarily until you find someone else. It will have to be after I get off work, so in the evening some time. Maybe a couple times a week."

"That's a fine offer, but I can't take it."

Stephen frowned. "Why?"

"I don't want to take advantage of you. I meant it when I said I can't pay much."

"I'll do it for free."

Moses gave him a half-smile. "You don't have any idea how much work there is on a farm, do you?"

"I'm not afraid of hard work."

Moses tugged on his silvery beard, looking Stephen up and down. "I'm sure you're not." He paused, still stroking his beard. "All right. But just until I find someone more permanent. And you won't do the work for free. I'll pay you something." He walked to Stephen and held out his hand. "Deal?"

Stephen took the old man's hand and shook it. "Deal. When do you want me to start?"

"Monday too soon?"

"Monday it is."

For the next hour Moses gave Stephen a small tour of the barn and part of the property, pointing out areas that needed fixing and sprucing up.

As the list grew longer and longer, Stephen wondered what he'd gotten himself into. He honestly didn't mind working hard, but as Moses talked, he could see even more clearly why the man was overwhelmed. Knowing that his help was needed solidified that he'd done the right thing, even though the decision had been impulsive.

They rounded the barn one last time, and the house came into view. Moses stopped and sighed. "Guess I better *geh* inside. Can't avoid the company forever. Martha was the one that liked having people over. Me, I could take 'em or leave 'em. Right now I'd like to leave 'em."

As they approached the house, Stephen saw Deborah sitting on one of two white plastic chairs on the front porch. Deborah's son was asleep in her lap, his head against her shoulder, his thumb dangling out of his mouth. When they neared, she turned her head toward her father before moving her gaze to him. She smiled shyly, but when he smiled back she glanced away. He stopped short of the porch steps. "Have you seen Elisabeth?"

"She went inside for a minute. She should be right back out."

Moses was already near the door. "Are you coming in?"

Stephen shook his head. "I should be getting back to work."

"All right. I'll see you on Monday, then."

When Moses went inside, Deborah said, "What about Monday?"

"I offered to come help your *daed* out with some of the work around here."

Deborah's eyes filled with surprise. "You did?"

He nodded.

"That's very kind of you. I hope you're not going to too much trouble."

He noticed she had a soft voice, almost lyrical. "I don't mind. I'm looking forward to it, actually. My *grossvadder* had a farm in Holmes County. We used to visit when I was growing up. I learned to break my first horse there."

"Is he still farming?"

"*Nee.* He retired, and now my uncle runs it. I don't get back there much anymore, though. Too much to do here."

Will suddenly lifted his head, his eyes opening halfway, wisps of his hair matted against the side of his head that had rested on Deborah's shoulder. He looked at Stephen, then buried his face in his mother's dress.

"He's a little shy around strangers." Deborah stroked his head. "He'll come around once he gets to know you."

"I'm sure he will. I better get going. Tell your *daed* I'll be here around five on Monday."

"I will."

Stephen turned around and started toward his buggy when he heard her call out his name. He faced her again. *"Ya?"*

"We usually eat supper around that time. Is there anything special you like?"

He almost laughed at her question. His appetite was legendary among his family, and they never failed to point out, not only how much he ate, but that he would eat almost anything his mother put in front of him. "Anything is fine. I'm not picky."

She nodded and Will looked up again. Stephen waved, then left. As he drove the buggy back to his *daed's* shop, he remembered about the desks he and his father and brothers had promised to build to replace the ones Zach Bender had destroyed the other day. He'd have to put twice as much effort into making the desks in order to have the time to work for the Coblentz family. Yet he had a feeling that in the end, it would be worth it.

Chapter Eight

Ruth looked at her reflection in the bathroom mirror and touched the small black-and-blue patch on her forehead. A little more than a week had passed since Zachariah had driven through the schoolhouse, and she was thankful the bruise was barely noticeable now, especially since she had a teachers' meeting to attend in an hour. Every other month, a group of teachers from around the district gathered together to exchange ideas and give encouragement. This would be Ruth's first meeting, and she had been looking forward to it for weeks.

After making sure the bobby pins keeping her *kapp* in place were secure, she smoothed out the white apron she had just put over one of her newer dresses. She left the bathroom and went to the living room, expecting Stephen to be waiting for her since she had asked him last week if he could give her a ride tonight. Instead, she found her mother sitting on the couch, crocheting a small light blue afghan. Frowning, Ruth left the living room and searched for Stephen. He wasn't in the kitchen, the barn, or the wood shop. She returned to the living room, annoyed. "Have you seen Stephen?"

"He left for the Coblentzes' a little while ago. I thought he mentioned something to your *daed* about helping Moses out with his farm in the evenings." Emma put down her crochet hook and yarn. "Why are you looking for him?"

"Because he said last week he would take me to Meadowlawn for my teachers' meeting."

Emma frowned. "Oh, dear. He must have forgotten."

Ruth's annoyance grew. Although it was admirable that Stephen wanted to help out Moses Coblentz, especially after the death of his wife, she really wanted to go to this meeting. "I suppose he took the buggy."

Emma nodded. "That he did. And your father took the other one. He went to Tobias's to help him finish up the front porch he's adding on to his house. I think Lukas and Sawyer are over there too." She pushed up her glasses.

Guess I won't be going to my meeting. Her disappointment was acute, but she held her frustration in.

"How's the *schulhaus* coming along?" her mother asked.

"Faster than I thought. I think just the painting is all that's left." She had been to the schoolhouse a few times over the past week to see how things were coming along, and she'd been surprised and impressed with Zachariah's progress. As far as she knew, other than erecting the wall, he had finished the repairs himself. "I'm hoping I can start school next week sometime."

"Will you be ready?"

"*Ya.* I'm ready." She felt like she'd been ready forever.

Emma looked at Ruth, then patted the empty spot next to her on the couch. Ruth joined her, unsure what her mother wanted to talk to her about.

Emma's blue eyes grew soft. "I know these past two weeks have been difficult for you. You've worked so hard to get this teaching job and to prepare for school. Then it was postponed. I know you're impatient to get started, but I'm sure there's a reason this happened."

"I know." But she hadn't been able to see it. She'd been taught all her life that everything happened for a reason, especially those things that were disappointing and difficult. It was the hardship in life that made God's faithful stronger. She had seen that in her own family when Moriah's first husband died and when Lukas and his wife, Anna, found out they would never have children of their own. Lined up against her siblings' trials, her problem seemed trivial. But it didn't make it less bothersome.

As if her mother had read her thoughts, she said, "I know you're struggling with this, but don't be too hard on Zachariah. He's the one who made the mistake. Now he's paying the consequences. From what I understand, he's financially responsible for the repairs."

Ruth looked at her mother. "He is, but that's his fault. You don't know him like I do. He was a troublemaker in school—"

"It's not our place to judge others, Ruth." Emma peered over her glasses. "It would do you *gut* to remember that."

Ruth stared down at her lap. "*Ya, Mami.* I will."

Emma smiled slightly. "Ruth, of all my *kinner*, you're the hardest worker. You're also a perfectionist. Even Lukas, with his high standards, is able to relax and enjoy life. I'd like to see you do that too."

"I enjoy my life. At least I will when it gets started. Right now I'm at a standstill until the *schulhaus* opens again. And there's nothing wrong with working hard. That's something you and *Daed* taught me."

"Don't get me wrong, I'm very pleased with your work ethic. Your father and I both are. It's just that we don't want to see teaching consume you the way your schoolwork did."

Ruth opened her mouth to say something but changed her mind. What her mother and everyone else saw as all consuming she considered enjoyment. She loved spending her extra time on her assignments for school, on reading books of all kinds, on poring over the resource section at Middlefield Library. Learning something new excited her, and nothing pleased her more than tackling a problem and coming up with the solution. Which was one reason waiting around for Zachariah to fix the schoolhouse frustrated her. Other than helping him out the day after the accident, there was little else she could do. When her career started was solely up to him, which made the situation that much worse.

"Where is the meeting?" her mother asked.

"Meadowlawn *schulhaus*."

"That's not too far." Emma picked up her crocheting again. "You could walk there."

"*Ya*, but I'd be late. The meeting starts at seven sharp."

Emma glanced at the small windup clock on the end table beside her. The delicate pink-and-white porcelain clock was the only fancy item in the room, a tenth anniversary gift from Ruth's father. It was a quarter past six. "You have forty-five minutes. If you left now, you'd probably be on time, or possibly a few minutes late."

"Teachers should never be tardy." At the sound of her mother's chuckle, she laughed. "You're right. I can certainly walk to Meadowlawn. It's a nice evening and the exercise will be *gut* for me. Did you know exercise has been proven not only to be beneficial for your body, but also your mind? There are scientific studies that show how physical activity boosts your mood." And lately, her mood definitely needed the boost.

Emma chuckled. "Spoken like a true teacher. Enjoy your meeting and be safe."

She told her mother goodbye, picked up her purse from the hook on the door, and headed toward the schoolhouse, which was a little more than four miles away. She walked at a brisk pace, almost panting. But when small trickles of sweat beaded on her forehead, she slowed down. It wouldn't do for her to show up at the meeting all sweaty. Still, she found the walk refreshing. White cotton-ball clouds floated against a backdrop of baby-blue sky. She walked by one of her neighbors' houses and waved at the couple as they sat on the front porch. Those studies about exercise were right. She felt better already.

She had trekked almost a mile when she heard a buggy coming up behind her. She didn't pay much attention to it, only on keeping a steady pace and staying clear of the cars on the side of the road. She expected the buggy to pass, but was surprised when it pulled alongside her. She was even more surprised to see Zachariah holding the reins.

"Hi," he said, slowing his horse to match her steps.

"Hello." She didn't slow her pace.

"Where are you headed on this fine evening?"

"To a teachers' meeting."

"Do you need a ride?"

"Nee." What was she doing? Of course she needed a ride. But she automatically rejected his offer.

"Are you sure? You seem to be in an awful hurry. My horse can barely catch up."

His ridiculous statement brought a small smile to her face. "If your horse was going any slower she would fall asleep."

He grinned. *"Gut* one."

She glanced at him, his compliment making her smile a little more.

"Why don't you let me drop you off wherever you're going?" He leaned forward in the seat. "Seems like we're heading in the same direction."

She'd be a fool to refuse him a second time. "Okay."

Zachariah brought the buggy to a stop and she

climbed in. Once she was seated, he tapped the reins against his horse's flanks and they began moving again.

"Where did you say you were going again?"

"Meadowlawn."

"Okay, I know exactly where that is."

They rode in silence for a while. With each minute that passed, she felt more awkward. Shouldn't they be talking about something? "Have you made any progress with the painting?"

"I wondered how long it would be before you asked me about the *schulhaus*."

"And?"

"I finished it." He turned to her and grinned.

Her mouth dropped. "You did? But I thought it would take the rest of the week."

He shook his head. "After I got off work yesterday afternoon, I went straight to the *schulhaus*. Just on my way back home now."

Ruth paused, absorbing what he just told her. She looked at his hands as they loosely held the reins, noticing for the first time the white paint spattered on them. Her gaze moved from his hands to his pale blue shirt, which also had spots of paint on it, then to his profile. His yellow hat was tilted back, exposing most of his forehead. She noted a shadow of a dark red beard on his cheeks and upper lip. As a single Amish man, he wouldn't grow a beard, as those were reserved only for married men, and he wouldn't grow a mustache at all.

Her eyebrows arched. "You stayed up all night?"

He nodded, glancing at her. "I took a cat nap here and there, but *ya*, for the most part I did. I know you're eager to start school so I finished up as quickly as possible. The only thing you won't have are the replacement desks. But I put a long table and some chairs in the classroom so the *kinner* will at least have a place to sit while the desks are being built."

She stared at him. How had she not noticed the fatigue etched around his eyes until now? Or the weary slump of his shoulders? "I can't believe you worked all day at your job and then all night on the *schulhaus*."

"My job at the buggy shop is just part-time."

"Aren't you tired?"

"*Ya*. But it's worth it. Now all I need is the school board's approval and you'll be open for business."

Her heart soared. That was the best news she'd gotten in the past two weeks.

"I still have some repairs to work on, but you'll at least be able to have students."

"That's what I was hoping for." Actually more than she hoped for. She looked at him again, squinting a bit at the evening sunlight behind him. She still couldn't believe he'd worked so hard to finish the school. Guilt prodded her, and she remembered what her mother said about being too hard on him. "I owe you an apology."

"You do?" He glanced at her, his green eyes reflecting his surprise. "For what?"

"I misjudged you. I…" She glanced away. "I didn't think you'd get the job done."

He chuckled, but it had a bitter edge to it. "You're not the only one. And you don't owe me anything. I just did what needed to be done."

She leaned back against the seat and started to relax a bit. Everything finally seemed to be back to normal, which was how she liked it. No more delays or surprises. She detested surprises.

Traffic was light as they made their way down the road. Ruth saw three children playing in a large front yard, a young boy pulling two small girls in a wagon down the driveway. Just as she smiled, a car sped by them, shaking the buggy. Three other ones did the same thing, honking their horns, as if they were all racing each other. Spooked by the traffic, the horse started to prance. Then the buggy lurched. Pitched forward, Ruth grappled for something to hold on to, her eyes darting to Zachariah. He yanked on the reins, his forearms straining with the effort.

Another car zoomed by as fast as the others, and that was more than the horse could take. She flew off at full gallop. "Whoa! Whoa!" Zach hollered.

Ruth grabbed the side of the buggy. "Make her stop!"

"I'm trying! Maggie! Whoa!" He jerked the reins, but with each pull the horse galloped faster. Zachariah turned his body to the side, his foot pressing against the inside of the buggy for leverage.

Ruth watched in terror as the landscape flew by. What if Zachariah lost control of the horse? She gripped the side of the buggy. "Zachariah!"

"Hang on!" He managed to steer the buggy onto a side road, getting them away from the cars, at least. That settled his horse a bit, but she still ran fast.

Maggie dashed into an abandoned field, Zach gripping the reins and Ruth clinging to the seat of the buggy so she wouldn't be thrown out. The wind stung her eyes. She felt the wheels stutter and skid. Then the buggy jolted and tilted to the left, barely balancing on two wheels. She lost her grip and slid across the seat, smashing into Zachariah.

With every ounce of strength he had, Zach held fast to Maggie's reins. He fought to keep control of his normally tame horse. She'd never been spooked before. But the crazy way those cars flew past them would have scared any animal, no matter how calm. He pulled on the reins as hard as he could, but she still refused to slow down. It was as if someone had put a torch to her hind end. All he could do was try to keep her from crashing the buggy until she wore herself out.

Maggie continued to flee across the field but then the buggy hit a huge bump. Zach's body rose off the seat, and the buggy tilted onto two wheels. Ruth slid into him and screamed. He took his eyes off the horse for a split second to see if she was all right. She gripped his upper arm with both hands, squeezing hard. He really needed that arm to help control the horse, but right now Ruth needed it even more because she had nothing else to hold on to.

The buggy slammed back down onto four wheels, but Ruth continued to clutch his arm. He yanked on the reins harder. "Whoa, Maggie, whoa!" Finally the reins went slack in his hand. Almost as quickly as she had sped up, she slowed her gallop to a canter, then finally to a walk, then at last to a stop.

He fell back against the seat, gasping for breath. Only then did he notice that Ruth hadn't let go of his arm. She stared straight ahead, her face whiter than the spot of hair between Maggie's eyes. "Ruth?" When she didn't say anything he asked again. "Ruth? Are you all right?"

She let out a small squeak.

He angled his body to the side, his heartbeat finally slowing. But he didn't try to extract his arm from her grip. "Ruth, it's okay. We're all right. Even Maggie's okay."

"I…" She looked up at him with round, bluish-gray eyes. "Wha?"

Something pulled at Zach, deep inside. Seeing Ruth this terrified worried him. He lowered his voice. "Ruth. You can let *geh* now. It's okay."

She wagged her head back and forth several times. "What if she takes off again?"

"Maggie won't. Those cars spooked her bad. I don't blame her; they were reckless." He looked at his horse, her sides pumping back and forth as she fought for breath. He glanced back at Ruth. "I need to check on her. I'll make sure she's really calmed down before we try to go anywhere."

She stared up at him again, intensifying the odd pull he felt toward her. He looked into her dark blue eyes, mesmerized by the mix of fear and total trust he found in them. She always seemed so guarded, but at that moment, her façade was gone. It was as if he was seeing the real Ruth, and it unnerved and attracted him at the same time.

Ruth slowly removed her hands from his arm.

He jumped out of the buggy and went to Maggie. He patted her brown flanks, talked to her a bit, and made sure she was okay, but his focus wasn't totally on his horse. As he pressed his hand against Maggie's side, he realized his body was shaking. Sure, he was tired after working twenty-four hours straight, and he was rattled after Maggie's fear-driven rampage off the road. But he also knew that he was shaking because of the spark of attraction he'd felt moments ago.

He snuck a glance at Ruth, making double sure she was all right. To his relief, the color was seeping back into her cheeks. And as it did, his senses seemed to return. He couldn't possibly be attracted to Ruth Byler. She wasn't anything near his type, especially her uptight personality. Whatever emotions he'd experienced had nothing to do with reality and everything to do with the fact that he needed sleep. And lots of it.

Satisfied that Maggie was okay, he took the opportunity to look around the field. Where were they? He didn't know how far the horse had taken them off the road. Giving her one last pat, he went back to the buggy, where Ruth was tucking stray strands of her dishwater-blond hair behind her ears.

"Where are we?" The tremble in her voice was almost undetectable, her stoic mask back in place. This was the Ruth he was used to.

"Not sure." He took off his hat and swiped his arm across his damp forehead.

"You mean you don't know?"

Exhausted, her curt question suddenly irritated him. "I was a little busy, remember? I didn't take time to notice where Maggie was dragging us."

"So you have no idea where we are?"

"*Nee*, but I'm sure we're not lost."

"That's the very definition of being lost." She climbed out of the buggy, moving steadily and purposefully. Any trace of the terrified woman he'd witnessed moments ago had disappeared completely. She strode away from the buggy and started looking around. "Where's the road?"

"From the buggy tracks, I think we came from that direction," he said, pointing west.

She looked up at him, shading her eyes from the weakening sunlight. "I'm going to miss my meeting because of this."

"Is that all you're concerned about?" He walked over to her.

"My teachers' meetings are important. It's a chance for us to get together and exchange knowledge and strategies for educating our students."

"Sounds scintillating." The words were out before he could stop them. Why couldn't she be more helpful instead of whining about missing her *dumm* meeting?

Her brows knit together. "That's quite a big word for you. Sure you know what that means, especially since you seem fuzzy on the definition of *lost*?"

His lips pressed together. Ordinarily he could appreciate skilled sarcasm, but not right now. "You might want to go easy on the charm, *fraulein*."

Her mouth formed a tight O shape, but she didn't reply. Instead she turned her back to him.

The horse whinnied behind Zach, and he walked over to her. He stroked her nose, relieved she was still calm and had finally caught her breath. It took him a few minutes to gather his composure. Flinging insults at each other wouldn't get them home. Once his emotions settled down, he called out to Ruth over his shoulder. "We should get back in the buggy. At least if Maggie takes off again, I can grab the reins and control her."

Ruth spun around and stared at him, her chin slightly lifted. And people told him he had a chip on his shoulder. "What if you can't?" she asked.

"Can't what?"

"Control her."

Was that a glint of anxiety he saw in her eyes? He softened his stance. "I won't let anything happen to you, Ruth. I promise."

She glanced away for an instant, then looked

back at him. "I'm not worried about me. I just wouldn't want anything to happen to your horse. She's a fine animal."

Zach fought a smile. "So you're worried about my horse?"

"Ya."

Sure you are. "C'mon, let's *geh*. We need to take advantage of the daylight that's left."

Ruth hesitated, but she climbed into the buggy, sitting as far away from him as possible. He picked up the reins and looked at her. "Don't fall out now."

"I won't."

He gently urged Maggie forward, relieved when she started moving without complaint. He held the reins loose in his hand, not guiding her in either direction.

"Aren't you going to steer?"

He shook his head. "Maggie knows the way home."

"You're putting an awful lot of confidence in your horse."

"Ya. Horses always find their way back home."

"You're not worried she'll *geh* the wrong way?"

"Nope. Haven't you ever been lost with a horse before?"

"Nee. I'm very *gut* with directions and orientation."

Figures she would be a human compass, although he didn't quite understand what she meant by orientation, and he wasn't up to figuring it out. All he wanted to do was go home.

He waited for her to say something else and was relieved when she didn't. For the next fifteen minutes Maggie wandered the field. Zach started to yawn. He kept glancing at Ruth, waiting for her to tell him Maggie was going in the wrong direction. She sat straight in the seat, her lips thinned, her hand gripping the edge of the seat, but she remained silent.

Finally the road came into view. He glanced at Ruth again. Her posture had relaxed, but only a tiny bit. Zach gripped the reins and directed Maggie onto the road, his body tensing in case she balked. But she calmly stepped onto the asphalt and dragged the buggy behind her. Even the few cars that passed them didn't affect her. He let out a deep breath, unaware he'd been holding it in.

It took Maggie twenty minutes to get to Ruth's, and by that time the sun was almost down. When he stopped in the driveway, he expected her to jump out. Instead she turned to him. She looked as drained as he felt. "If need be, you can let Maggie have a drink before you *geh* home."

Zach lifted a brow in surprise. That was the last thing he'd expected from her, an invitation to water his horse. "*Danki*, but she'll be fine until I get home."

She nodded, then moved to get out of the buggy.

"Wait." When she turned around, he said, "Sorry you didn't get a chance to *geh* to your meeting."

She paused for a moment. "It's okay. It was an adventure."

He watched her climb out of the buggy, his lips forming a half-smile. The woman was an odd duck. Hard as glass, but just as fragile too. He didn't know what to make of her. Worse yet, he didn't know what to make of himself, his own temperament bouncing from irritation to attraction like a Ping-Pong ball. He never thought being around Ruth Byler would be this exhausting. Or interesting.

"You're back already?" Emma set down her knitting. A frown appeared on her face. "*Gut* heavens, what happened to you this time?"

Ruth brushed away the loose strand of hair resting on her cheek. She knew she had to look a sight. "You wouldn't believe me if I told you."

Emma stood. "I'm sure I would. You look like you've been riding in one of those fancy convertible cars." Her frown deepened. "Please tell me you weren't doing that."

"I wasn't." As she told her mother about Zachariah's horse running scared, her expression mellowed.

"Then you never made it to your meeting."

Ruth shook her head. "*Nee*. I didn't."

"Well, there's always the next one. I'm just glad you're okay. Where's Zachariah now?"

"He went home." He'd looked so tired when he left, and she couldn't blame him. She felt a tiny stab of guilt for arguing with him over getting lost. She knew it hadn't been his fault, and because of his quick thinking and strong arms, he'd saved them from serious injury, or worse. But she hadn't been thinking about that at the time. She'd been terrified, then frustrated that she'd shown him that weakness. Then once the buggy had come to a stop, she couldn't let go of his arm, partly out of fear, but partly because she didn't want to. Even now, she could remember the calmness she felt being that close to him. It made her feel safe when only moments earlier she had felt anything but. But she had to be rational about what had happened. She'd been afraid, and her mixed-up feelings had been a result of that fear. Simple cause and effect.

If that was true, then why couldn't she stop thinking about the way he'd looked at her before she'd let go of his arm? His green eyes had narrowed slightly and darkened to an almost emerald color, making her breath hitch.

"Ruth?" Emma moved closer to her. "Are you sure you're all right?"

She shoved the memory away and looked at her mother. "I'm fine. I didn't hit my head again, if that's what you're worried about."

"I thought for a minute you might have. You're acting a bit dazed."

Ruth frowned, then blanked her emotions. "Really, I'm okay. And I have *gut* news." She told her mother that the school was ready, but left out the part about Zachariah working all night long. Even mentally acknowledging that piqued her feelings, something she didn't need, not when she had to force herself not to think of him at all.

Emma planted a kiss on her cheek. "Your *daed* should be home soon. I think I'll wait for him upstairs. One thing's for sure, *dochder*. Your life hasn't been boring lately." She winked at Ruth and left the room.

Ruth sighed, plopping down on the couch. The lock of hair dislodged from behind her ear again, but she let it fall against her cheek. Her mother was right. Things hadn't been boring lately. But she *liked* boring. She preferred predictable. And orderly. And ever since Zachariah had plowed into the school, her life had been a lesson in disorder.

Chapter Nine

"You've done a fine job, Zach." Gabe Miller nodded as he strolled around the schoolroom. "A very fine job."

Zach couldn't hide his smile. He, Gabe, and his father had arrived at the schoolhouse a short while ago. As members of the school board, his father and Gabe were there to approve Zach's repairs. If they did, Gabe would make an announcement tomorrow after church that the school would open on Monday. Zach hoped it would happen, not just for his sake, but for Ruth's too.

But while Gabe seemed pleased with the results, his father had said nothing so far. The ride in the buggy to the school had been filled with silence. Zach even tried a few times to start a conversation, bringing up his work at the buggy shop. But he soon got tired of his father's one-syllable answers and kept his mouth shut the rest of the way.

He stood by Ruth's desk and watched his father stare at the new wall and stroke his beard. He couldn't see his father's expression, but from the way he had slowly walked back and forth, stopping at times to examine the floor or look up at the ceiling, Zach could guess what his father was thinking.

"There's paint on the floor." He marked the spot with his foot.

"Where?" Zach zipped between two of the rows of desks. He'd set them up in even rows, thinking Ruth might want them that way. If she didn't, she could rearrange them. He reached his father and bent down to see the paint spots. They were more like paint flecks. He rubbed them off with his thumbnail. "There. Satisfied?" The biting words were out before he could stop them.

His *daed* turned to him, green eyes snapping. "Satisfaction comes from a job *well* done."

Zach stared at his father. He'd spent almost two weeks working on the school, sweating in the heat, making sure he not only finished the job early, but that he did it well. And all his father could do was complain about a few stray paint flecks?

"I don't see why we can't open school Monday."

Gabe moved to stand between the two men. "Unless you have an objection, Gideon?"

Zach held his breath as his father continued to look around, taking his time before answering. Finally he said, "*Nee.*"

Gabe glanced at Zach, giving him a quick smile. With that one gesture Zach knew Gabe not only recognized what was going on between father and son, he also understood. He was glad someone did, because he certainly didn't understand his father's behavior.

Moments later they were on their way home. It had been overcast all day, and the scent of impending rain filled the evening air. Dusk cast a purplish haze on the grassy fields and on the white houses lining both sides of the road.

They were halfway home when Zach couldn't take the silence anymore. "Why are you being so hard on me?"

His father remained silent.

Zach slid down in his seat, feeling like a kid of eight instead of an adult of eighteen. "I don't understand. You said you wanted me to be responsible. To be a *mann.* And now that I've proven myself to you, you won't acknowledge it."

"You've done *one* thing, Zachariah. One small thing."

"Repairing the *schulhaus* wasn't a small thing!"

His *daed* gripped the reins. "It will take more than that to make you a *mann*."

Anger surged through Zach. He clenched his fists until his fingernails dug into the palms of his hands. "Nothing's ever *gut* enough for you, is it?"

"And you've never understood what I've been telling you all these years. Mostly because you haven't listened."

"I'm listening now!"

His father stared straight ahead but didn't say another word.

Zach clenched his teeth. He couldn't remember being this furious before. Couldn't his father see he was trying? Did he even care? He seemed to think more of Johnny Mullet, the kid he'd hired to work in his shop, than his own son. More than once Zach heard his father say how pleased he was with Johnny's work. Each compliment dug at Zach. When he was younger, his brothers had been praised by his father, and Zach had hoped one day he would be praised too. But after to-night, that seemed impossible.

"Are you sure you want to get here this early?" Stephen asked.

Ruth looked at her brother, who had agreed to give her a ride this morning. She frowned at him.

Her nerves were already frazzled. "*Ya*. I want to get here this early."

Stephen held up his hand, his expression wary. "Sorry for asking."

She let out a long sigh. "*Nee*, I'm sorry."

"You're not nervous, are you?"

"Of course not." She fumbled with her purse and her satchel, both of them slipping from her grip. She picked them up again. "Can you pick me up this afternoon?"

He nodded. "What time?"

"Four?"

"See you then."

She got out of the buggy.

"Ruth?"

She turned and looked at him. He gave her a smile. "*Gut* luck. You'll do a *gut* job with the *kinner*. If anyone was born to be a teacher, it's you."

She nodded and managed a smile as Stephen drove away. Despite her brother's vote of confidence, she felt a stab of doubt. She'd spent most of her life preparing for this day, and she'd prayed over each and every one of her students last night before going to bed. Yet in spite of that, it felt like a hundred butterflies were dancing a jig inside her stomach. She reassured herself that everything would go smoothly today. She had formulated a contingency plan for every problem she could think of, and her lessons were ready. As long as nothing unexpected happened, everything would be okay. Yet she couldn't get rid of those annoying butterflies.

As Stephen drove off, Ruth balanced her purse and the heavy satchel on one arm and fished for her schoolhouse key. The weight of both bags threw her off balance. Her purse and satchel fell off of her arm, hitting the ground. The satchel had been fastened shut, but the contents of her purse were scattered on the small concrete stoop. She squatted and placed everything neatly back inside. Once everything was where it belonged, she grabbed her bags and stood up, reached for her key—

Oh no! Where was her key?

She dropped her satchel and riffled through her purse. It wasn't there. She knelt and searched the ground where she'd dropped her things. The key must have bounced off the concrete and fallen in the nearby grass. She ran her hands through the blades on both sides, expecting to see a glint of gold winking at her. When she didn't, panic set in, and she searched again, frantic this time. Fifteen minutes later she stood up. Her key was nowhere to be found.

Surely she hadn't left it at the house. She racked her brain as she mentally went through her evening and morning rituals. Last night she had cleaned out her purse, something she did every Sunday evening. Was the key in there at that time? Her hands pressed against the sides of her head. Why couldn't she remember?

Over and over she went through her routine, but nothing jogged her memory. How could she be so thoughtless? How could she have not paid attention to where she put the key to the schoolhouse?

She started to pace, trying to figure out what to do. Maybe she could climb in a window. She couldn't believe she was even contemplating it, but she was desperate.

Ruth walked to the window on the side of the small white building. Hopefully Zachariah hadn't locked it after finishing his repairs yesterday, which is what she would have done. She hadn't seen him since the runaway horse incident, and she'd spent the last few days preparing for school and trying to forget about him. She had nearly succeeded, but last night he'd had the nerve to pop up in her dreams. When she woke up, she couldn't remember the specifics of the dream, only that he had again slipped into her subconscious.

She shook her head to clear her mind. Why was she thinking about Zachariah at a time like this?

She stretched her arms up and tried to shove

open the window. At five foot four, she couldn't reach it easily. On her third try, she managed to lift the sash enough for her body to squeeze through. Now she just had to figure out a way to crawl in.

She looked around for something to stand on, but there was nothing in sight, not even an old pail or a large rock. Somehow she'd have to scramble inside on her own. Gripping the window ledge, she counted to three, then jumped and pulled up her body. Leaning forward, she stuck her head through the opening, only to bump it on the bottom of the sash.

"Ow!" Several drops of perspiration ran down her face. It might be morning, but it was still hot, even during the beginning of September. Her dress started to cling to her skin in the heat. Ruth breathed in and steadied herself. *Lord, I promise I will never, ever forget my key again! Just help me get through this window!* Ducking her head further, she started to climb through when she felt something land on her back, pinning her against the ledge and knocking the wind out of her. "Oof."

She gasped, then shifted and tried to open the window by bowing her back. The *dumm* thing wouldn't move. Then she tried to climb the rest of the way through the window, but the sash pinned her in place. A bead of sweat trickled down her nose.

Panicked, she tried to budge the window again, but no matter how she twisted her body, it wouldn't move. She was wedged in tight. Kicking out her legs, she searched for leverage on the outside of the building, but the rubber soles of her shoes slid right off the wood siding.

Her face was aflame. Soon her students would show up, and she couldn't let them see her with half her body hanging out of the window. This was not the way to make a professional impression on her class.

But her students were the least of her problems; the pressure from being sandwiched between the window and ledge was putting a strain on her back and stomach. Becoming more desperate, she tried everything she could think of to break free. She kicked, pulled, arched, flexed, groaned, grunted, and nearly burst into tears as she tried to move the window resting on her back. Nothing worked, and now she could barely breathe. Light-headed and gulping air, she ended up doing the only thing she could. Cars and buggies traveled up and down this road all the time. Closing her eyes, she started to pray that someone would see her and come to her rescue.

"Ma! *Ma!*"

The sound of Will's voice brought Deborah out of a heavy sleep. She opened her sticky eyes and squinted at her son across the room. He was standing in his new crib, gripping the side and looking at her with an expectant expression. "Ma!"

"All right, *sohn*, I hear you." She sat up in bed, and her long braid tumbled over her shoulder, the end landing in her lap. She blinked a few times, struggling to wake up. She'd gone to bed early last night, at the same time as Will, suffering from a pounding headache. Thankfully, her head didn't hurt anymore. Glancing at the window, she saw a bright ray of sunlight streaming through the glass. She frowned. There wasn't a clock in the room. How long had she slept?

Will started to grunt, spurring Deborah to get up and take him out of the crib. She changed his diaper and carried him out of the bedroom. Maybe Naomi might let her help with the meal this morning, although she doubted it. Over the past two days she had offered to help out so many times she lost track, but each time her sister refused. Naomi had staked the house as her domain.

As she made her way downstairs, sadness seeped into her. Her aunt was leaving today. The only person Deborah could talk to about her mother. Her father had been subdued since the funeral, saying very little and retiring early. Deborah was worried about him, but she didn't know what to do. The only person who didn't seem affected by everything was her sister. Naomi hadn't even mentioned their mother one time.

The scent of bacon frying made her belly grumble. Naomi had already started breakfast without her. Deborah sighed. She wondered if their relationship would ever be repaired.

But when she walked into the kitchen, it wasn't Naomi standing at the stove. *"Aenti?"*

Sadie turned around, both hands covered in quilted oven mitts, one hand holding a spatula. Her wardrobe was more subdued than usual: a white pair of pedal pushers topped with a bright pink T-shirt that said *Growing old is mandatory, growing up is optional.* She wore a turquoise kerchief on her head, but Deborah didn't know if she was sporting it as a fashion accessory or in deference to staying in an Amish home. "Good morning, sunshine!" A bright smile formed on her red lips.

Deborah frowned, suspicious. "What's going on, *Aenti*?"

Sadie's curled black lashes batted up and down. "Nothing, dear. How would you like your eggs? Overly sunny-side, or hard up?"

"What?"

"I meant sunny-side up or overly hard. Or is it overly easy?"

"Maybe scrambled would be easier." She took

a slice of homemade bread from the plate on the table, tore it into pieces, and put them on a paper napkin in front of Will. He started stuffing the bits into his mouth. "I can make breakfast, *Aenti*."

"You'll do no such thing." Sadie put her oven-mitt-covered hand on one ample hip. "I might only cook once a decade, but I can handle this myself. It's only eggs and bacon. How hard can they be?"

"The bacon's burning."

Sniffing the air, Sadie whirled around. Deborah moved beside her, spotting four pieces of black, shriveled meat in a frying pan of smoking grease.

"Dear heavens." Sadie fumbled with the knob on the gas stove, which was turned up to high, but she couldn't get a grip on it with the oven mitt. Deborah reached over and turned the burner off, but clouds of smoke hovered over the stove.

Sadie sighed. "Oh well. I never was a big fan of bacon anyway. Guess we'll have to settle for eggs and bread."

Deborah took the spatula from Sadie. "Why don't you sit down with Will and I'll make us all something."

Sadie nodded, slipping off the oven mitts and putting them on the counter near the stove. "Can't say I didn't try."

"And I love you for it." Deborah smiled and turned to the stove.

"Wait, don't worry about fixing anything for me," Sadie said from behind her. "I already ate."

"Oh?" Deborah glanced over her shoulder before picking up a brown egg and cracking it into the cast-iron skillet. The clear liquid immediately turned white. Deborah swiftly turned down the burner. Knowing her aunt preferred not to rise very early in the morning, she asked, "Did you go out to eat for breakfast?"

"Um, not exactly."

Her aunt's strange tone made Deborah turn all the way around. "What do you mean?"

"What she means is that I already had it made." Naomi came into the kitchen, carrying a small stack of folded kitchen towels. "At six a.m. The proper time for breakfast."

"There's no proper time for breakfast, Naomi." Sadie poured Will a glass of milk from the pitcher on the table and held it for him while he drank. "People eat when they're hungry."

"In an Amish home there is." She yanked open one of the cabinet drawers and put the towels inside. "We don't have time to lounge around all day in bed when there's so much work to be done."

Deborah glanced at the clock on the wall opposite the sink. 7:00 a.m. Had she really slept that long? Normally she was up by five every day. Naomi did have the right to be irritated. "I'm sorry. I didn't realize I'd slept so late."

"You've got nothing to apologize for." Sadie took the empty glass from Will and stood up. She glared at Naomi's back. "Obviously you needed the sleep."

Naomi turned around but didn't look at Sadie. Instead she scanned the kitchen, her expression growing harder by the second. "I just cleaned up and now look. The kitchen stinks from the bacon you burned, there are crumbs all over the table—"

"I burned the—"

"*Aenti,*" Deborah said, holding up her hand. She flicked off the burner under the eggs before they overcooked and faced Naomi. "You're right, I should have gotten up earlier. I'll clean up the mess."

Naomi crossed her arms over her tiny waist. "I'll do it. I've seen the way you clean." She walked over to the stove, picked up the pan of partially cooked eggs, and dumped them in the wastebasket by the back door. Before Deborah could say anything, her sister had put the pan in the sink and was running water over it.

"Why would you—" Sadie started for Naomi, but Deborah stepped in front of her. The last thing she wanted was for her aunt and sister to argue in front of Will.

"It's okay," Deborah said in a low voice.

"No, it's not," Sadie whispered back. "She did that on purpose." Sadie looked around Deborah's shoulder at Naomi, who had her back to them while she scrubbed the frying pan.

"Probably, but I'll talk to her." Deborah guided her aunt to the table and continued to whisper. "Will needs more than bread for breakfast. I've got some raisins in my bag. He can have those until I can fix him something else."

"Never mind the raisins." She picked Will up and perched him on her hip. "We're going out to breakfast." When Deborah shook her head, she held up her free hand. "No arguments." She tilted her head toward Naomi. "Let her stew by herself."

"You and Will go ahead. I have to stay and talk to her."

"Suit yourself. I think you're wasting your time. She's past reasoning with."

When Sadie and Will left the kitchen, Deborah turned to Naomi. "You and I need to talk."

Naomi didn't say anything, just rinsed the pan and set it in the dish drainer. When she moved to go to the stove, Deborah touched her arm. "I don't want to fight anymore, Naomi. I'd like us to be friends."

"Friends?" Naomi rolled her eyes and pulled from her grasp. "We're sisters. We don't have to be friends."

"Then at least we have to be civil to each other. For *Daed's* and Will's sakes."

"If you don't like how things are here, you're free to leave." She grabbed the dishrag and started wiping down the table. "It's not like you haven't done it before."

"I don't want to leave. I want to stay and help out you and *Daed*."

"We don't need your help." She scrubbed the rag against the table. "We've been doing fine since you've been gone."

"But now that I'm here, I can take some of the load off of you."

Naomi hurried to the sink and shook out the rag. Bread crumbs fell into the soapy water, and Deborah wondered why her sister hadn't dumped the crumbs into the trash can like she normally did. Then Naomi dropped the rag in the sink and faced Deborah. "Your *sohn* is needy and sloppy and messy. All he does is make more work for me."

"He's a *boppli*, Naomi. Of course he's going to need things and be sloppy. I don't expect you to watch after him anyway."

"*Gut*, because I won't take care of him. He's your responsibility, not mine."

"I know that." She didn't understand where Naomi's vehemence was coming from. She was acting as if Will was an unwanted animal instead of her nephew. And as committed to the Amish as her sister was, she should understand that children, all children, were to be treasured and nurtured. "I'll try to keep Will out of your way."

"See that you do." She looked straight at Deborah. "We're living under the same roof, and that's it. So don't try to be friends with me, or involve me in your problems, or act like you want to be helpful. I'm not interested. I have my own life to live." She stalked out of the room.

Deborah stood in the kitchen, dumbfounded by what had just happened. Maybe Sadie had been right; her sister was beyond reasoning with. She just didn't understand why.

Chapter Ten

Zach tapped the reins lightly against Maggie's flanks. She picked up her steps and trotted down the road. Thankfully she'd recovered from her scare the other day. Ruth had called flying over a meadow in a runaway buggy "an adventure." It certainly had been an adventure all right, one he didn't care to repeat.

Normally he'd be on his way to the buggy shop, but he remembered last night that he'd planned to fix the window in the schoolhouse before Ruth and her students arrived this morning. Last week, it had fallen down without warning several times, and he'd told himself he needed to fix it before school reopened. It just kept slipping his mind. So he'd left home early, planning to stop at the school, fix the window, then head over to Kline's for half a day's work.

He was grateful for his new job. The supplies

to repair the school hadn't been cheap, and he had purchased them all on credit. He intended to pay everyone back as soon as possible. That meant working as many hours as he could. It would help if he had another job. He'd even thought about asking his father if he had any extra work, but after their conversation Saturday night, Zach wouldn't bother. His *daed* would rather pay someone who wasn't a part of the family than pay him.

He forced the thoughts from his mind. He didn't want to think about how his father was still disappointed in him. He wasn't about to let his *daed* or anyone else spoil today.

Zach started whistling a church hymn, taking in the bright sunshine and cloudless sky. This kind of day breathed from the heavens, his grandfather used to say. He never paid much attention to the phrase before, but now he understood what his grandfather meant. Something was changing inside Zach. He had worked harder than he ever had in his life, and the sense of accomplishment brought a joy he'd never experienced before. He finally understood what his father meant by gaining satisfaction through a job well done, even if his *daed* refused to recognize Zach's accomplishment.

He passed by a large white Amish house set far back from the road, its dirt drive winding through a green field of short grass. Just past the house was a huge field filled with leafy, green cornstalks that had been picked clean and left to turn brown. Everything around him was bathed in sunlight, which warmed him in the black buggy. He pushed back his hat, letting the breeze cool his damp forehead. Hot already. It was going to be a scorcher today.

His thoughts skidded to a stop when he saw the schoolhouse. As his buggy neared, he gave his head a quick shake. Was he seeing things? Had to be. There was no way a woman's legs were dangling out the window of the schoolhouse.

He blinked again, but he still saw them. Black shoes, black knee socks, and a light gray dress draped over her calves. Good grief, was that Ruth? He spurred Maggie onward. When he whipped into the drive, he couldn't keep his eyes off the window and the slender woman hanging halfway out of it.

He reined his horse to a stop and dashed out of the buggy. "Ruth!"

The legs started kicking harder, making her dress sway. "Help!" came a muffled voice from inside the building.

He yanked up the heavy window, put his hands on her small waist, and pulled her out, placing her on the ground in front of him. The window immediately slammed shut.

Ruth bent over, gasping for air. He moved closer to her. "Ruth, are you all right?"

She stood and pressed her hand against her stomach. A few seconds later, she took a couple of deep breaths then turned and faced him. To his relief, she seemed okay. How had she climbed in the window anyway? He looked around, expecting to see the metal tub from the shed underneath the window, but it wasn't there. She must have stood on something, unless she'd hoisted herself on her own. Her cheeks were flushed, and her skin was shiny with perspiration. Her white apron was twisted to the side, and strands of her hair had loosened from her *kapp*. But she wasn't hurt. This was the second time he'd seen her looking disheveled, and he had to admit he kind of liked it. She looked pretty...cute.

Her surprised gaze met his as she took a couple more big breaths. "Zachariah?"

A lock of her hair lay partly over her left brow bone, almost covering her eye. Without thinking, he reached up and brushed it back, the side of his hand gliding against her heated cheek. His breath hitched. He meant to sweep it behind her ear, but before he could, she caught his hand in hers, holding it for a second before pushing it away.

His face grew hotter than a gas heater in

winter. What in the world had gotten into him? She moved away from him until she was pressed against the schoolhouse. He steeled himself for her anger. If she'd ever had a reason to be upset with him—and lately he'd given her plenty of reasons—it was now. He had no right to touch her, and yet he'd done it twice. She probably thought he was a complete *dummkopf*. Or that he was trying to take advantage of her.

But she didn't say a word, and her expression didn't reveal anything close to anger. At first he saw confusion in her eyes, then an emotion he couldn't immediately define. Then he saw...nothing.

She straightened, adjusted her apron, and tucked another loose strand of hair behind her other ear. "*Danki*, Zachariah." No longer breathless, her tone was formal, as if she were addressing a stranger. "Why are you here?"

He rubbed the back of his neck, his skin growing slick not only from the heat of the day, but from trying to hide his embarrassment at being so impulsive. He wasn't like Ruth, who apparently could turn her emotions on and off with ease. He needed more than a few seconds to compose himself. "I, uh, I was on my way to, um, work." Great, now his tongue wasn't cooperating. He was making an all-out fool of himself. "I stopped by to, uh, fix the window."

"Fix the window?" Her eyes narrowed ever so slightly. "You knew the window was broken?"

"Ah, *ya*. I meant to repair it the other day but I, um, forgot. But I can fix it now." He tried to smile, but he was only half successful.

Her chin rose. "It's…" She cleared her throat. "It's all right."

But Zach didn't believe her. "It's not all right. I should have fixed that window long before. Why were you hanging out of it anyway?"

Her eyes darted downward. "I forgot my key."

"I have mine. I can let you in." Glad to do something useful, he walked around to the front of the school. Ruth followed right behind him. He dug inside the pocket of his pants and pulled out a key ring with two keys: one belonging to the school and the other for the buggy shop. *Herr* Kline had given him the key on Saturday when he had arrived at work. Zachariah had taken that as a sign that Kline thought he was responsible. But where had that responsibility been when it came to fixing the window? If he had remembered to repair and lock it, Ruth would have been waiting outside the door instead of hanging out of the window. And if he hadn't come by when he had…he didn't want to think about that.

He turned and looked at her as she picked up her purse, then reached for a big, black leather bag. "I can get that for you."

"I've got it." She grabbed the bag and headed for the entrance.

"All right. It should only take me a minute to fix the window." He started to go inside, but she stopped him.

"I need to prepare for my class," she said. "Could you come back later today and fix the window?"

"Are you sure? It's going to get hot in there."

"I'll leave the door open."

"Hang on a minute." He dashed into the school and breathed in the lingering scent of fresh paint. He inspected the window on the opposite side of the room, then called out, "Do you have a ruler?"

"Wooden or plastic?"

He smiled. Leave it to her to have both kinds. "Wooden will work." When she handed it to him, he opened the window and stuck the wooden ruler upright in the corner, letting the window rest on top of it. After he checked to make sure it would hold, he turned and faced her. "That should stay open until I come back."

She peered at his quick fix and nodded.

He moved toward her but made sure there was a decent amount of space between them this time. "I'm really sorry about the window. I promise I'll take care of it this afternoon."

"School ends at three o'clock. You can come after then." Ruth walked over to her desk. "Now, if you'll excuse me, I've got to get started. I'm behind as it is."

"Right." He walked toward the door, giving the schoolroom a quick scan as he went. With the freshly painted wall, new flooring, and a couple of secondhand but high quality wooden bookshelves he'd gotten for a decent price, he had to admit everything looked pretty good. He had one foot in the doorway when he heard her speak.

"*Danki*, Zachariah."

He turned and looked at her. She stood behind her desk, her hands folded in front of her white apron, which was slightly wrinkled but still looked nice on her. "Zach," he suddenly said.

"What?"

"I wish you would call me Zach. Zachariah is too much of a mouthful."

Looking unsure, she said, "All right…Zach."

He thought she might say something else, but instead she pulled out her chair and sat down. She opened a desk drawer and pulled out a stack of file folders and placed them on her desk.

Looks like I'm dismissed. But as he turned to walk out the door, out of the corner of his eye, he caught her glancing at him. He grinned. Maybe she wasn't as emotionless as he thought.

After Zachariah—*Zach*, she had to remind herself—left the school, Ruth fluttered around the classroom making sure everything was in place but feeling like her life was completely out of control. Getting stuck in the window had thrown off the rhythm of her day. But that wasn't the only thing flustering her. She had Zach to thank for knocking her completely off-kilter.

But he'd showed up just when she needed him. While she wanted to be irritated with him for not repairing the window, she couldn't. In fact, she couldn't stop thinking about him. He had actually touched her cheek. Not a simple touch either, more like a tender caress. And to her surprise, she *enjoyed* it. That didn't make sense at all.

She put her fingertips to her temples, as if the pressure could derail her thoughts. She had no business thinking about Zach that way, or in any way. She couldn't possibly be attracted to him, much less like him. They were complete opposites; anyone could see that. She must've been oxygen-deprived while she'd been trapped in the window.

Fifteen minutes before school was scheduled to start, she could hear voices outside. Forcing her mind to focus on her job, she walked over to the window and looked out onto the playground, where a simple wooden play set stood to the right. Several students romped around the yard, many of them barefoot, their shoes lined up near the schoolhouse. Watching them running around calmed her down. She was finally getting the chance to teach. She said a quick prayer and called for the children to come inside, pleased when they complied.

She directed the younger children to the desks near the front. Once those were filled, she told the older students to sit at the long table Zach had set up, apologizing for the lack of desks and promising they would have their own as soon as possible. When everyone was seated, she moved to the front of the room and faced the class.

Suddenly her mouth went dry. All eyes were on her. Expecting her to say something. To do something. Her gaze darted around the group of children, who ranged in age from six to thirteen. Twenty children. Eight grades. What made her think she could do this? When she didn't say anything right away, they started to whisper.

Dear Lord, help me. Take these nerves away.

The prayer calmed her enough to say, "*Gut morgen, kinner.*" She moved over to the board where she had written her name. "I'm *Fraulien* Byler. B-Y-L-E-R." She touched each letter as she spelled it out. "I'm your new teacher this year." She looked at them and smiled.

"We already know your name." Eight-year-old Billy Stoltzfus rubbed his nose.

"We always see you at church," Sarah, Billy's six-year-old sister, added.

Ruth paused. "Um, *ya*, you do. But since this is our first day of school, I thought a formal introduction would be appropriate." Her students stared back at her, confused expressions on their faces. "And, uh, we're going to have a great time learning to be *gut* and diligent students."

Lori Fisher raised her tiny hand. The towheaded girl was her youngest student, barely six. "What does *dilibent* mean?"

"Not 'dilibent.' *Diligent. Diligent* means to take *gut* care of your work. To do it to the best of your ability, thoroughly, and turn it in on time."

"And what if we don't?"

Ruth looked up at an older boy sitting as far in the back of the room as possible. He was slouching in his seat, his arms crossed over his chest, a sullen expression on his face. She didn't recognize him. "What if we don't what?"

"Be diligent. What happens if we aren't?"

The question threw her off guard. She wasn't expecting this on the first day, and certainly not within the first five minutes of class. Actually she wasn't expecting the question at all. "Well..." She put on her reading glasses, then picked up her seating chart from her desk. Jacob Kline. Now she remembered him, the son of the owner of Kline's Buggy Shop. "Jacob, if you're not diligent, then you'll have to face the consequences."

"What consequences?"

"I was just about to explain those to all of you." Taking the segue, she explained the classroom rules to her pupils, most of whom listened with interest, or at least pretended to. She glanced at the back of the room a couple of times and noticed Jacob had put his head down on his arms, which were lying on the table.

"Jacob, I would appreciate if you give me your attention while I'm talking."

"I'm paying attention." With his face covered by his arms, his voice was muffled.

"It doesn't look that way to me. When you're paying attention to someone, you're looking directly at them."

He lifted his head and stared at her with belligerence, his gray eyes piercing her. "Better?"

She didn't speak for a moment, confused by the anger she saw in his eyes. "*Ya*," she finally said slowly, trying to figure out the best way to react to him. "*Danki.*"

He tilted his head to the side and continued to stare at her, as if in challenge. She pulled her gaze away and tried to focus on the other nineteen students who were being more cooperative.

She spent the rest of the morning passing out textbooks and giving a writing assignment. Fortunately that process went smoothly. When she finished, she said, "I'd like you to spend the next several minutes writing about your summer break. You might have noticed each of you has a brand-new spiral notebook and pencil on either your desk or the table."

Jacob had put his head back down, refusing to touch the notebook. Not knowing what else to do, she ignored him. "These are your writing journals. You can put your first assignment in them. First graders, I want you to draw a picture of something fun you did on your summer vacation. The rest of you will write at least a paragraph." She went to the blackboard and picked up a piece of white chalk. "I'd like you to write this heading at the top of the page: your name, date, Writing Assignment 1." She heard the sound of something hitting the floor and she turned around. "What was that?"

Billy raised his hand. "Jacob shoved his notebook on the floor."

Ruth expected Jacob to refute Billy's claim, but he didn't. Instead he stared at her with utter defiance. Her blood pressure started to spike and she fought to remain calm. "Jacob, please pick up your journal and start your writing assignment."

He looked at her for a moment, then stomped his foot on top of the journal. "Oops." Sarcasm dripped from the word. But he didn't pick up the notebook.

Ruth wasn't sure what to do. Should she yell at him? The books she'd read about classroom management and discipline warned that yelling would only escalate the problem. She'd never met a child like this. Amish children were taught to be respectful to their elders. Although she wasn't more than a few years older than Jacob, she still deserved his respect. "*Kinner*, please start on your assignments. Jacob, I'd like to see you outside for a moment."

Jacob sauntered to the front of the schoolhouse, then out the door. Ruth followed. But Jacob didn't turn around or stop like she expected him to. Instead, he kept on walking.

"Jacob," she said loudly, but he continued to walk away. She started after him but realized she couldn't leave her other students to chase after him. "Come back here!"

He kept on walking toward the road.

Her eyes widened, and something inside her started to roil. How dare he? Struggling to slow her heart rate, she balled her fists and counted to ten. Then twenty. Finally when she hit thirty-five, she was calm enough to go inside.

School had only been in session for two hours, and already she felt like a failure.

Zach steered his buggy toward the schoolhouse at three o'clock sharp. Before he turned in the driveway, though, he watched the students pour out of the building and head off in different directions. Some of the little ones ran in the grass on the side of the road while the older ones hovered behind them, making sure they stayed out of harm's way.

Zach grinned, wistful. As much trouble as he'd had in school, he missed some of those carefree days, when he used to race his friends down the street or stop off in an open field and play a pickup game of baseball. He usually arrived home late, but the trouble he got in was worth it. Sometimes.

He tied his horse to the hitching post and got out. What he saw when he walked inside stopped him in his tracks. The schoolhouse was pretty much the way he'd left it, and the ruler had remained in the window, letting in the fresh air. But what surprised him was seeing Ruth at her desk, her head resting in her hands. He frowned and took a step forward. She jerked up her head at the sound of his boot heel hitting the floor.

"Oh!" She sat up and turned to him, her arm brushing against a stack of spiral notebooks on her desk. The stack tilted, then fell to the floor.

In three steps he was beside her desk. She had jumped out of her chair, and they both knelt down and picked up the notebooks, grasping the last one at the same time. His fingers slid across the top of her hand. Even though the contact was quick, he could feel the smoothness of her skin.

His gaze met hers. There it was again, the vulnerability he'd seen after his horse got spooked. At that time she'd been afraid. What was she afraid of now?

She shot to her feet and put the notebooks on her desk. When he handed her the three he'd picked up, she took them from him, saying thank you in a small voice. But she didn't look at him. She kept her focus on the pile of notebooks, rearranging and straightening them into a perfect stack. He noticed a slight tremble in her hands.

"Is everything all right?" He took a step toward her, and at the same time, she moved away.

"*Ya*, everything is fine. How long will it take you to fix the window?"

"Not long." He had carried his tool belt with him, and after a brief pause, he walked by her desk on the way to the window. He set his tools on the floor then stole a glance at her. She was still standing, gazing at the stack of notebooks. "Are you sure you're okay?"

"I'm fine." She looked up at him. "Please fix the window, okay?"

He still didn't believe her, but he'd been around Ruth enough to know that if something was bothering her, she wouldn't admit it. He removed the ruler, catching the window before it slammed down.

Behind him he heard the sound of chair legs moving against the floor. He turned and saw that she had sat down on her chair and was looking through one of the notebooks, a red pen in her hand. She picked up her glasses from the desk and put them on. He hadn't seen her wear them very often, and he thought they flattered her face. He was starting to like a lot of things about Ruth Byler, and he couldn't decide if that pleased or disturbed him. Right now it was a good mix of both.

Focusing his attention on the window, he discovered the problem and groaned. It would have to be replaced. He picked up his tool belt and walked over to Ruth. "Done for the day."

She looked up at him, her blue eyes filling with surprise behind her glasses. Wow, she really did look pretty in those things. "Already?"

"*Ya*. The frame is splitting. I could try to repair it, but it will start falling again. I'll bring a new one in tomorrow."

She peered at him. "You don't have to do that."

"I do. There's also a two-inch gap around the sash. In the winter it will let in a draft—"

"That's not what I mean." She removed her glasses. "The window isn't your responsibility. It wasn't damaged in the accident, so you don't have to replace it. I can let Gabriel know it's broken and the school board will take care of it."

Zach waved off her suggestion. "Don't bother them with it. It's not a big deal to pick up a window and put it in."

"But you shouldn't have to pay for it."

"I don't mind."

Her brow lifted. "Did you get a raise at the buggy shop?"

She had him there. "Ah, *nee*. But I know where I can get a good window at a fair price, so it's fine. I can take care of it."

"All right. If you're sure."

"I'm positive." And he was. So what if it cost him a little more money and time? It was worth the good feeling he had right now. "Let me show you how to prop it open for tomorrow morning."

She followed him to the window, and he opened it with one hand, keeping it up. With the other, he handed her the ruler. "Just put it in the corner."

"Here?"

"Yep."

Ruth placed the ruler in the corner as he instructed, and he let go of the window. As soon as he did, the ruler snapped in half. Ruth's hand was still on the ledge, and he grabbed and moved it before the window slammed down on it. He started to let go, but then he felt the light pressure of her fingers on his, as if she didn't want him to let go. Then she slipped her hand out of his grasp.

Had he imagined it? No, he hadn't. His hand tingled from the memory of her warm touch. "I'm sorry, Ruth. I didn't know that was going to happen."

"I must have put it in wrong. Or the wood weakened from the pressure of holding it up all day." She turned away from him. "Or…"

The way her voice faded pulled at him. It wasn't like her to express self-doubt. "Ruth." He touched her shoulder, not caring if she shrugged him off. When she didn't, he asked, "Did something happen today?"

She shook her head, then turned around, her expression strained. "I said everything's fine."

"It doesn't seem that way." He dropped his hand from her shoulder. "Is there anything I can do to help?"

Ruth opened her mouth, but nothing came out. She pressed her lips together and shook her head. "I've got to *geh*." She brushed past him and hurried to her desk, grabbed her purse, then ran out the door.

Puzzled, he walked to her desk, noticing she'd left her satchel and glasses behind. Not to mention the door wide open. That wasn't like Ruth at all.

He picked up her glasses and gently folded the

arms, taking care not to touch the lenses. Something was going on with Ruth, and he intended to find out what.

Chapter Eleven

"I told you I'd come pick you up." Stephen cast a glance at Ruth as he started the buggy moving again. "Why were you walking home?"

Ruth didn't answer him right away. She'd walked almost a mile down the road when she saw Stephen heading toward her. He pulled over and she ran to the buggy. But maybe she should have kept going instead. She'd been walking to avoid Zachariah and his questions, only to have to hear them from Stephen. She closed her eyes. Would this day never end?

"Ruth, what's going on?"

"Nix." How many times did she have to say that before someone would understand?

"I don't believe you. I know *mei glee schwester* and—"

"Don't call me that! I'm not a *kinn*, I'm a grown

woman!" She balled her fists and fought the burning pain in her throat.

"I'm sorry." Stephen's deep voice was nearly inaudible. "I didn't mean anything by it."

She knew he didn't, but right now she was so upset she couldn't speak. From the time she forgot her key, the entire day had spiraled into a waking nightmare. After Jacob left, she'd had to keep two brothers from fighting with each other, she caught one girl copying math answers from the boy sitting next to her, and little Lori Fisher frequently burst into tears because she missed her *mami*. By the end of the day she hadn't completed a single objective in her lesson plan, and she was ready to drop with exhaustion. If she couldn't be successful on her first day, how was she going to manage her classroom for an entire school term?

And then there was Zachariah Bender. As if her reaction to him this morning hadn't been enough, this afternoon she had to fight more conflicting emotions than she knew what to do with. His offer to replace the window, the way he snatched her hand before the window slammed on it, the low, concerned tone of his voice when he asked her if she was okay. She'd even squeezed his hand! She'd never touched a man's hand before, much less squeezed one while wishing she didn't have to let go. None of it made any sense.

"Ruth? I really am sorry. I didn't mean to upset you."

She looked at her brother, taking in the uncomfortable expression on his face. It was unfair for her to take her frustration out on him. "I know, Stephen. I've just had a bad day."

He paused. "Want to talk about it?"

"Nee."

"Okay. But if you do, let me know." He gave her an encouraging smile and focused on the road ahead.

She leaned back in the seat and closed her eyes. They flew open a second later when she realized she'd left her satchel at the schoolhouse. And the notebooks she was supposed to grade. And her glasses. They were halfway home by now, so she couldn't ask Stephen to turn around, even though he probably would if she did. She would have to trust that Zachariah would lock the schoolhouse. After all, he had been keeping his word lately. She said a quick prayer that he would remember.

By the time they reached home, she had calmed down, for the most part. Tonight she would regroup and make sure she was completely prepared, key and all. Then she would try to relax a little bit. But that thought flew out of her head when she remembered Jacob Kline. She had to talk to his parents tonight. Walking out of school the way he did today was inexcusable. She turned to Stephen. "Are you using the buggy tonight?"

"*Ya.* I'm going to the Coblentzes' again. Moses has had a hard time of it lately."

Ruth's mood turned even more somber. The problems of her life were insignificant compared to losing a loved one.

Stephen made a right turn onto their road. "Why?"

"I have to *geh* somewhere after supper." She didn't want to reveal the details, and she was glad he didn't ask for them.

"I know *Mami* and *Daed* are planning to visit Aaron and Elisabeth tonight." Stephen scratched his cheek. "Where do you have to *geh*? Maybe I can drop you off?" When she told him he shook his head. "That's in the opposite direction of the Coblentzes' farm. Do you have to *geh die nacht*?"

"I guess not." Hopefully Jacob would be in school tomorrow and the two of them could work this out. Perhaps she wouldn't have to get his parents involved just yet, although she fully intended to let them know about his behavior as soon as she could.

After Stephen left, her parents invited her to come with them to Aaron and Elisabeth's, but she wasn't in the mood. Once they were gone, she went upstairs and tried to relax, but she couldn't, her mind still racing from the day. Her bedroom suddenly became stifling, and she went down-stairs to the front porch and sat in the swing, hoping the fresh air of the evening would help. She'd been there only a few minutes when a buggy turned into her driveway, pulled by a chestnut-colored horse with a white spot between her eyes. Maggie.

She left the swing and met Zachariah as he pulled his buggy to a stop. "What are you doing here?"

He looked at her, a smirk on his face. "Hello to you too."

Her cheeks heated. "I'm sorry. I'm just surprised to see you."

"I was on my way home and thought you might be needing this." He handed her the satchel through the buggy opening. "Your glasses and the notebooks are in there too."

She took it from him, shocked. "*Danki*. You didn't have to make a special trip out here."

"I didn't mind. It's a nice evening. I figured you didn't mean to leave that stuff behind."

She wasn't sure what to say. Who would have thought Zachariah Bender could be so considerate? She certainly hadn't. "I did need these. I can't read without my glasses."

"Then I'm glad I got them to you." He smiled.

Earlier in the day she had marveled at his eyes, but they were nothing compared to his smile. Her stomach started fluttering and her mouth suddenly went dry, as if she'd had sawdust for dessert.

"Well, now that I've made my delivery, I'll be on my way." But as he reached for the reins, she decided she didn't want him to go.

"Would you like some lemonade? *Mami* just made some before she and *Daed* left to visit Elisabeth. It's *appeditlich*."

His brow lifted. "*Danki*, I am thirsty. I'll take some for the road."

"Actually, I wondered if you might like to stay. For a little bit," she quickly added, surprised by her boldness. Where had that invitation come from?

He hesitated for a moment. "I guess…sure."

She hid a frown. He didn't have to sound so excited about it. Of course he was probably only being polite. Now she wished she hadn't said anything. "It's all right. You don't have to."

"*Nee*, I want to."

Her gaze flew to him. His tone was a little more eager, but not by much. She'd never felt so awkward in her life. If only she'd kept her mouth shut.

"Where should I park?"

"There's a spot behind the house, near the barn." She directed him down the asphalt driveway, which lay between her house and her father's woodworking shop. Zachariah and Maggie disappeared behind the house.

Ruth took a deep breath and went inside. As she poured two glasses of lemonade, she fought the discomfort spreading through her. She and Zachariah had nothing in common. What would they talk about? Her palms grew slick. Hopefully he would drink the lemonade quickly and be on his way. Never, ever would she be this impulsive again. The embarrassment was unbearable.

"I wish you didn't have to leave." Deborah fought back tears as she gave Sadie a huge hug. Her aunt had delayed her departure for most of the day, but now she was ready to head back to Paradise.

"I wish I didn't have to go either. But I can't take any more time from work. You have no idea how crabby my boss can be when he's short employees." She shook her head. "I work in a little grocery store, for Pete's sake. The world won't end if I'm not there."

"You're not in trouble, are you?"

"No, I'm fine. He's like a firecracker. All pop, very little sizzle."

She stepped back from her aunt. "*Danki* for everything you've done. I couldn't have gotten through this without you."

Sadie cupped Deborah's chin, tears welling in

her eyes. "I didn't do much. Not near enough." She looked past Deborah's shoulder to the front porch.

Deborah followed her gaze to see her *daed* sitting on the front porch. He'd brought the hickory rocking chair outside yesterday evening, and now he had Will on his lap. Moses put his hat on the boy's small head, but Will kept yanking it off, bringing a ghost of a smile to his grandfather's face.

"I told you that child would be good for Moses." She looked back at Deborah. "He's having such a hard time now. Make sure you look after him. I don't trust Naomi to do it."

"I will." Her eyes filled with water, turning her aunt's face into a blurry blob.

"Now, don't you cry. I don't want my mascara running everywhere. It takes time to put on this face, you know."

Deborah chuckled and sniffed, wiping her eyes with her fingers. "I don't know what I'm going to do without you."

"You'll be fine. You're needed here, no matter what your sister says. And that big young man your father hired. What's his name?"

"Stephen."

"Yes, that's right. Never was good with names, you know. He's going to be a huge help. That will take some of the burden off your father."

Deborah nodded. Although Stephen had only worked one evening, he'd made a big difference already. He had cleaned out both the chicken coop and goat pen, and still had enough time to replace the warped wood on the bottom porch step.

Sadie patted Deborah's cheek. "Now, if I don't get on the road I'll never leave. I'll be praying for you, and Will, and Moses. I'll even pray for Naomi." She made a face. "That might be the hardest thing I've ever done."

She hugged her aunt one more time. "Have a safe trip back."

"Will do. Now don't hesitate to call if you need anything. You know my number."

"I will."

Sadie walked around and opened the door to her car. "And write me. I'd ask you to send pictures of Will, but I know you can't do that."

"I'll tell you everything he's doing, though."

"You better. But I may just have to make a trip back and see for myself." She blew Deborah a kiss with her big red lips. "Love you, sugar."

"Love you too."

Deborah waved goodbye to her aunt as she pulled out of the driveway. Then she crossed her arms in an effort to keep herself together. Emptiness filled her. The loss of her mother was acute now, and an overwhelming sadness fell over her. Her aunt had confidence that she would be okay, but Deborah wasn't sure. *Dear God, give me strength to do this, to take care of* Daed *and Will, to forge some kind of truce with Naomi.*

When Sadie had disappeared down the road, Deborah walked up the porch steps and smiled at Will and her *daed.* Her father had just put his hat back on Will's head, but Will tossed it on the ground and burst into a fit of giggles. She scooped it up and handed it back to her father.

"Gotta get that boy to wear a hat." *Daed* plopped it back on Will's head, and Will threw it down again.

"He thinks it's a game, *Daed.*"

"Oh, I know. Why do you think I keep doing it?" He set Will down on the front porch. Will toddled past Deborah and over to the playpen they'd purchased when they went to pick up the crib. Deborah had wanted to pay for the playpen herself, but Sadie wouldn't hear of it, and Deborah had to admit she was relieved. She had saved a little money from her job, but it wouldn't last very long. Deborah lifted Will and put him inside, where he started playing with his toys.

"He'll get used to wearing the hat when he's older." *Daed* stood up from his chair. "Got to check on the cows. I let them out in the pasture this morning. They're probably ready to come in by now. Might do some clean up in the barn too.

Don't want to leave everything to Stephen. What time did Naomi say supper would be?"

"She didn't."

"All right, I'll go in and ask her." He moved to go inside, then stopped and looked at her. "How are things between you two?"

Deborah glanced away. "All right." She refused to elaborate, knowing her father became edgy whenever she and her sister fought. He'd always let their mother referee their arguments. She didn't want to put any more of an emotional burden on him than he already had. She and her sister were adults. They could settle their differences themselves. That was her prayer anyway.

He nodded, seeming satisfied with her answer. "If I haven't said it before, I'm glad you're here. I'm sorry I didn't give you a proper welcome the other day."

Deborah's lip trembled. "You don't have to keep apologizing for that, *Daed.* I understand."

"Still, I shouldn't have been so harsh. I don't know what got into me that night."

"You were grieving." He still was. They all were, but he seemed to be handling it a little better now. She liked to think her aunt was right and that Will had something to do with it.

Her father looked at her. "I thought you might have gone back to Paradise with Sadie. Seems

like you were getting pretty settled back there.
I'm glad you decided to stay."

When she'd first arrived, she had thought
the same thing. But seeing her father with Will
and the way he acted toward her now made her
change her mind. She and her son were needed
here.

Thomas suddenly came to mind. She hadn't
had a chance to write and tell him what had happened. As soon as everything settled down, she
would tell him that she was staying in Middlefield, at least for the time being. She owed him
that much.

"I better hunt your *schwester* down and find
out about supper time. She doesn't abide lateness,
you know."

After her father went inside to find Naomi,
Deborah sat down on his chair and watched Will
in the playpen. She closed her eyes, stifling a
yawn. She should go inside and see if Naomi
needed help getting supper ready, but knowing
her sister would refuse, she stayed outside with
Will. Later they could go check on the garden or
take a walk to the barn and look at the cows. Will
had never seen any up close because her aunt
lived in a subdivision on the outskirts of Paradise.

The sound of a buggy approaching made her
open her eyes. She stood up and saw a black ve-

hicle turn into her driveway, drawn by a beautiful palomino horse. Stephen had arrived.

Stephen brought the buggy around and parked it next to her father's. He jumped out and tied his horse to the hitching rail then walked toward them. As he neared, she was again struck by his size. He had to be the tallest man in Middlefield. Even in Paradise she'd never seen an Amish man close to his height. But even though he was tall, he wasn't thin or lanky. His broad shoulders and solid torso made sure of that. She was most curious about why he held his hand behind his back.

When he was a few feet away, she averted her gaze, not wanting him to catch her staring at him. She picked up Will from the pen. Only when he stopped in front of her did she look up at him.

"Hello," he said, smiling.

His grin was so genuine she couldn't help but smile back. "Hello, Stephen."

"Is your *daed* around? I'm a little early but I wanted to get going on the barn."

"He's inside. You can come in while I *geh* get him."

Stephen shook his head. "*Nee*, I'll wait out here."

Deborah saw Will tilt his head back to look at Stephen, his eyes wide. Stephen turned his attention to the boy, reaching out his large hand. "Hello, Will."

She didn't expect Will to respond. When Stephen joined them for supper last night, Will had only stared at him. Spending most of his life almost exclusively with his mother and Aunt Sadie had made him wary of others, especially of men. The only man he'd taken to so far was his grandpa. But to her surprise Will tentatively grasped the tip of Stephen's finger, and the contrast between the sizes of their hands was striking. Then Will released Stephen's finger and laid his cheek against her shoulder.

"I brought something for Will." He brought his hand out from behind his back. In his palm was a small wooden horse on wheels. "I made this awhile back for Moriah and Gabe's *kinner*. But they keep having *maed*, so I thought Will might like it." Stephen looked at her. "If it's all right with you."

Deeply touched, Deborah nodded. "*Danki*, Stephen." She looked at the toy. "You didn't have to do that."

He shrugged, but the glint in his eyes told her he was pleased. He held out the horse to Will. "*Gaul*."

Will slowly reached for the horse, then snatched it out of Stephen's hand. Stephen chuckled.

"He says *danki* too," Deborah said as Will clutched the toy to his chest.

At the squeak of the screen door opening, she turned around. Her father walked over to them. He held out his hand to Stephen. After Stephen shook it, her *daed* looked at Deborah. "Naomi says supper will be done in half an hour."

"Does she need any help?" Although Deborah knew the answer, she still wanted to offer.

"Not that she said. You know your sister. She's like your mother was, a marvel in the kitchen." A flicker of sadness crossed his features, then disappeared as he looked at Stephen. "I suppose you're ready to get started on that barn."

"*Ya.* Just tell me what you need me to do."

Deborah watched as they walked toward the barn together, Stephen's height overshadowing her father. She smiled again. It was comforting to know someone else was here to help out. She was glad her father didn't have to take care of the farm on his own.

She looked down at the horse Will held. She was no expert, but she could tell the quality of the workmanship. It must have taken him quite a while to make it. Will was already sitting up in her arms, running his fingers over the wheels. He laughed and held it up to Deborah. *"Gaul!"*

Deborah smiled. By giving him such a simple gift, Stephen had made them both happy.

Stephen had joined Moses in the loft of the barn. They were straightening up and counting the square bales. Moses picked up a sixth hay bale to put on top of a stack, but he struggled to lift it high enough. Stephen took it from him and completed the task with ease.

Moses nodded, looking impressed. "Must be nice to be so tall."

"It has its advantages." Being able to reach things was one Stephen appreciated. But there were also numerous disadvantages. Folding himself into buggies, sitting in chairs that were meant for people half his size, finding size six-teen shoes, which he usually had to special order, especially the work boots. And those were just some of the problems he faced.

"You're strong as an ox too." Moses leaned against the hay bales, his chest heaving. "Ah, to be young again."

"Do you want me to finish this?" Stephen looked at Moses with concern. The man was breathing pretty hard.

"Nah, just let me catch my breath. I'll be fine in a minute."

As he waited, Stephen looked around the huge barn that housed several different animals. One side was dedicated to the cows, while the other half of the barn had been divided into three sec-tions—a stall for the horse, a gated area for the pigs, and a small area for the goats, which he'd cleaned yesterday. He hoped to have the rest of the barn finished tonight. The Byler family had a much smaller barn that only held two horses and had an extended roof to shield the buggies from the elements. Usually it took him less than an hour to clean it out. It wouldn't be the same for this barn.

"All right, I'm *gut* now." Moses moved to stand by Stephen. He scratched his chin. "Gotta decide what to tackle next."

Stephen thought the old man sounded overwhelmed. "What about the pigpen?"

"Sounds *gut* to me."

They had both just climbed down the ladder leading to the loft when he heard a woman speak. "*Daed*? Supper is ready."

Stephen turned around and saw Deborah's sister, Naomi, standing in the barn doorway. Over the years he'd seen Naomi at church, but she was older than he was and he never paid her much attention. But when he'd arrived yesterday, he'd been struck by how different she and Deborah looked. Deborah's face was round with rosy, prominent cheeks, and Naomi's was long, almost rectangular, with flatter cheeks and a tight mouth. But the real difference was the eyes. They were the same brown color, yet while Deborah's were soft, Naomi's had a hard glint to them. Those eyes narrowed as she turned her gaze on him. "Will you be staying for supper again?"

Just the mention of food made his stomach growl. Yet he should say no. He'd eaten supper with them last night, and he didn't want them to think they owed him food. He was here to help, not to be an extra mouth to feed. "I don't want to impose." Stephen turned to Moses.

"You're not an imposition. We have plenty." Even though Naomi's words had sounded like she wanted him to stay, her expression said the exact opposite, and he wondered if she resented him being here. That strengthened his resolve. He could eat leftovers when he got home. "*Danki*, but I'm fine." He turned to Moses. "*Geh* ahead and eat. I'll get started on the pen."

Moses looked to his daughter, then to Stephen. "Are you sure?"

"*Ya.*"

"All right. You'll find the shovel and wheelbarrow over by the horse's stall. I'll be out as soon as I can."

"Take your time." Stephen moved to get the tools as Moses and Naomi left. But before she walked away, she gave him a strange look, then followed her father back to the house.

He looked at the horse, who was poking its head out of the stall. "Wonder what's got her so out of sorts?"

Chapter Twelve

Zach rubbed his damp palms on his pants. As soon as Ruth asked him to stay, his pulse had ramped up ten notches. It had taken a great effort for him to sound nonchalant, and he couldn't tell if he'd been successful or not. Ruth's expression had been difficult to read, as usual.

He clenched his hands a couple times. What was wrong with him? He'd talked to girls before. He'd even been on a couple of dates, although they hadn't been anything special, and usually by the end of the date, whatever attraction he'd felt had disappeared. He couldn't say the same about Ruth. The more he was around her, the more attracted he became. Normally that wouldn't be a problem, but this was Ruth Byler. The only reason she'd even invited him to stay was because it would be impolite not to do so. And if anyone was a stickler for rules it was Ruth. He doubted she'd ever broken a rule in her life. As for him, he'd spent his childhood smashing rules to bits.

He tied up Maggie, trying to get his hammering heartbeat under control. He took off his hat, ran his hand through his hair, and put the hat back on, making sure it was straight. Not that she would notice. He knew she saw him as little more than the *dummkopf* who ruined her school, made her miss her meeting, and caused her to get stuck in the window. Still, that didn't stop him from tucking in his shirt.

When he walked to the front of the house, he saw Ruth on the front porch, her posture stiff, holding the glasses of lemonade in a tight grip as if they were toxic. He should have told her no when she asked him to stay. That would have saved her from pretending she wanted to be around him.

"Can't stay long," he said as he skipped up the short steps to the front porch. A look passed over her face, and he couldn't tell if she was glad or disappointed. The woman was impossible to read.

She handed him the lemonade, barely making eye contact with him. "I hope you enjoy it."

But as he reached for it, the glass started to slip from her hand. He grabbed it as she pushed it forward. Half of the lemonade splashed on the front of his shirt.

She set the glass down on the porch railing. "Oh no! I'm so sorry, how clumsy of me. It's all over your shirt now."

He glanced down to see the wet spot spread across his stomach. "It's not that bad, Ruth. It will dry in no time."

"I should have been paying attention." Her voice was barely above a whisper. "That was so *dumm*."

Zach noticed the hand holding the other glass was shaking. He took the glass from her and set it next to the half-empty one on the railing. "Ruth, it's okay, really. It's just lemonade."

"I can't do anything right." She looked up at him for a moment, her eyes filled with defeat, then turned away.

His heart went out to her. He recognized that look. How many times had he identified with that emotion, had said those exact same words? More than he could count. But they were true for him, not for Ruth. "Don't say that."

She faced him, her expression a little more composed, but not much. "I'm a failure."

"You just spilled a little lemonade. Accidents happen, Ruth. I should know. I'm the *keenich* of them."

"I'm not talking about the lemonade. Well,

maybe I am. A little." She walked over to the porch swing and sat down, her shoulders slumping. "I don't even know what I mean."

He gazed at her for a moment, taking in her slouched posture, the way her chin nearly touched the top of her chest, the tight grip she had on the hem of her white apron. He'd never seen her like this. Self-defeating. Unsure. *A lot like me.*

Zach sat down next to her, half expecting her to tell him to leave. She didn't. But she didn't look up or say anything either. "Ruth, you're not a failure. I don't see how that's even possible."

"You weren't in my class today." She lifted her head and glanced at him. "Nothing went right. Not a single thing."

The beaten-down look on her face made him want to put his arms around her. "I'm sure it's not as bad as you think."

"Oh, it was. How many teachers have their students walk out on them?"

That bit of news surprised him. "Really? Some *kinn* actually left school?"

She nodded, her lips tugging into a deep frown. "*Ya.* Walked right out and never came back."

He sat back in the swing, stunned. He'd had his problems with school, and he'd exasperated more than one teacher over the years. Actually he probably irritated every single one. But not once did it dawn on him to walk out of school. That wasn't done. "Did you try to talk to him?"

Her eyes flashed. "Of course I did! I asked him to step outside so we wouldn't disturb the other *kinner*. That's when he left. But it wasn't just him."

As she explained her trials of the day, he began to understand why she was so frustrated. "I think you're entitled to a bad day or two, don't you? Everything can't be perfect."

"But it's supposed to be." She angled her body toward him. "I've spent my entire life dreaming of being a teacher. I studied for hours and hours to make sure I had good grades. I made sure I *learned* the material, not just memorized it for tests. I read books about teaching theory, about child development. I spent half my summer on lesson plans alone!" As she spoke, the irritated spark in her eyes and voice grew. "And for what? I lost control of my class on the first day. That makes me a horrible teacher."

He let out a chuckle. "It makes you human."

"I can't believe you're laughing at me." She crossed her arms over her chest.

"*Nee*, I'm not laughing at you. Believe it or not, I know exactly what you're talking about."

"You do?"

"*Ya*. The day you had today? That pretty much describes my life. Minus the whole school part." He shifted his body so he faced her, resting his bent leg on the swing. "My driving into the school is just one example. Now *that* was a bad day."

Her expression softened slightly. "For both of us. But you had the worst of it."

"And it was my fault. I shouldn't have been driving Rick's truck. I'm a *gut* buggy driver, but not that experienced with cars. I made a bad decision. Just one of many."

"Maybe becoming a teacher was a bad decision."

"C'mon now. You don't believe that." He leaned toward her, looking straight into her eyes. "No one has more passion for learning than you do. I remember seeing that when we were in school together, even though I didn't understand it then. All I wanted to do was get out of there, and I thanked God every day I didn't have to keep going after eighth grade."

"And I would have gone on through high school, if I could."

She didn't have to say what they both knew. The Amish restricted school to age fourteen. If she had made the choice to go to high school, she might not have been able to join the church. He suspected Ruth was just as passionate about her faith as she was about her job.

"But that doesn't matter right now." She sighed.

"Ruth. You love school, don't you?" When she nodded he continued. "And you love teaching."

"You can tell that?"

He nodded. "You wouldn't be so upset about what happened if you didn't."

She took a deep breath. "I do love it. But I'm not *gut* at it. Today proved that."

"Ruth, you've spent one day as a teacher. One day. How can you know if you're any *gut* or not?"

Her fingers fumbled with the hem of her white apron. "You're right," she said softly.

He cupped his hand over his ear. "Excuse me? I didn't quite hear that."

"I said you're right." She looked up at him, her mouth lifting at one corner.

It was only a half-smile, but he'd take it. "That's better." He sat back, grinning.

Ruth was amazed. Zach was able to do something no one, not even her family, had been able to do—understand her. It wasn't his words that proved that. She could imagine her mother, her sister Moriah, or anyone else telling her the same things—that she wasn't a failure, that she hadn't given the job enough time, that she was meant to be a teacher. But it was the way he said them, the sincerity and empathy in his eyes that made her believe he had slipped into her skin, if just for a brief moment. She'd spent her life hiding her doubts and insecurities, fearing others would find her weak or incapable. Yet in the past few minutes, Zach had scaled that invisible wall she'd erected around herself, and instead of feeling fragile, admitting her fears gave her strength.

Letting go of her apron, she looked at Zach, as if seeing him for the first time. Yes, he still had the most beautiful eyes she'd ever seen. And the more she saw him smile, the more affected she became by it. But now she saw past all that. Because while she had let down her defenses, he had let down his too. She wondered if he even realized it.

His grin faded, replaced by a serious expression. "You're not still feeling like a failure, are you? Because if you are, then my pep talk skills need serious work."

She shook her head, giving him a full smile. "*Nee*. Thanks to you, I'm feeling inspired."

"You are?"

"*Ya.*" She stood from the swing. It swayed back and forth, then stilled. "Like you said, I can't let one day determine my capability as a teacher. I need to learn to be flexible. Roll with the punches, so to speak."

He looked up at her, the swing moving again as he pushed against the porch with his toe.

"Why do I think that might be easier said than done?"

"Because it will. I'm not the most spontaneous person in the world."

"I hadn't noticed." His smile widened.

She smirked. "That doesn't mean I shouldn't try. In Colossians it says we should be kind and humble, and persevere. I think I need to work on all three."

"Don't we all."

"I think you're right on track." She said the words with all sincerity.

His bright expression dimmed. "I don't know about that."

"Now who's being self-deprecating?"

His brow lifted. "What does that mean, Ms. Smarty?"

She sat down next to him, a little closer this time. "It means you're not thinking highly enough of yourself. Which is a shame."

His mouth tugged downward. "Now I'm the one getting the pep talk?"

"Do you need one?"

He paused, then shook his head. "*Nee.* I'm fine. And enough about me anyway, I'm boring."

She thought nothing of the sort, but she didn't say that.

"Let's get back to you persevering. What are

you going to do about the *kinn* who left your class?"

"Jacob Kline?"

Surprise lit up his face. "Jacob did that? I knew his *daed* was having trouble with him at home, but…" He shook his head.

"You know Jacob?"

"The buggy shop I work at? The Klines own it. Part of the reason I was hired is because *Herr* Kline can't count on Jacob to help out." He looked down at his lap, then up again. "Kind of reminds me of someone I know."

"Who?"

"Me."

Ruth shook her head. "You never walked out of school."

"*Nee.* But I was tempted. Knowing my father would have my hide if I did is what kept me from it. I wonder if the Klines know about this."

"I doubt it. I was planning to talk to them tonight, but I didn't have a ride. I'll speak with him about it tomorrow. I must be doing something wrong."

"There you *geh* again."

"*Nee,* I'm not speaking out of self-pity. Merely stating a possible fact. There's something going on, and if I can adjust the way I react to him, plus try to figure out what motivates him, then maybe I can at least keep him in the classroom."

Zach didn't say anything for a long moment. Then he looked at her. "You want me to talk to him? I might be able to find out something. Though I can't make any guarantees."

"You'd be willing to do that?"

He nodded. "I can see how much you want to help him. And he's my boss's *sohn*. *Herr* Kline has been *gut* to me. If I can help him out, I'm willing to."

Ruth could have hugged him at that moment. "I'll take any help I can get. *Danki*, Zach."

"*Gut*, you remembered."

"Remembered what?"

He leaned forward. "To call me Zach. You know, I think there might be hope for our friendship after all."

She was thinking the exact same thing.

Deborah held a small piece of white meat to Will's lips. He turned and shook his head, pressing his little lips together. All through the meal, she'd tried to get him to eat the chicken, but he'd refused. She'd have to be satisfied with the mashed potatoes and cooked carrots he'd devoured earlier. She cleaned him up as Naomi finished clearing the table. Deborah gave him the toy horse to play with while she took a plate from the cupboard. She selected a fried chicken leg and put it on the plate, then added a large scoop of potato salad.

"What are you doing?" Naomi was filling the kitchen sink with soapy water. When the bubbles rose to the edge, she turned the faucet off with a hard twist.

"Fixing a plate for Stephen." She had thought he would join them for supper, but he hadn't. She knew he had to be hungry, so she thought she'd take a bit of dinner out to him after Will went to bed, just in case he wanted a snack.

"I hope he doesn't expect us to feed him every time he comes here."

"I think it's obvious he doesn't, since he didn't eat with us tonight."

"Then why bother giving him food?"

A sarcastic remark perched on the tip of her tongue, but she swallowed it. Naomi was touchy enough as it was. All through dinner her sister had been sullen. As usual, her father pretended to be oblivious to the tension, keeping his head down as he ate quickly, then went straight back outside. She didn't blame him.

"I don't see why he's even here." Naomi grabbed the three plates from the table and took them to the garbage can, where she scraped off the extra food. "We don't need his help."

Deborah tore off a piece of aluminum foil and

covered the plate. "*Daed* needs his help. Haven't you noticed how tired he is?"

"Of course he's tired. It's the end of the day and he works hard. Unlike other people I know."

Deborah was growing weary of her sister's digs. "I've offered to help you, but you won't let me. You can't do that one minute and the next minute complain you've got too much work to do."

Naomi paused, holding one plate suspended over the garbage can. Then she finished pushing off the food and took the plates to the sink, slipping them into the dishwater. She didn't say anything else, but her silence told Deborah everything she needed to know.

But she could play the ignoring game just as well as her sister. Deborah pulled Will out of his high chair, another gift from Aunt Sadie, and went into the living room. They sat in the rocking chair. Will yawned as Deborah rocked back and forth, and before long he was asleep, the horse pressed against his tiny chest.

Once she took him upstairs to bed, she came back down and went into the kitchen. As she expected, it was spotless, and Naomi was nowhere in sight, which was fine by Deborah. She wasn't in the mood to talk to her anyway.

Outside the kitchen window, she could see the side of the barn. Stephen came out pushing a wheelbarrow piled high with manure. He dumped it in a large pile a few feet from the barn, then went back in. Deborah walked outside to tell him about the plate she had fixed. She had just reached the barn when he came out with another load of smelly manure.

"Hey," he said, wiping his forehead with the back of his grimy hand. "If you're looking for your *daed*, he's out in the pasture. One of the cows decided she didn't want to come in, so he's trying to coax her back."

"There's always one stubborn one." She looked at him. "When you're finished, I have some lemonade and a plate of food left from supper."

She glanced at the huge pile of manure he'd brought out of the barn. "Wow. You've done all that tonight?"

"*Ya*. Thought I'd clean out the horse's stall real quick before I leave."

"I'm impressed. I've helped *Daed* clean out the barn a time or two and it would have taken us twice as long to get that much done." At his surprised look she added, "It was just us *maed* here and he sometimes needed the help."

"It's not a fun job, for sure."

"I don't mind it." She looked around the property. "I missed this place while I was gone."

"It's a *gut* farm."

"That needs a lot of work."

He put his hands on his hips and gazed in the direction of the pasture. "I'm finding I really enjoy the work. Being cooped up in the shop can get to me sometimes." He looked back at her. "Where's Will?"

"He's sleeping. I should *geh* check on him."

"All right." He nodded at her, then bent down and grasped the handles of the wheelbarrow. "I think I'll take you up on the food, if that's all right. I'm just about done here."

Deborah smiled. "I'll have it ready for you."

After she went back inside and quickly checked on Will, she poured a glass of lemonade for Stephen and put it and the plate of food on the table. At the same time she heard a knock on the door. She went to open it, seeing Stephen through the screen door.

"Where should I leave my boots?" he asked.

"Right outside the door will be fine."

She watched as he slipped off his muddy boots, revealing the white socks he wore underneath. He put them a few feet from the front door and walked inside. Deborah led him to the kitchen. "You can wash your hands here."

"Danki." He flipped on the faucet.

She stood behind him as he washed his hands. He was bent slightly over the sink, the countertop edge hitting below his waist. His huge presence filled the small kitchen. She glanced down at his feet, then looked at hers in comparison. His were almost twice as long as hers. Her head was still down when he turned away from the sink, so she didn't see him coming until he bumped into her, knocking her backward. He grabbed her shoulders and steadied her.

"Sorry about that." He looked sheepish.

"*Nee*, it was my fault. I stood too close." She glanced at his hand, still on her shoulder, his palm almost completely covering it. The warmth of his touch seeped through the thin material of her dress, causing her heart to skip a beat. Warning alarms sounded in her head. She stepped out of his grasp, disturbed that his innocent touch had affected her so much.

His gaze met hers, then a puzzled look crossed his face. "Sure you're okay? I didn't step on your foot or something?"

She shook her head and walked to the table. She pulled off the foil from the plate and smiled. "I'm fine."

"*Gut*. I can be clumsy sometimes." He pulled out a chair and sat down. He bowed his head for a minute, then picked up the fork. "Looks *appeditlich*."

"Naomi's an excellent cook."

"Where is your *schwester*?" He scooped up a large forkful of potato salad and put it in his mouth.

"Upstairs." Since Deborah's arrival, Naomi had gone to her room after supper each night, not reappearing until early morning. She had no idea what her sister was doing cooped up in her room. Maybe working on a quilt or sewing project. But she could do that downstairs in the front parlor, like their mother used to do. It was obvious to Deborah that Naomi wanted to avoid her.

Stephen didn't pry, and she was glad for that. He took another bite of salad and followed it with a gulp of lemonade. Then he held out his hand toward the chair next to him. "Care to join me?" He quickly added, "Unless you're busy."

She wasn't busy, but she wasn't sure she should join him either. She wanted to, and not just because of that flash of attraction she'd felt moments ago. She realized how lonely she felt, especially since her aunt left. Looking at Stephen now, she didn't feel anything, and that calmed her. That one second of intense emotion must have been a fluke. And with Naomi refusing to speak to her and her father consumed by the farm, she had little company other than Will. It would be nice to sit down and have a conversation with an adult, and Stephen was easy to be around. Smiling again, she pulled the chair out from the table. "Sure."

He picked up the chicken leg and took a bite. "You're right," he said, after he finished chewing. "She is a *gut* cook." He picked up his glass and drained the lemonade in nearly one gulp.

Deborah moved to stand, glad he was enjoying the meal. "Do you want some more? We have plenty."

"*Nee*, I'm fine. I have to get back home soon." He polished off the potato salad. "Let your *daed* know I'll be back tomorrow."

"Are you sure? He said you'd be working only a couple days a week."

"That's what we agreed to, but I think he needs me more than that." Stephen finished off the chicken and wiped his mouth and hands with the napkin.

"*Ya*, but he won't admit it. And I don't think he'll agree to you coming out here every day for free."

"Then you'll just have to pay me in lemonade." He winked.

Another jolt of attraction went through her. He was so different from other men she knew. There was a gentleness about him that contrasted with his large size. And now that they were sitting at eye level with each other, he was even more handsome.

She halted the direction of her thoughts. She'd fallen for a handsome man before. Chase had not only been good-looking, but charming and a smooth talker. He said what she wanted to hear, and she'd fallen for him. But she wouldn't make that mistake again. She had to keep her thoughts pure, especially since Stephen would be here often. It would be a good idea to keep her distance from him in the future.

Chapter Thirteen

When Zach arrived at work the next morning, he still wasn't sure what he was going to say to *Herr* Kline. Or Jacob, when he had a chance to talk to him. Just because he understood the boy didn't mean he knew what to say. But he didn't want to let Ruth down. After their talk yesterday, if she had asked him to walk on broken glass barefoot for two miles, he would have done it. He'd come to the realization that—as Rick would say—he had it bad for her. For the past couple of weeks, he'd teetered on the edge between attraction and irritation. But seeing the real Ruth, catching a glimpse of the fire in her eyes as she talked about helping Jacob, had sent him over that edge.

But he needed to keep his feelings hidden. He mentioned friendship yesterday, and to her, that's what it was and would always be. Ruth Byler was destined to be with someone like her. Smart, clever, responsible. He was none of the above, just a part-time worker in a buggy shop whose father still refused to speak more than four syllables to him at the supper table. Ruth could have her pick of men in the community. The thought made his gut twist with envy. But his feelings didn't matter here. He would be satisfied with friendship. He'd have to be.

He walked into the buggy shop. As usual, *Herr* Kline had already started work, nailing pieces of a buggy frame together with a pneumatic nail gun. A long blue tube snaked from the gun and attached to a large, black air compressor tank. As Zach approached, he looked up and nodded. *"Guten morgen."*

"Guten morgen, Herr Kline."

"I think you've worked here long enough to call me David."

Zach nodded but stayed behind the counter, still unsure what to say. How could he tell his boss that his child had run away from school?

"Something wrong?" David straightened, letting the hand holding the nail gun dangle at his side.

Zach let out a deep breath. "Something happened at the school yesterday."

David shook his head, but he didn't look surprised. "Let me guess. Jacob got in trouble."

"You could say that." When Zach explained

about Jacob running off, David's face grew red. But he didn't say anything, just set down the nail gun, then rubbed the back of his neck. "I don't know what I'm going to do with that *bu*."

Now those were familiar words. Zach moved from behind the counter and walked over to him. "You have any idea why he would have done that?"

"*Nee*. I didn't even know he left. He came home from school at the usual time. I thought he'd been there all day." He looked at Zach. "How did you know about it?"

"*Mei freind* is his teacher. She told me about it last night." There, it wasn't so bad calling Ruth his friend. Maybe someday he'd get used to it. Like in ten years or so.

"Ever since we moved here, he's been taking off. He'll be gone all day, then sneak back in the house. Problem is, I can't be with him all the time. I have my business to run, and my *frau*... well, she's got a soft spot for him. She thinks if we love him more, he'll start behavin'. I love my *sohn*, but I don't know how to talk to him. Even when I do, he won't listen." David looked at Zach. "He's almost fourteen years old. How long are we gonna have to wait for him to straighten himself out?" Before Zach could answer, he added, "As soon as Jacob's home, I'll take him right over to the school to apologize. Maybe I should do that right now. I can check and see if he's even there."

Zach held out his hand to stop him. "I don't think that's a *gut* idea."

David's gaze narrowed. It was the first time Zach had ever seen the mild man agitated. "Why not?"

"Because he'll be embarrassed, and that won't help the situation."

"Embarrassed?" David stomped his foot. "Do you think I give one whit whether that *bu* is embarrassed? He's humiliated me enough times."

Zach experienced a strange sense of déjà vu. David Kline couldn't be more different from Zach's father in physical appearance and temperament, but at that moment Zach could hear his father saying those exact words. "I know," he said. And he did. More than David would ever realize.

His boss's tone mellowed. "I'm sorry. I don't mean to take it out on you. I know you mean well. You're a *gut mann*. You don't need to get involved in this."

David's words touched him deeply. "I think I can help, though. I understand Jacob."

"You do?"

"*Ya*. I understand him because…I am him. Or at least, I was."

As she had hoped, Ruth's second day of school was better than the first. She had prayed for God to help her relax, to be firm but not inflexible. The approach worked. There were no fights, no cheating attempts, and little Lori only cried once and had been easily soothed with a hug. The only disappointment was that Jacob Kline hadn't shown up. She hoped Zach would be able to talk to him, to find out how that young man ticked.

She had thought about Zach throughout the day. It was hard not to, as nearly everything in the *schulhaus* triggered a memory. Even the scent of the new wood and fresh paint brought his image to her mind. She couldn't escape him and, she admitted to herself, she didn't want to.

At the end of the day, she dismissed the class. When the last student exited the schoolhouse, Ruth breathed a sigh of satisfaction. *Thank You, Lord.*

For the next half hour, she graded papers while she waited for Stephen to pick her up. She had just finished checking the last math assignment when she heard a knock on the door. Looking up, she saw Zach standing in the doorway.

"Just checking to see how your day went." He didn't come in the door.

"Gut." She removed her glasses and smiled. "Exceptionally well, actually."

He leaned against the doorjamb. "I'm not surprised." His gaze went to the window. That morning she had stuck a tin can on the sill. The window wasn't open as wide as before, but the prop was steadier. "Nice fix. I'll come by later tonight and put in the new window."

"There's no hurry. We can manage for a few days without it."

"All right, but I'll get it done this weekend."

"I know you will." The smile he gave her, along with the light redness she saw on his freckled cheeks, made her heart flip. "Jacob wasn't at school today."

"He wasn't?" He stood straight and walked in the schoolhouse. "I had a talk with his father today. He said since they moved here from Iowa in June, he's had trouble with Jacob. Said he left behind a lot of *freind*. And he thinks that's why Jacob's been running off all summer."

"That's not a reason to run away from school or be disrespectful. There are a couple of other students new to the area too."

Zach shrugged. "I don't know what to tell you. David believes that's the problem, and he's not sure what to do with him. He's got his hands full trying to make the shop a success and support his *familye*."

"What do you think he does all day?"

Zach shrugged. "Fishing? Hiding in the woods? I don't know."

Ruth stood, pushing her chair out from behind her. "Then we should *geh* find him. Tell him how important it is that he attend school, and that he has to be respectful to his parents."

He let out a bitter chuckle. "If only it were that easy." He looked down at her. "Ruth, we could scour Middlefield until midnight and we wouldn't find him. He doesn't want to be found. He'll come home tonight, and his *daed* will talk to him again. Matter of fact, he said he'd walk Jacob to school in the morning to apologize."

Ruth nodded. At least that was something. But it still didn't give her much insight into Jacob and how to reach him. That would take a lot of prayer and a lot of patience, and she was willing to invest both. "I appreciate you stopping by and letting me know."

"No problem. If I get a chance to talk to him, I will. But he's not one for listening, according to his *daed*. Hate to say it, but I know what that's like too. I was never one to pay much attention to what my *daed* told me." He shrugged. "Change of subject. Do you have a ride home?"

"*Ya*. Stephen's picking me up."

"All right, just making sure." He moved to leave. "But if you ever need a ride, just let me know. I'll be glad to give you one." With that he walked out of the schoolhouse.

Ruth smiled. *I definitely will.*

The next morning Ruth was writing math problems on the blackboard when David and

Jacob Kline walked in, thirty minutes before school started. "*Fraulein* Byler?"

She had seen David Kline at church a few times, but they had never formally met. The Klines usually left right after the service. There was a resemblance between father and son. Both had the same hooded gray eyes, thin lips, and hair so dark it was nearly black, although David's had started to thin. She set down her chalk and walked to them. "Hello, *Herr* Kline." She moved her gaze to the surly young man next to him. "Jacob. I'm glad to see you here today."

When Jacob didn't respond, David nudged him forward. "*Guten morgen*," he said in a flat tone, not looking at her.

"Jacob's got something to tell you. Don't you, *sohn*?"

Jacob crossed his arms over his chest. "I'm sorry." He practically mouthed the words.

"She didn't hear you."

Ruth started to say she did, but she remained silent.

"I'm sorry. There. Can I *geh* now?" When his father gave him a curt nod, he dashed out the door.

David's expression grew somber. "I'm sorry for that, *Fraulein* Byler. And I'm sorry Jacob's missed school these past two days. It won't happen again."

"*Danki*. I appreciate you coming to let me know. I'll try to talk to him about the importance of education sometime today."

Shaking his head, David said, "You can try, but like I told Zach yesterday, my *sohn* isn't too *gut* of a listener." An embarrassed look crossed his face. "I guess the apple don't fall too far from the tree. I was never much for school, although I see the importance of it now." He tilted his head in the direction of the blackboard. "If I'd paid more attention to that, it'd be a lot easier to run my business. But when I try to tell that to Jacob, he doesn't want to hear it. Anyway, I've got to get back to work. Let me know if you have any more problems with him."

"I will." She walked him to the door, then stepped outside. A few other students had arrived at the playground, and she could see Jacob running after a ball so fast that his hat flew off his head. He ran back to get it and plopped it on his head. The tension in his face was gone. It had been replaced with a grin as he played with two other boys near his age. Jacob seemed to fit in seamlessly with the other kids. But maybe that was just a fluke today, and he was fighting homesickness more than she realized. People masked their pain in different ways.

Her mind went back to her school days, which were only a few years ago but seemed longer.

The younger children playing tag under a clear blue sky, with the bright sunshine glinting off their yellow straw hats and white prayer *kapps*. Then, as now, a few girls were standing in a small group, taking turns whispering to each other behind cupped hands. Jacob and his friends were punching a volleyball back and forth even though there wasn't a net, the same way Zach and the other boys had done.

And her standing apart.

Although now she didn't look at this group of kids and wish she could be a part of them. She *was* a part of this group. They were her class, and they would learn and grow together. That included Jacob, God willing.

She called out to the students, telling them to come inside. They all ran toward the *schulhaus*, those who were barefoot grabbing their shoes and carrying them inside. Jacob was the last one, and he dragged the toes of his shoes on the ground as he walked. He moved to go inside the schoolhouse, but Ruth stopped him.

Ruth said a quick prayer, asking God to give her the words to reach this child. "I'd like to talk to you for a moment before we start the day."

He looked up at her, his hooded eyes barely open. "I already said I was sorry. What more do you want?"

"Jacob, there's no need to be angry. I'm trying to help you."

"I don't need no help." He wiped his nose with the top of his forearm. "Especially from you. I'm only here because *mei daed* made me come. But I ain't gonna learn nothin', and you can't make me."

"You're right. I can't make you."

Surprise crossed his face, and he opened his eyes a little wider. "What?"

"I can't force you to learn. My job is to help you learn. I can't do that when you're not in school."

Although he was just thirteen, he was nearly equal to her in height. "I don't wanna be here, and don't act like you want me here."

"But I—"

He walked inside, leaving her with her mouth dangling open. So much for reaching him. But at least he went inside and didn't run away. *Thank You, Lord, for small favors.*

For the next week, Stephen went to the Coblentz farm every evening. Just as Deborah had warned, Moses wasn't happy about it.

"You're here again?" Moses growled as Stephen approached him in the barn at the end of the week.

"Now that's a fine greeting." Stephen grinned,

but it faded when he saw the old man's stern expression.

"We agreed you'd help out for a couple of days. Temporarily. Remember?"

"I know. But Deborah and Naomi are busy canning vegetables from the garden, and you need to get the corn in. Plus there's the fence that needs fixing, the roof in the barn is leaking—"

"You think I don't know all that?" Moses leaned against the horse stall. The dappled mare whinnied and took a step back. The old man looked up at Stephen, weariness seemingly permanently etched in the lines and crags on his face. "Maybe I should just sell it."

"Sell the farm?" Stephen looked at him, incredulous. "Why would you do that?"

"I can't keep relying on your charity."

"It's not charity—"

"And I know *mei dochders* can't take care of the place themselves." He looked down at the ground. "It would be different if they were married. But I can't see that happening any time soon."

Stephen wondered if exhaustion combined with grief over Martha's death had clouded Moses's mind. It was unusual for a woman Naomi's age to still be single, but that didn't mean she'd never get married. And as for Deborah...he had no doubt she'd get married. There was something special about her. The way her eyes filled with love when she looked at her son. Her thoughtfulness in making sure Stephen had something to eat, despite him refusing supper before. Then there was the shy way she'd looked at him the other evening in the kitchen, when he'd accidentally bumped into her. He hadn't realized how pretty she was until that moment. No, she didn't have to worry about not getting married. Any man would be lucky to have her.

Moses's deep sigh brought him out of his thoughts. "You don't need to give up yet, Moses. Helping you isn't work for me. I enjoy it. And I'm learning a lot. So don't worry about not being able to pay me or taking advantage of me." He looked down at the man. "I don't know what else I can say to convince you, other than this. Think about your *grosssohn*. If you sell the farm, what will his legacy be?"

Moses blinked a couple times, and Stephen thought he saw his lip tremble. "I hadn't thought about that. You're right. This will all be his someday, Lord willing." With renewed energy he stood up. "Let's get back to work."

Relief ran through Stephen. He followed Moses outside to the south end of the barn. He looked up to see several five-inch gaps and holes in the roof.

"There's the ladder." Moses pointed to the six-foot-tall metal ladder leaning against the side of the barn. "You're not afraid of heights, are you?"

"As tall as I am, I better not be."

Moses laughed, making Stephen grin. The speed with which the man could switch moods was amazing, and in this case, he was glad to see Moses had snapped out of his melancholy.

After checking that his tool belt was secure, he fetched the ladder and started to climb. Once on the roof, he looked down and saw Moses heading for the pasture. Stephen noticed he spent a lot of time out there, repairing the fence, which was broken in a few places. Seeing the sudden slump in the old man's shoulders, Stephen frowned. Maybe he hadn't shaken off his sadness after all.

Chapter Fourteen

Deborah sat in the old hickory chair on the front porch, watching her father trod to the back pasture again. Over the past week, he had spent every evening out in that pasture, and tonight was no exception. She saw him disappear beyond the gentle slope, and she sighed. Stephen had mentioned that the fence needed repairing, and undoubtedly her father was doing that. But the memory of finding him disheveled and partly out of his head with grief when she first arrived in Middlefield was never far from her mind. She wanted to talk to him, especially about her mother. No one mentioned *Mami* anymore, as if she'd never existed. Her connection to her mother was slipping away, and she was trying to cling to it. But like Naomi, her father went to bed right after dark and rose early, often heading outside before sunup.

The pounding of a hammer pulled her gaze to the roof of the barn. Stephen was crouched on the steep incline, working on one of the holes. Even at this distance she could see the strength in his arm as he brought the hammer down, the muscles visible because the short sleeves of his white shirt were rolled tightly above his upper arm. She jerked her head away from the view of the barn, bothered by the sudden surge of attraction she felt.

She forced herself to ignore Stephen and focus on the job she needed to do. She had been in Middlefield for two weeks and she still hadn't written to Thomas, mostly because she was busy, but she also had to admit that she had been avoiding the task. After she'd put Will to bed, she sought out some of her mother's stationery, then grabbed a ballpoint pen and came outside. She ran her finger across the delicate rose drawing at the top of the paper, fighting back tears. Deborah had received many letters from her mother over the past two years, written on this same paper. She brought the tablet to her chest. Would this pain ever go away?

Wiping her nose, she took a deep breath and began the letter. *Dear Thomas…* But for some reason the rest of the words wouldn't come. Even his image was fuzzy in her mind. She hadn't thought about his marriage proposal since she'd come back home. If he barely entered her thoughts, how could she even consider marrying him?

She looked at Stephen again. He had moved to another part of the roof. He was still crouched but leaning back, almost to a sitting position. He took off his straw hat and wiped his forehead with the back of his arm, then ran his fingers through his hair, making it mussed and a bit wild-looking. He put the hat back on and went back to work.

She had yet to see Stephen angry or frustrated about anything. Even Will had taken to him, toddling over to him earlier that evening right after he'd arrived. Stephen had scooped him up in one arm and carried him back to her, tickling Will under his chubby chin before handing him over. He was a natural with her son, and she knew he would be a wonderful father someday. If only things were different, then maybe she'd have a chance with a man like Stephen.

But things weren't different. By now, like in Paradise, everyone knew about Will's father, about how she had foolishly ignored her Amish faith to be with a Yankee man. Maybe there was a man in Middlefield who could overlook that, like Thomas was willing to do. But what if there wasn't?

She glanced down at the letter in her lap, then closed her eyes and prayed. She sensed the Lord telling her what was already in her heart—she couldn't marry Thomas. He might be able to live without love, but she couldn't. She put the pen to paper and forced herself to write. After quickly signing her name, she took a matching envelope from the box, slipped the letter inside, then sealed it. She hurried to the mailbox at the end of the driveway, placed it inside, and lifted the red flag. As she made her way back to the house, a heaviness settled over her heart, even though she knew she'd done the right thing.

She went back to the porch, intent on gathering the stationery and going back inside. But when she climbed the steps, she heard Stephen call out to her. "Deborah."

Deborah turned and faced him. The hot and muggy evening had taken its toll on him. Beads of perspiration slid down the sides of his face, and his shirt was soaked. "Can I get you something to drink?" she asked.

He nodded, removing his hat. His face was flushed from the heat. "That would be *wunderbaar.*"

She dashed inside and fixed him some ice water, using the largest glass she could find. When she came outside he was squeezing himself into one of the plastic chairs on the front porch. "Sit here," she said, touching the hickory rocker, which was bigger than the chair.

"I'm fine right here." He smiled and sat down. "See? No problem."

But he looked uncomfortable, his knees rising up to the level of his chest. She couldn't help but smile. "Don't be ridiculous. You can have the rocker. I'll take the chair."

He hesitated, then tried to get up, but the chair stuck to his back end.

A laugh escaped her lips. Mortified, she covered her mouth, hoping she hadn't offended him.

He let out a low, rumbling chuckle. "Guess the chair wants to come with me." He grinned and set the chair on the porch, then sat in the rocker.

She dropped her hand from her mouth. "I'm sorry. I didn't mean to laugh."

"Why not?" He shrugged, still smiling. "It was funny. And it's not the first time I've tangled with a chair."

Giggling, she handed him the water. He gulped it down. "*Danki*. That hit the spot." He set the glass down on the small table next to the rocker. "I was hoping it would cool down a little tonight. Too bad it hasn't." Removing his hat, he ran his large hand through his hair again, making the ends stick up in damp clumps. Then his expression grew serious. "I wondered if I could talk to you about something."

Deborah sat and watched him, mesmerized. His hair was thick, the locks covering his ears, and she started to wonder how it would feel against her hand. She clasped her fingers together and squeezed them tight. When she realized he was waiting for her answer, she said, "Um, sure."

"It's about your *daed*. I'm a little worried about him."

A thread of panic wound through her. "Why? Did something happen?"

"*Nee, nix*. He's fine, although he seems pretty tired."

"*Ya*. I noticed that too."

"Understandable, considering the circumstances. But I'm more concerned with something he said to me." Stephen angled his body toward her and leaned forward, resting his forearms against his knees. "He mentioned selling the farm."

Deborah frowned. "He did?"

Stephen nodded. "Has he talked about that before?"

"*Nee*, not that I know of." She paused. "But I was gone for a while and haven't been back long." She looked down at her lap, feeling a familiar twinge of guilt. "I could ask Naomi. But I can't imagine him selling this place. It's his whole life."

"He's worried he can't keep up with the place. And you were right the other night about him not wanting me to come out here so often. But I think

I convinced him that it's not a bother to me. I like doing the work." He sat up straight. "I told him I'd help him out as long as he needed me. But he still seems to have some doubts about handling the farm himself."

She sat back in her chair, dumbfounded. "Do you really think he wants to sell?" Just the thought of it triggered panic.

"I don't think so, not right now anyway." At the sound of her relieved sigh, he smiled and said, "Thought you'd be happy about that."

"I am." She rubbed her left earlobe. "But I also understand how he feels. I wish I could do more to help him, but keeping up with Will takes up a lot of my time."

"As it should. Don't feel guilty for taking care of your *sohn*, Deborah. That's what *gut mudders* do."

She looked at him, a lump lodging in her throat. He'd said exactly what she needed to hear. "What did you say to make *Daed* change his mind?"

Stephen leaned back in the rocker. "I told him to think of Will. That was the clincher. But I'm not sure the thought of selling won't cross his mind again. That's why I'm telling you about this. I figured you'd want to know."

Deborah nodded. Despite her efforts, tears

slipped out of the corners of her eyes. She averted her gaze and wiped them away.

"Deborah?"

She turned at the sound of Stephen's deep voice, unable to resist his gentle tone. "I'm all right."

His brows furrowed. "You're crying." He moved forward again. "I'm sorry."

She shook her head. "It's not your fault." More tears flowed, and she fisted her hands. "I feel so stupid."

"Why?"

"Crying in front of you." She sniffed, wishing she had a tissue. Even more, she wished she could control her emotions, but the more she tried to stop the tears, the more they betrayed her. She squeezed her eyes shut, as if the action would cease the flow.

She heard the squeak of the porch floor as he got up from the rocker. She didn't open her eyes, knowing that he was walking away. Her father could never abide his wife's or daughters' tears, always leaving the room whenever the waterworks started. She certainly couldn't blame Stephen for doing the same.

"Deborah. Look at me."

Opening her eyes, she saw Stephen kneeling in front of her. It was a strange feeling, looking down on a man she had always looked up to.

His dark blue eyes were filled with compassion. "Don't apologize. You just lost your *mudder*. You have a right to grieve."

His kind words touched her soul, making her more vulnerable. "It's not just that. I'm worried about *Daed* too. He's not the same since *Mami* died. Not that I expect him to be, but he's so distant sometimes. Then the next minute he seems almost fine, like *Mami's* still here but she's gone to town for the day." She brushed her cheek with the palm of her hand. "And then there's Naomi…" She gazed down at him. "Never mind. I shouldn't be telling you all this."

"Why not?"

"Because it's not your problem. It's mine." She wiped her face and tried to force a smile. "I'm sure I'm boring you to death with my self-pity."

He shook his head. "I'm not bored at all. I wish I could help you somehow."

"You have, more than enough." She sniffed and straightened her shoulders. "I'm okay, really."

Worry creased his forehead. "I don't think you are."

He was right, but she didn't want him feeling sorry for her. "*Danki* for telling me about *Daed*. I'll let Naomi know, and together we'll watch out for him." She moved to get up from the chair, but he was in her way.

Taking the cue, he stood, allowing her to stand.

She looked up at him, moved by his concern, which only made her want to cry more. Why couldn't she get her emotions under control? She expected him to step aside and let her pass, but for some reason he remained there, staring down at her with kindness. If she didn't get away from him, she would break down completely, and she didn't want him witnessing that. "Did you need something else to drink?" she asked, trying to sound unaffected. But the tremble in her voice gave her away.

"*Nee*. Deborah, I—"

"Then I should get back inside, in case Will wakes up." Before he could say anything else, she ran inside and upstairs to her room. Not wanting to disturb Will, she gently sat on her bed, lowered her head into her hands, and sobbed in silence.

At the end of the first two weeks of school, Ruth finally felt like she had established a routine. Her days hadn't been without a few hiccups, but now she had command of her students and the curriculum. With each passing day, her confidence grew, and the doubts she'd had on that disastrous first day had disappeared. But there was still one problem that she couldn't solve. She had yet to find a way to teach Jacob.

She had tried a few different methods with him. Being nice. Being harsh. Telling him to stay after school, which he wouldn't do. But even through the problems, she could see his potential. He'd made a couple of jokes in class that were clever, and he'd given a right answer or two, which meant he was paying attention to some degree. But she had no idea how to talk to him, to discipline him, or to teach him.

Though she'd wanted to handle Jacob herself, she had to get his father involved. She had driven herself to school that morning so she could go to the buggy shop and speak with David Kline when school was over.

As she made her way down Hayes Road, she thought about Zach. True to his word, he had replaced the window with a new one, and he had done so in time for the first rain they'd had in September. The stifling heat had ended and was replaced by cooler air and less humidity. But Zach had made himself scarce, which disappointed her. Now that the schoolhouse was finished, the window replaced, and the new desks delivered, there wasn't a reason for him to come around. She wondered what he was doing with his time, other than working at the buggy shop. She missed him, more than she thought she would. She thought she might see him at the shop today, but then she remembered that he worked in the mornings.

When she went inside Kline's Buggy Shop, another customer stood at the counter, a man who appeared to be near her father's age. A few moments passed but no one came to help him. Ruth turned to leave, deciding to stop by the Kline house and hopefully catch Jacob's mother.

Then Zach appeared from a room in the far back of the shop, his head down as he maneuvered his way through the buggy parts toward the front. He approached the counter and looked up at the man in front of her. Obviously he hadn't noticed her yet. He and the customer were speaking in low tones, and when Ruth moved forward a few steps, she could hear parts of the conversation.

"So you want to add a blinker to the buggy?" Zach asked.

The older man nodded. "My *sohn's* been driving it. Let's say he's not as careful as I'd like him to be. I think the blinker will help. You know how fast some of these cars *geh* around here. Plus people don't pay no attention anymore. Driving around here's not like it used to be back in the day."

Zach nodded. "I know exactly what you mean."

Ruth thought she detected a small smile on Zach's face, but she wasn't sure. If anyone understood about the consequences of reckless driving, he did.

"Okay," he continued. "Leave the buggy with

us and you can pick it back up tomorrow. It should be done by then."

The man nodded. "Sounds fine by me." When Zach started to walk away, the man added, "Aren't you gonna write me a ticket or something?"

Zach froze. "Oh. Um, yeah."

Ruth frowned at the change in Zach's demeanor. So far he'd handled the customer with confidence. Now it was like he didn't know what to do. Then he saw her. Their eyes met, and his expression turned to confusion.

He looked away from Ruth and back to the customer. "Need to find the tickets first." He fumbled around underneath the counter and pulled out a pad of paper. As he reached for a pen in the cup on the counter, he knocked it over, spilling the contents.

"Sorry." He scrambled to pick up the pens and shove them back in the cup. One fell out, but he let it go. He looked down at the paper, squinting. "Um, okay," he said. "So you want blinkers, then."

The man crossed his arms over his chest. "*Ya*. We just covered that."

Zach put the pen to paper hesitantly, then scribbled something on the sheet. Ruth tried to peer around the man's shoulder to see what he'd written. When she caught a glimpse, she couldn't make out anything but the price.

"I need you to sign here." He turned the paper over to the man.

The man picked it up and looked at it. "I can't make this out."

"It says that you agree to pay for the blinker upon pickup."

"It does?" He looked at it again, then put the paper down. He signed it and handed it back to Zach, leaning forward as he did. "You might want to work on your penmanship. I couldn't make heads or tails over what you just wrote."

Once the man left the shop, Ruth stepped forward. Zach didn't look directly at her. Instead he took the paper and stuffed it underneath the counter. "Surprised to see you here." He kept his gaze averted.

He sounded agitated, which was unusual. "Is everything okay?"

"It's fine." Now his tone turned curt. "Did you need something?" He finally looked at her, his eyes hard. Then he started fidgeting with the pencils and pens in the cup.

"I came to talk to David. I'm still having trouble with Jacob in my classroom."

"He's not here. I'm all by myself today. Anything else? Because I have a lot of work to do."

"Have you had a chance to talk to Jacob?"

His jaw clenched. "I've been busy."

His agitation reminded her of when they were

in school together, memories of the teacher telling him to settle down, only to see him become more restless. She never understood why he wouldn't comply with the teacher's request. Jacob often reacted the same way to her. "Zach, are you sure everything is—"

"It's fine, all right? Now stop bugging me so I can get back to work."

She stepped back, trying not to be hurt by his tone, but failing. He'd never talked to her like that before. "All right. I'll leave."

Once outside, she took a deep breath, swallowing the lump that formed in her throat. Why was she so upset? So what if he yelled at her. It wasn't like she'd done anything wrong. Whatever he was mad about had nothing to do with her. Or did it? Forgetting about Jacob, she climbed in her buggy, trying to figure out if she had said or done anything to make Zach angry. Then again, why should she even care? They were barely friends. She blinked, aware of the growing dampness in her eyes. It shouldn't matter this much. But it did.

"Ruth?"

She wiped her eyes and turned to Zach. He was standing on the opposite side of the buggy, his expression contrite. "What?" She tried to keep the bite out of her voice, but it came out anyway.

He hung his head for a moment, then looked

at her again. "I shouldn't have talked to you that way. I'm sorry."

"It's okay." And it was, sort of. His apology helped.

"*Nee*, it's not." He glanced around the driveway, then back at her. "Can I sit with you for a minute?"

His request surprised her. "Sure."

Zach climbed in but didn't sit close to her. He leaned forward, his elbows on his knees. "I did try to talk to Jacob earlier this week. The conversation was going great, as long as we stuck to fishing and baseball. But as soon as I brought up school, he clammed up."

Ruth knew exactly what he meant. She'd seen the same thing happen with Jacob in her classroom.

"So I'll try again. And again. As long as it takes." He tilted his head toward her. "I'm starting to understand what my father went through with me."

"What helped you?"

"*Nix.*" He sat up and sighed. "It didn't matter what he said. How he punished me, or threatened to punish me. I still screwed up everything."

"You're not screwing up now."

He let out a bitter laugh. "Give me some time. It will happen."

She didn't know what to say. He'd been agitated before, but now he seemed almost despondent.

"I've got to get back to work. Like I said, David's gone, but his *frau's* inside. You can talk to her about Jacob if you want."

"I will." She pulled her glasses out of her purse and slipped them on. She noticed Zach staring at her. "What?"

He looked away. *"Nix."*

She frowned, ready to press him again, but decided to drop it. He started to leave but she stopped him. "I've been reading a book I got from the library. It's in my bag under your feet. It's called *Quirky Kids*. I'd like to show it to Jacob's *mudder.* There are a few ideas the authors bring up that I want to discuss with her. Can you hand it to me?"

He looked at her for a moment, his eyes widening.

His hesitation puzzled her. He acted like she'd asked him to walk a tightrope without a net. "Zach?"

He licked his lips and picked up the satchel, which held several books. "What did you say the title was?"

"Quirky Kids." She gave him the authors' names too.

He shuffled through the bag. Finally he pulled

out a book and handed it to her, then scrambled out of the buggy.

She looked at the cover. It was an English book. The title wasn't anything close to what she had told him. She started to point out that he gave her the wrong book, but he had already headed to the shop. Then she remembered how the customer couldn't read his handwriting. Her mind traveled even farther, back to school. The way Zach usually cracked a joke instead of giving the correct answer. How he used to get in trouble for not turning in homework. At the time she'd thought him lazy. A troublemaker who didn't take his education seriously. Now she realized the real reason behind his behavior.

He couldn't read.

Chapter Fifteen

Ruth walked into the shop and saw Zach behind the counter. She took a deep breath and slowly approached him. "Why didn't you tell me you couldn't read?" He flinched but didn't say anything. "I don't know how you made it out of school without learning to read. How are you making it through life?"

He didn't look at her. "I've been getting along just fine." His voice was brittle, like clumps of charred wood after a fire.

"But how do you do your job?"

"I don't have to read to fix buggies."

"What about writing tickets? You have to read to do that."

"Look, I can read some, okay?" He looked down at the floor and scuffed his shoe against the black splotches of paint on the concrete. "I just have trouble with it. Always have."

"Maybe if you'd paid more attention in school—"

"Don't." He held up his hand, then balled it into a fist and let his arm drop to his side. "Don't judge me." He looked down at her. "Perfect Ruth. Doesn't have a single flaw but always eager to point out everyone else's."

Ruth couldn't believe what she was hearing. "That's not true."

"Isn't it?" Zach's hot glare made her take a step back. "You've always had a low opinion of me. Especially after I crashed into the *schulhaus*."

Shame coursed through her, because she couldn't deny it was true. She was guilty of pointing out the splinters in other people's eyes, especially his, before pulling out the plank in her own. But she had changed, at least she thought she had. "I'm not perfect, Zach. You know that better than anyone. And I don't have a poor opinion of you…not anymore."

"I know. Now you just feel sorry for me."

She shook her head, walking toward him until there were only a few inches between them. "Listen to me, Zach. I don't feel sorry for you. I feel—" She stopped herself, suddenly afraid. She'd come so close to admitting her true feelings for him, something she'd tried to keep tucked deep inside.

But he wasn't making it easy for her. He leaned

down close. "What do you feel, Ruth?" His words were low, his voice deeper than she'd ever heard it.

"I feel…" She still had on her glasses, and being this close to Zach, she could see every freckle on his cheeks, the way his emerald eyes darkened to a deep green. Her breath caught as she focused on his mouth, the image of kissing him flooding her mind.

At the last second, she reined herself in and backed away. How could she be thinking about kissing at a time like this? He had admitted something that pained him deeply, and all she could focus on was her desires. She turned away from him.

He sighed and leaned against the counter. "Leave me alone, Ruth."

She whirled around and looked at him. Fatigue etched his features. "Zach, I can help you. I can teach you—"

"I said leave me alone." His eyes held hers. They were no longer soft but like hard chips of green ice. "I mean it."

At a loss to say anything else, she turned around and rushed back to the buggy. When she got inside, she covered her face with her hands. Tears spilled over, and there was nothing she could do to stop them.

* * *

Zach gripped the side of the counter until his knuckles cramped. He'd heard Ruth's buggy drive away, but his body was still trembling, and he struggled to calm himself. Sending Ruth away was one of the hardest things he'd ever done. But he'd had to. There was no hope for their friendship, which was questionable anyway. And any outside chance he had of developing their relationship into something else had fizzled, now that she knew the truth.

He shut his eyes. He'd almost kissed her, and when he looked into her eyes, he thought she wanted him to. Then she backed away, and he knew he'd made a mistake. She didn't want him. And her offer to help him? To teach him? He didn't want to be one of her pet projects.

He raked his hands through his hair. In school he'd lived in fear of being found out. First graders read better than he did. And it wasn't like he didn't try. But what he saw on the page didn't match what the teachers told him. Letters seemed backward. Mixed-up. If he took the time to puzzle the words out, sometimes he could read a little. But the effort wasn't worth it, not when everyone else was smarter than him.

After he'd finished school, he didn't worry about it as much. He just avoided anything that required reading and writing. Obviously, he didn't need to read to paint a buggy—or repair a school and replace a window, he thought bitterly. He never had to fill out a job application anyway. The only thing he had to do was sign his name. Until today, when he had to fill out the ticket. He'd never been so humiliated.

Opening his eyes, he released his grip and walked to the partially completed buggy he'd been working on before Ruth came. He started to pick up the spray gun but kicked at a buggy wheel instead.

"My *daed's* not gonna like that."

Zach jumped at the sound of Jacob's voice. His gaze narrowed. "Where did you come from?"

"Out back. When *Fraulein* Byler showed up, I hid behind the shop." He looked dead-on at Zach. "I thought she was here for me. But she was here for you."

"*Nee*, she wasn't. She came to talk to your *daed*. About you and the problems you've been giving her in school."

Jacob shrugged, his expression empty. "Whatever."

Zach stormed toward the boy. "You're a fool, you know that? You've got a teacher willing to do anything to help you. You've got parents who love you and want you to succeed. And what do you do? Treat them like garbage and act like a spoiled brat."

The boy's hooded lids flew open wide. "You don't know anything about me."

"You don't think so?" Zach leaned in close, years of frustration and anger pulsing through him. "I used to be just like you."

Jacob's nostrils flared. "At least I can read."

Zach froze. He took a step back. "What did you hear?"

"Enough to know you can't read. And that it doesn't matter if you can. You made it through school just fine."

"I *barely* made it through school. And it wasn't 'just fine.'"

"I'm almost fourteen. I have one more year to *geh*, then I can get a job. Who cares what happens in school anyway?"

"A lot of people. People that matter to you. Like your parents."

Jacob glanced away. "If they cared about me, they wouldn't have moved away."

Hearing the melancholy in the boy's voice released some of Zach's tension. "Is that what all this is about? The move?"

He faced Zach. "All my friends are back in Iowa. And my aunts, uncles, cousins. There's nothing here. Middlefield stinks."

"But there are plenty of *kinner* around. You can make friends."

"You sound just like them. I should have

known you wouldn't get it. I bet you've lived here all your life." When Zach nodded, Jacob scowled. "As soon as I'm done with school, I'm going back to Iowa."

"How?"

"What do you mean how?"

"I mean how are you going to get there? Do you have a buggy?"

Jacob frowned. "*Nee*. But I can get a bus ticket."

"With what? Do you have any money?"

After a pause, the boy shook his head. "I can get a job."

Zach held out his hands. "Where are you going to find a job? You won't even help out around here. Your *daed* had to hire someone else because he can't rely on you."

"That's not my fault. Besides, who wants to work in a *dumm* buggy shop? I'll find a job somewhere else."

The irony of the conversation was unreal. Everything Jacob said echoed Zach's conversations with his own father. And he was on the verge of saying the exact things his father had told him. *Help me here, Lord. Give me the words to say to Jacob. I don't want to mess this up.* "Jacob, you're making everything harder on yourself."

"I don't care."

"I know you don't care now. But let me tell you

something. When you're done with school, you'll start to care. Do you know why I'm working here at the buggy shop?"

He shook his head.

"Because my *daed* wouldn't hire me. He doesn't trust me enough to give me a job." Saying it out loud hurt, but if admitting his failures would help Jacob, it was worth it.

"Like that's my problem."

"And that's my point. If you keep causing trouble for other people and yourself, that will be your problem. I can't get work anywhere else. I don't have the best reputation around here because of the stuff I did as a kid. Because of the bad decisions I made. Some of those decisions have cost me money, like the *schulhaus*. I'm in debt up to my eyeballs over that. But others have cost me the respect of people who are important to me. I don't want to see that happen to you."

"It won't."

"It already is."

Jacob looked at him with belligerence. Zach worried that he wasn't getting through, but then the boy said, "If it's so important I *geh* to school, then how come you told *Fraulein* Byler to get out of here?"

Zach frowned. "If I'd known you were out there, she would've been talking to you."

"*Nee*. I'm not the one who needs to talk to her. You do."

"What?"

"I guess you don't think school is that important either. Especially reading."

"Now wait a minute. My problem with reading has nothing to do with you."

"I heard her say she could teach you. I bet she could; she is a *gut* teacher." Jacob curled his upper lip into a sneer. "But I guess you're better at giving advice than taking it." He turned on his heel and walked out of the buggy shop.

Zach stood there, stunned. Jacob's words hit him hard. Zach didn't have the right to tell Jacob anything. Not when he wouldn't give Ruth a chance. He'd rather hang on to his pride than have her see how dumb he really was. He'd been trying so hard to change these past few weeks, and he thought he had. But it took the words of an obnoxious kid to show him that, deep inside, he hadn't changed much at all.

That evening, Zach walked into the kitchen where his parents had already started to eat. He put his cooler on the counter, his hat on the peg, and washed his hands before sitting down. After a quick, silent prayer, he reached for the bowl of potatoes and put a spoonful on his plate. But he didn't touch it. His appetite was gone.

"Aren't you going to eat?" His mother looked at him, a worried expression on her face.

He didn't say anything for a moment, then shook his head. "*Nee.* I'm not really hungry."

"Your *mudder* worked hard to prepare this food." His father gave him a harsh look. "Don't waste it."

Zach looked at the potatoes, then at his father. Even though they tasted like cardboard in his mouth, he finished off the potatoes, and the glass of iced tea his mother had poured earlier.

He excused himself, saying he needed to clean out Maggie's stall. He escaped to the barn, and when he'd finished his task, he still wasn't ready to go inside. His mind mulled over what Jacob had said. What Ruth had told him. And how he responded to both of them. He sat down on a hay bale and let his head drop into his hands.

At the sound of footsteps entering the barn, he looked up. His father was walking toward him. Zach popped up from the hay bale. He must have done something wrong again, although he couldn't imagine what. Not that it mattered. In his father's eyes, almost everything Zach did was wrong.

But his father didn't say anything right away. He didn't even look at Zach at first. He walked over to Maggie and patted her, then peered over the top of the gate and inside the stall. Suddenly

Zach realized his father was checking on his work. When his father didn't speak, Zach turned around to leave.

"Zachariah."

Zach didn't think he could take another insult or admonition from his father. Not tonight. He should ignore his father and walk away, save himself from more pain. Hadn't he experienced enough shame for one day?

But something kept him in place. Whatever his father had to say, Zach needed to face it. After his conversation with Jacob, he knew what it was like to have your words ignored, your advice questioned and rejected outright. He turned around and looked at his *daed*. *"Ya?"*

"Gabriel Miller came by today. He was looking for you."

"Is something wrong with the *schulhaus*?"

His father shook his head, then reached into his pants pocket. He took out a few folded bills. "He wanted to give this to you."

Zach stepped forward and took the money. It was over a hundred dollars. "What's this for?"

"Apparently Ruth told him that you paid for the replacement window out of your own pocket. He wanted to make sure you were reimbursed." His father scratched his beard. "I didn't know you did that."

Zach looked down at the money. It was more

than the window had cost. Far more, and it would make a small dent in the debt he'd accrued. But he handed the bills to his *daed*. "You can give it back to Gabriel."

Surprise registered on his father's face. "What?"

"I don't need the money." At his father's dubious look he added, "*Ya*, I need the money, but not this way. I said I was going to take care of the repairs for the school, and I meant it."

"But the window has nothing to do with that."

"Then consider it a contribution to the school. I'm sure the board can figure out a better way to use the money."

His father looked more perplexed than before as he pocketed the money. "Your *mudder's* worried about you. It's not like you not to eat her supper."

"I wasn't hungry."

"You're always hungry."

Zach looked at his father and shrugged. "Not today." He turned away, and when he'd taken only a couple of steps toward the other side of the barn, he heard, "You've done *gut*, *sohn*."

Zach looked up, hearing the crack in his father's voice. The light inside the barn wasn't on, but there was still enough daylight for him to see his old man's expression. His father's bottom lip quivered for a moment but he turned around before Zach could see any more.

As his father walked out of the barn, it felt like a boulder had lodged in his throat. For the first time since he could remember, his father had praised him.

Chapter Sixteen

After her talk with Stephen, Deborah spent the next few days keeping an eye on her father as much as she could. He seemed all right, although the few times she'd approached him alone he was too consumed with farmwork to exchange more than a few words. He also stuck with his routine of leaving the house early and coming inside after dark, which made her wonder if he was avoiding her and Naomi. As of yet, he hadn't done or said anything to alarm her, but she would continue to watch him.

When she'd resolved to look after her father, she'd also vowed to avoid Stephen. On the night she'd cried herself to sleep, she'd tried to make sense of her feelings toward him. She was afraid she was falling for him. Then again, what woman wouldn't in her situation? He had shown so much compassion toward her and her family. And no one could deny he was a very handsome man. But could she trust her heart? She wondered if her attraction to Stephen was driven by her loneliness. Her worry over her father had kept her tied to the house, and other than attending church the previous Sunday, she didn't interact with too many people, not even Elisabeth, who was busy with her own life. Deborah didn't begrudge her that. At the moment, Stephen was the only other adult she could talk to.

She decided her feelings toward Stephen didn't matter. There was no spark of attraction in his eyes when he looked at her. No desire. He was her best friend's brother and a friend to her family. Nothing more than that. And her yearning for more from Stephen just kept her from trusting herself. She'd rather stay away from him than spend so much time second-guessing herself. Between Will, her father, Naomi, and the farm, she had enough to deal with.

Shortly after supper she tried to play with Will inside, but he was antsy and wouldn't behave, especially with the weather so beautiful outside. The temperature was mild, not stifling hot as before, and Will wasn't the only one who didn't want to be cooped up inside. She scooped him up and took him to the backyard, hoping she could avoid seeing Stephen. When she walked out the back door, though, she was surprised to see Naomi standing by the vegetable garden. She thought her sister was still upstairs.

Will squirmed. Deborah put him on the grass but hung on to his hand and led him to the tire swing. The swing had been there since she and Naomi were children. She put him in the center of the tire and knelt down, one hand on his waist as she gently pushed the swing back and forth.

She kept her gaze on Naomi, who was still standing at the edge of the garden, staring at the ground. Deborah frowned. It wasn't like her sister to be so still. She was constantly moving, always doing something. Deborah knew there were still a few green bean plants that needed picking and a couple of tomato vines that were still bearing fruit. Yet instead of tending the garden, Naomi remained as motionless as a cement figurine.

"Ma!" Will called out, trying to climb out of the swing. Deborah sighed. His attention span was so short that he flitted from activity to activity like a bee in a flower garden.

Naomi had jumped at the sound of Will's voice, her expression startled. Without looking at Deborah, she headed back to the house.

Deborah called, "Naomi, wait."

Her sister took a few more steps forward, and for a minute Deborah thought she would ignore her again. To her surprise, Naomi looked at her. "What?"

"I need to talk to you. It's about *Daed*." She picked up Will and balanced him on her hip as she walked over to Naomi. Will held his arms out to Naomi, but she ignored him.

"What about *Daed*?" she said, folding her arms over her skinny chest.

Deborah noticed the movement. Her sister had always been thin, but she seemed to have lost weight since Deborah's arrival. "Are you eating enough?"

Naomi's eyes clouded. "What does that have to do with *Daed*?"

"*Nix*. It's just that you look like you've lost weight."

"I don't want to be fat like you."

The words dug in deep. True, Deborah had never been as slender as Naomi, and her hips had widened since giving birth to Will, but she wasn't fat. She put Will on the ground next to her, partly to shield him from her sister's wrath. "That was mean."

Naomi lifted her chin in response, peering down her nose.

Deborah sighed. "I don't want to play this game anymore. If it makes you feel better, insult me all you want. I don't care. What I care about is *Daed*. I think there's something wrong."

Her sister's chin dipped a quarter inch. "I haven't noticed anything."

"Has he talked to you about the farm? What his plans are for it?"

She shook her head, her gaze narrowing. "Why? Has he been talking to you about it?"

"*Nee*. But a few days ago he mentioned to Stephen that he might sell the farm."

"*What*? Why would he do that?" Naomi spoke through clenched teeth, her arms falling to her sides. "Doesn't he know how important this farm is?"

"He's overwhelmed, Naomi. There's a lot of work to do around here."

"If you'd do your part instead of chasing that *kinn* around all the time, he wouldn't have to work so hard."

Deborah struggled to let the comment slide. *Lord, help me!* "Naomi, this isn't about me. Or you. This is about taking care of *Daed*."

"He can't sell this place," Naomi shouted. "I won't allow it."

"I don't see how you can stop him, if he's set on it. And it may not even come to that. Stephen reminded him how the farm is Will's legacy. That seemed to change his mind—or at least give him something to think about."

Naomi looked ready to explode. "*His* legacy? Your illegitimate *kinn* doesn't deserve any part of this land." Her acidic tone dripped with anger. "Not a single blade of grass."

Deborah could take insults about herself, but not about her son. She picked him back up and held him close. "He is my *kinn*, and he's as much a part of this *familye* as you and I are!" She took a deep breath and said, "Naomi, we need to focus on *Daed*. If the farm's too much for him to handle…maybe he should sell it." From the way Naomi's face reddened, Deborah regretted voicing the thought out loud. And it hadn't been easy to say. But it was something she'd prayed about the last few days since her talk with Stephen. At first, the idea of letting go of the farm had pained her, but she couldn't ignore how exhausted and withdrawn her father had become. "We have to be realistic. Trying to keep the farm running isn't worth ruining *Daed's* health or spirit."

"I can't believe this. I *refuse* to believe it." She stared at Deborah. "Stephen told you all this? He's lying to you, but you're such a fool you can't see it."

"Why would he lie to me?"

"Ever think he might want the farm for himself? He shows up here all of the sudden, offering to help *Daed*. He's here every night checking out the property, assessing the value, calculating its worth."

"That's not true." Deborah couldn't accept Naomi's theory. "Stephen wouldn't do something like that."

Naomi scoffed. "Pathetic. That's what you are. All a *mann* has to do is say a few nice words and you'll believe whatever he tells you. You'll do whatever he wants." She looked at Will, disgust coloring her features.

Deborah stepped away from her, pierced by her sister's anger. "What did I do to make you so angry with me?"

Naomi glared at her, her eyes blazing. Then she spun around and stormed off.

Stephen stood near the barn, unable to move as he watched Deborah and her sister argue several yards away. Neither woman had noticed him. He couldn't make out what they were saying, but from his vantage point, he had a clear view of Naomi. Anger radiated off of her; he could sense it from this distance. Will clung to Deborah, his chin resting on her shoulder. He saw the fear in the child's eyes, and that spurred him to move.

Just as he reached the backyard, Naomi stormed into the house, Deborah watching her go. Will's eyes met his and the toddler lifted up his chin. *"Da!"*

Deborah spun around, and the look on her face made Stephen halt his steps. Stricken didn't begin to describe her expression. Her lips were a slash of red against her stark white skin, and her body trembled all over.

He rushed to her. "Are you all right?"

She looked up at him, opening her mouth but not saying a word. Will twisted in her arms, pushing against her shoulders as he tried to get out of her grip.

Stephen held out his arm to the boy. "Let me take him for a minute."

She shook her head and took a step back. "*Nee.* He's fine. I'm fine." Her words ran together in one breath.

"Look, I don't know what happened with you and Naomi, but you're not fine." This time, when Will held out his arms, Stephen took him. "You need to sit down."

Her breathing came in spasms, and she shook her head.

"No arguments." Tucking Will against his side, he put his other hand underneath Deborah's arm and led her to a small wooden bench on the edge of the garden. "Sit."

She looked as if she would refuse, then she lowered herself onto the bench. Stephen sat beside her, balancing Will on his knee. He bounced the child up and down as he looked at Deborah. "Take a deep breath." He watched her try to calm herself. "That's it."

Her breathing slowed, her shoulders dipping as the tension eased from them. "I don't understand it," she finally said, not looking at him.

"Understand what?"

"Why she's so angry with me." She looked up at him this time. "It's like she…hates me."

"That's not true. It can't be." Growing up Amish, he'd been taught not to hate, not to even utter the word. He knew Deborah and Naomi had been raised the same way.

Her gaze went to Will, and Stephen thought that she might take him. But she didn't. Instead she stared at her child, her eyes filling with sorrow. "Then why does she insult me? Insult my *sohn*?"

He couldn't answer that. Naomi hadn't said much to him these past two weeks, even though he had tried to make conversation with her. He gave up after a while. Bitterness flowed from the woman. Moses never discussed his daughters, other than the one time that he'd mentioned they might never get married. The more he learned about Naomi's brittle personality, the more convinced he became that their father had been right.

His heart ached at the pain on Deborah's face. Her eyes were dry, but he would rather see her tears than the heavy sorrow she couldn't release. He'd never felt so helpless in his life. Without thinking, he put his arm around her shoulders. "It'll be all right, Deborah."

She leaned against him, resting her head on his shoulder. His arm tightened around her. He closed his eyes. Something pulled at him, deep inside. Having her close to him felt *right*. As if he were meant to be there for her at that moment, comforting her while he held her son. When she looked up at him, his heart halted, his gaze lost in the deep brown of her eyes, his fingers suddenly longing to glide across the flawless skin of her cheeks.

Then, in a movement so swift he barely had time to respond, she pulled away and took Will out of his arms. She popped up from the bench and began to walk away. He followed her and put his hand on her shoulder. "Deborah—"

"Don't." She kept her back to him. "Don't touch me, Stephen."

His heart ripped at her words. "I'm sorry, I didn't mean…" He swallowed. "I want to help you. That's all."

"I don't need your help." She looked at him, her expression raw. "Naomi was right about one thing. I am a fool." Then she ran back to the house.

Stephen stilled, floored by her rejection. What did she mean by that?

"Now if he gets upset, you can give him his little brown bear. That seems to calm him down." Deborah handed Elisabeth her diaper bag. It was Saturday afternoon, and her friends had stopped by for a visit, then insisted on taking Will for a couple of hours so she could have a break. Deborah had refused at first. Will had never been away from her before, and she wasn't sure he could handle it. It took almost fifteen minutes for Elisabeth to convince her to agree.

As they walked out the door, she saw Aaron standing at the bottom of the porch stairs. "You did it," he said, grinning. "Congratulations."

Elisabeth gave her husband a warning look, and his smile disappeared, replaced by a guilty expression.

"What was that about?" Deborah said, holding Will as she watched Aaron slink back to the buggy.

"Oh, *nix*."

"C'mon. I know you better than that. Aaron wouldn't have disappeared like that if he hadn't said something he shouldn't."

Elisabeth grimaced. "All right. He said I wouldn't be able to convince you to let us keep Will this afternoon."

"I'm still not sure it's a *gut* idea." She held on to Will a little tighter. He arched his back in response.

"Now hold on a minute. First off, Aaron always underestimates my powers of persuasion. You'd think someday he'd figure out that I can talk—I mean encourage—anyone into doing anything."

"Yes, your badgering—I mean encouraging—skills are pretty *gut*."

Elisabeth laughed, which made Deborah grin. It felt good to smile, even for a moment. The past two days had been awful. Naomi was colder to her than ever before, though Deborah hadn't thought that was possible. And the guilt over running away from Stephen wouldn't go away. He hadn't stopped by in the past few days, and she couldn't blame him. He had been so caring, and she had treated him so poorly. Yet what choice did she have? He had put his arm around her in a friendly way, and she had turned into a puddle of mush, laying her head on his shoulder and soaking in his comfort, her mind traveling beyond that moment and thinking about what it would feel like to be wrapped in his huge arms, to feel his kiss—

Her smile disappeared as her emotions warred inside. She was hopeless. And as her sister said, a fool.

"Deborah?" Elisabeth snapped her fingers once. "You're not changing your mind, are you?" She held her hands out to Will. "Here, *yung mann*, let me take you before your *mudder* backs out." The toddler went to Elisabeth without protest.

Deborah watched her friend and son for a moment, listening as Elisabeth cooed a few nonsense words to Will. "You'll be a *gut mudder* when the time comes, Elisabeth."

"I'm not sure about that." She sighed. "But Aaron's terrific with *kinner*." She lowered her voice. "He's ready to be a *daed*. But God hasn't seen fit to let it happen, at least not yet. I think it's my fault."

"Why would you think that?"

"I have a lot of doubts about having a *boppli*. I've been praying about it a lot, asking God to help me have more confidence about being a *mudder*. I don't think it will come naturally to me, like it did you."

Deborah was flattered by her words, but she shook her head. "It will, Elisabeth. I was terrified before Will was born. What did I know about having a *boppli*? I didn't have any nieces or nephews to watch, and I was all alone."

Elisabeth sobered. "I'm sorry. Here I am whining about my *dumm* doubts while you had to *geh* through this all by yourself."

"They're not *dumm*, Elisabeth. I'm sure if I had been married I would have had the same fears. But God helped me through it, and He'll help you, when you have your children."

Restless, Will wiggled in Elisabeth's grasp.

"You better get going, or else *he'll* change his mind," Deborah said.

"Will do. *Danki* for the advice." Elisabeth smiled. "We'll take *gut* care of him for you."

"I know you will." But even though she felt reassured that her son was in safe hands with Elisabeth and Aaron, it didn't make watching them leave any easier. After the buggy disappeared, she didn't know what to do next. Naomi had left for Middlefield earlier in the day to do some shopping, and her father, as usual, was out working, this time in the cornfield, double checking that all the good ears had been picked and collecting the ones that never fully matured for the pigs. For the first time since before Will's birth, she was completely alone.

A cool breeze kicked up, making the ribbons of her *kapp* flutter. A couple of orange and red leaves skittered across the porch. Noticing the dust on the porch, she picked up a broom and started sweeping. The mundane task helped keep her mind off Will. But it would take a lot more than sweeping to put Stephen out of her mind.

Chapter Seventeen

As Stephen made his way to the Coblentzes', he saw Aaron and Elisabeth's buggy on the opposite side of the road. He slowed, and when he waved, he saw Will sitting on Elisabeth's lap. His sister had been talking about taking care of Will and giving Deborah a break, but he was surprised to see Aaron with her. Then again, his sister had never been confident in her babysitting skills. Aaron must've taken the day off to lend his support.

He directed Trapper down the dirt road to the Coblentz farm. He had missed being here. Two days ago, Byler and Sons had gotten a huge order for bookcases from a Yankee customer, and he had spent the past couple days helping his father and brothers with it. But the whole time he'd been in the shop, he'd itched to come back to the farm. Something strange had happened in the three weeks he'd been helping the Coblentzes. He had fallen in love with farming.

As a kid he'd visited his grandparents' farm in Holmes County, and he'd always enjoyed it, but this was different. Now he felt connected to the land. He loved soaking up the sunshine while working in the field. Spending the end of the day looking across the pasture, listening to the cows lowing and the chickens clucking as they settled in for the night. Breathing in the fresh air, feeling the warm, soft earth in his hands. All that filled him with happiness, much more so than working as a carpenter in a wood shop. He'd never been dissatisfied with his work as a carpenter until now. And the more he thought about it, the more he wanted a farm of his own.

But he knew that dream was far off. He had a lot of hurdles to overcome first. He'd have to save up enough money to purchase the land. God wasn't going to drop a farm in his lap. Then he'd have to tell his father he was leaving the family business. That would be harder than anything he'd ever done, and he wasn't sure he could go through with it. He had to put the matter to prayer before he made any decisions.

As he drove, he also thought of Deborah. She hadn't been far from his mind since his last visit to the farm, and putting his confusing feelings about Deborah into prayer was more difficult. He wasn't sure how he felt about her. He liked her, a lot. He also respected her and admired how she took care of her son and her father. Her nurturing nature appealed to him. It didn't help at all that she was pretty and seemed to become more so each time he saw her.

The special order for bookcases had come at a good time, because while he missed working on the farm, it gave him time to figure out what to do about Deborah. He had to honor her wishes. If she didn't want him to help her, he wouldn't. He'd focus on Moses and the farm exclusively, no matter how hard it would be.

When he turned his buggy into his usual parking place, he saw that the Coblentzes' buggy wasn't there. He wondered if anyone was home. He'd never come on a Saturday, but he'd gotten the time off from the shop to make up for the days he'd missed at the farm. Working so many hours this week had taken its toll on him, and he had to admit he was pretty tired. But once he stepped out of the buggy, a cool blast of air refreshed him, and he was ready to dive into work.

Stephen walked inside the barn and checked on the animals. They were all fed and content, so he headed for the back of the pasture to check on Moses's progress on the fence. He hadn't been back there since he'd first started helping at the farm, as Moses always said he had the repairs under control. But after he'd stamped through a field of shorn timothy grass, he came to the fence and frowned, noticing that the rips in the wire hadn't been touched. He walked farther along, inspecting the fence, until he reached the very back of the pasture. Not a single repair had been done.

Stephen scratched the back of his neck. What had Moses been doing all this time back here? It didn't make any sense. Had he run out of fencing, or out of money to buy it, and hadn't mentioned it to Stephen? If that was the case, he wasn't all that surprised. But still, he wished Moses would've said something. Stephen would have bought the materials himself if he had to.

Some needle-nose pliers and a little elbow grease could fix a couple of those holes. Stephen turned to head to the barn to get his tools, but something caught his eye several feet away. He went to investigate, and as he neared the dark form, he realized it was a person. He sprinted forward when he recognized who it was.

When Deborah heard Stephen's buggy approach, she gripped the handle of the broom tightly and kept right on sweeping. Her palms started to sweat, and she forced herself to keep her back to the barn until she finished the chore. After the porch was swept cleaner than she'd ever seen it, she leaned the broom against the railing. At that exact moment, Stephen left the barn and walked out to the pasture. She couldn't help but watch him as he went, his long stride and confident gait mesmerizing. She snapped herself back to reality and went inside. It was safer there. She didn't have to worry about seeing him again.

But what was she supposed to do in here? Naomi had cleaned every single inch of the house, so she didn't have any housekeeping to do. She'd finished her laundry yesterday, since Naomi only washed her and her father's clothes on Mondays. All the canning was done, and the breads had been baked for the week. She thought about picking up her knitting, but she wasn't in the mood. Maybe she should go work in the garden. There were always weeds to pull. But then she'd probably see Stephen again, and she didn't want that. At least she tried to convince herself that she didn't want to see him.

She plopped down on the couch in the living room and saw a copy of *Family Life* magazine on the coffee table. She thumbed through it and set it back down. She missed Will. A glance at the clock on the fireplace mantel told her he wouldn't be home for another hour.

Deborah sat there for a few moments before her eyes drooped. She stretched out on the couch and was just about asleep when the screen door burst open. She sat up and saw Stephen rushing in, her father in his arms.

"Daed?" She jumped up from the couch. "What happened? What's wrong with *Daed*?"

Stephen laid her father on the couch. His skin was ashen, and she couldn't tell if he was breathing. She whirled and faced Stephen, fear climbing in her throat. "What's wrong with him?" she shrieked.

"I don't know! I found him lying by the fence when I went out there." He looked at Deborah, his chest heaving up and down. "Call an ambulance!"

Deborah ran to the call box at the end of their drive. She knew a doctor who made house calls; she'd call him first. Fear tried to numb her legs and thoughts. Would her father be okay? She couldn't take it if she lost her *daed* too.

Deborah hugged her body as she stared out of the picture window in their living room. It was dark outside, and there were no street lamps by their house. All she saw was her own shadowy image reflected back at her, with a background of inky darkness behind her. Worry coursed through her, so strong she could barely contain it. The doctor had arrived quickly after Deborah's call. Just before his arrival, her father had regained consciousness, and at the doctor's request, Stephen had helped *Daed* to his bedroom. The doctor was in there now, examining him. Deborah knew she should be grateful that he was awake, but until she heard the doctor say her father was all right, she couldn't let go of her dread.

Adding to her worry was the fact that Will hadn't returned. Elisabeth should have been back with him by now. What if something happened to her baby? The thought brought tears to her eyes and compressed the air out of her chest. She couldn't even find the words to pray.

"Deborah?"

She turned at the sound of Stephen's voice. He had disappeared outside after helping *Daed* to the bedroom. Now he walked toward her, concern etched on his features, weariness creasing the corners of his dark blue eyes. She automatically went to him, drawn by his compassion.

When they were inches from each other, they both halted. He looked down at her. She breathed in the faint scent of hay and animals. It was a smell she'd grown up with, one she never minded and found comforting. They looked at each other for a long moment, not saying a word. Then he held out his arms to her. Without hesitation she walked into them.

"He'll be okay, Deborah."

Stephen's soft voice cloaked her like a warm

quilt on a frigid day. She wanted to believe him. But the longer the doctor stayed in the room with her father, the more the doubts set in. "I can't lose him," she said, choking on the words.

"You won't. I prayed that it wouldn't happen."

She stepped back and looked up at him. "You prayed for him?"

He nodded. "Just now. While I was in the barn."

She marveled at how he was able to pray to God when she wasn't able to. *"Danki."* A tear rolled down her cheek.

He reached out and brushed it off with his thumb, then jerked away. "Sorry."

"Don't be." She looked up at him, moved to the core by his gentleness. There wasn't a single man kinder or gentler than Stephen Byler, she was sure of that. And right now she needed that feather-light touch more than anything.

Stephen knew he shouldn't have touched Deborah. The gesture of wiping her tears was meant to be innocent, to offer comfort. Yet the emotions churning inside him from that brief contact were anything but innocent. Her skin was so smooth against his thumb. And now she was embracing him. Out of her own grief, he knew. But deep inside he wished she were embracing him for a different reason. She smelled sweet, the scent of the outdoors still in her hair. Powerless to stop himself, he stroked her back, and leaned down and rested his cheek on top of her head.

The front door opened and she jerked out of his embrace. "Will?" she cried, spinning around.

His arms were still stretched out in front of him, feeling empty, his body suddenly cold from the absence of her warmth. He saw Naomi come through the door. She froze, staring at them.

"What's going on here?" Her disapproving gaze traveled from Deborah to Stephen. Her eyes were cold, her tone frosty.

"*Nix*," Deborah said, going to her. "Naomi—"

"You were hugging him." She snapped her eyes to Stephen, distrust radiating from her. "I saw you. Don't deny it." She glared at Deborah. "I can see he's helping himself to more than the farm."

Deborah clenched her fists. "You don't know what you're talking about."

"Oh, I think I do."

Stephen could feel his blood pressure spike. No wonder Deborah had been so distraught over Naomi. The woman was meaner than a ticked-off bull. But before he could say anything, Deborah moved closer to her sister and spoke.

"Listen to me, Naomi. Something's happened to *Daed*."

Naomi's flaming red cheeks suddenly paled. "What?"

"He's in the bedroom now with the doctor—"

Naomi shoved past her, hurling a black glare at Stephen. "What did you do to him?"

Stephen held out his hands. "I didn't do anything—"

But she had already moved past him, too, heading straight for her father's bedroom.

"Naomi, don't *geh* in there." Deborah started after her. "The doctor is still examining him."

"Don't tell me what to do!" She spun around and faced Deborah. "If something happens to him, I will never forgive you. Ever!" Naomi hurried away in a flurry of anger.

Stephen's ears burned from the woman's words, and he wasn't sure they were even directed at him. He looked at Deborah, who seemed more weary than shocked. He started to go toward her, but stopped, unsure he'd be able to keep a safe distance from her.

"I'm sorry you had to hear that." Deborah crossed her arms over her chest, maintaining space between them.

Before he could respond, there was a knock on the door. Deborah turned around and opened it. Elisabeth stood on the front porch, holding Will, who was asleep on her shoulder.

Deborah cried out with relief. "Where have

you been?" She took the sleeping child from Elisabeth's arms and hugged him close, then began to walk away.

"Deborah?" Elisabeth said, but when Deborah didn't turn around, she looked at Stephen, her blue eyes wide with bewilderment. "What's going on?"

Deborah had moved to the corner of the room, her face buried in her son's neck. Stephen motioned for Elisabeth to go outside. He met her on the front porch.

"Stephen, what's wrong with Deborah?"

He looked down at his sister, barely making out the white hue of her prayer *kapp* in the darkness. "Why were you late bringing Will home?" His tone was sharper than he intended.

"We stopped off at Aaron's parents' house for a short while. Aaron was helping his *daed* move some furniture out to the shed. We stayed a little longer than we thought." Her voice sounded small. "I didn't mean to make her mad. I should *geh* talk to her..."

Stephen cut in. "Now's not a *gut* time. Where's Aaron?"

"He's waiting for me by the barn. Stephen, are you going to tell me what's going on?"

He told her about Moses's collapse and that Deborah was worried about Will. "She'll be okay, once she finds out her *daed* is fine."

"Is he going to be fine?"

He glanced over his shoulder, making sure Deborah wasn't near the door. Lowering his voice, he said, "I don't know."

Elisabeth drew in a breath. "Should I stay? I can tell Aaron to *geh* home without me."

Stephen shook his head. "I'll stay."

She nodded. "Make sure you keep an eye on her. I've never seen her so upset, not since she was…well, just look out for her, okay?"

"I will." He wondered what his sister was referring to, but he didn't ask.

Once Elisabeth left, he walked back inside. Deborah was sitting on the couch, Will leaning against her. He was still asleep. Stephen sat next to her, glad when she didn't tell him to go away.

"Elisabeth and Aaron must have worn him out." She touched her lips to the top of Will's head. Then she looked at Stephen. "I owe her an apology."

"*Nee*, you don't. I explained everything to her. She understands."

"I'm glad. She's a *gut* friend." She turned to him. "I'm sorry about what Naomi said. She was just upset over *Daed*."

He knew it was more than that. "It's forgotten. No harm done."

She gave him a half-smile and looked down at Will. "I was so worried about him." She put her hand on his back. "I'm worried about *Daed*." Her smile disappeared, and her lower lip trembled.

He wished he knew the right words to comfort her, but he didn't. He held out his hand to her. She looked at it for a long moment before entwining her fingers in his.

"What do you mean he's had a heart attack?"

Deborah clenched her jaw at Naomi's shrill question. It had been nearly an hour since the doctor had arrived. She had already put Will to bed, and Stephen was waiting outside in the living room. She threaded her fingers together, remembering the warmth of his hand. The comfort of his embrace. She couldn't have made it through this without him.

Deborah looked at her father, taking in his pale complexion and gray lips. He seemed to have aged a decade since she'd seen him this morning. A blue-and-white quilt was draped across his chest and tucked under his arms. His eyes were closed, and she asked, "Is he asleep or unconscious?" She made sure to keep her voice at a normal level.

"Asleep. I gave him a mild sedative." The young doctor turned to Naomi. "To answer your question, I don't know for sure if he had a heart attack. I need to admit him to the hospital for tests."

"Then do it!" Naomi clasped her hands together. "Do whatever you have to do!"

Dr. Williams held up his hand. "Ms. Coblentz, you'll have to keep your voice down. I don't want your father to get upset." When Naomi nodded, he continued. "I asked him to go to the hospital, but he refused. He said he was just tired, which of course is common for cardiac arrest, or he could just be extremely fatigued. But he did complain of chest pain, and I think he should have an EKG to make sure. However, I can't force him to go to the hospital."

"Then what are we supposed to do?" Deborah looked at the doctor, who had to be in his late twenties or early thirties. Was he even old enough to practice medicine?

He rubbed his dark brown mustache and glanced at her father. "Other than try to convince him to come to the hospital for tests, make sure he rests for the next few days, longer if possible. Keep his stress level low, and under no circumstances is he to do any physical labor for a while."

Deborah thought about the farm. All her father did was physical labor. How were they supposed to keep him from doing that? "Anything else?"

"Call me if he gets worse. Short of breath, any more fainting, or complaints of chest pain." He picked up his jacket, which had been lying on a rocking chair in the corner of the room. "Don't hesitate to call 911 too."

"We won't," Naomi said, casting another glare at Deborah.

Deborah didn't acknowledge it. She didn't have the time or the energy to deal with Naomi right now. "I'll walk you out, Doctor." She left the room, leaving Naomi with her father. Deborah hoped she wouldn't wake him up.

When she and Dr. Williams walked into the living room, Stephen was leaning forward on the couch, his head hanging down. He stood up. "How is he?" When she held up one finger and mouthed the words "just a minute," he nodded and sat back down.

She walked Dr. Williams to the door. "How much do I owe you?"

He waved her off. "Don't worry about it. I'll bill you." He gave her a small smile and opened the door. "The good thing is that your father seems okay. Once he regained consciousness he didn't have trouble breathing and the pains in his chest were gone. But if you can convince him to come in for tests, that would be the best thing."

"Thank you." She closed the door behind him and went back into the living room. Then she sat next to Stephen and faced him. He looked so tired, his expression filled with worry. "You didn't have to stay," she said. But she was glad he had.

He looked at her for a moment. "I wanted to see how your *daed* is."

"He might have had a heart attack."

Stephen's eyes grew wide. "Really?"

"But we can't know for sure because *Daed* won't go to the hospital and get tested. Which doesn't surprise me. So Dr. Williams asked if Naomi and I could convince him to do it." She stared at the coffee table in front of her. "But I don't know if we can."

"Your *daed* can be a little *obsenaat*."

"*Ya*, I know. But getting him to the hospital isn't the hard part. We also have to make sure he rests and doesn't do any physical exertion. That's going to be impossible."

"I'll take care of it. I can come by twice a day if you need me to."

"I can't ask you to do that." She looked up at him. "Naomi and I can handle this."

"But—"

"Deborah's right." Naomi came in the room. "She and I will take care of our *daed*. And of *our* farm." She looked at Stephen, her expression set in stone.

Stephen moved his gaze to Deborah, as if he expected her to disagree with Naomi. In this case, she couldn't. She couldn't ask Stephen to take on any more responsibility than he already had. She and Naomi had to work together to take over the farm responsibilities.

"It would be best if you left." Naomi pinned him with her glare.

"Naomi, that's enough." She'd had it with her sister's rudeness, especially to Stephen. Her accusing him of taking advantage of her had been insulting, and he didn't deserve that.

"He's not needed here."

Before Deborah could protest, Stephen rose from the couch. She could see anger flitting across his face, but he didn't express it. "I'll be back by tomorrow to check on Moses. For now I think it's best I leave." He glanced at Naomi, his lips thinning. Naomi lifted her chin, meeting his gaze directly. He turned to go.

Deborah followed him to the door. "Stephen?"

He turned, his frustration still evident.

She lowered her voice, aware that Naomi was standing behind them. "Please, don't let her get to you."

His eyes softened. "Deborah, don't worry about me. I don't want her getting to you. I'm serious about what I said. Anything you need from me, or your *daed* needs, let me know. I'm here for you."

Deborah took a deep breath, almost overwhelmed with emotion. She nodded, unable to speak, then closed the door. She leaned her forehead against the door frame, her body shuddering from weariness.

"Why didn't you call an ambulance?"

Deborah looked up to see her sister's face turn the shade of a plum. "What?"

"*Daed* would be getting the medical care he needed if you had done that instead of calling the doctor. We'll never get him to the hospital. You know that."

"The doctor was quicker," she said, her voice weak with fatigue. "I thought he would be the best bet."

"You don't know anything, do you? I don't know how you expect to raise your child if you can't make a simple decision." She looked around. "Where is he, anyway?"

The shock of her sister acknowledging Will directly for the first time barely registered. "He's upstairs, asleep. He spent the day with Elisabeth and Aaron."

"Figures you'd want him gone." She pointed her finger at Deborah. "That way you and Stephen could be alone together. I bet you were messing around while *Daed* was having his heart attack."

Deborah clenched her fists. "I can't believe you'd say that. Stephen's not that kind of *mann*."

"But you're that kind of *fraulein*," she sneered.

"You proved that to everyone, didn't you?" Naomi turned away and went to her father's bedroom.

Deborah stood there, shaking with anger. How dare her sister say that to her? But she dared, because it was true. She closed her eyes. "Lord, help me," she whispered.

She didn't know how long she stood there in the living room, but when she stopped shaking she moved to the couch and prayed. The words she couldn't find earlier poured out of her. She prayed for her father, for herself, for her son, and even for Naomi, asking God to soften her heart. If she and her sister didn't manage to work together, they could lose everything.

Chapter Eighteen

The third week of school had been the busiest yet for Ruth. She and her students had settled into a routine, and now that she knew them better, she was able to tailor her lessons to how they learned. Individualizing her plans took more work on her part, but she thought it was worth it.

At the end of the school day, Ruth dismissed the class. "Now remember, fifth graders, you have a math test tomorrow. Be sure to study. And third graders, practice your spelling words."

"We will, *Fraulein* Byler," several students said at the same time.

Ruth smiled. Then her gaze met Jacob, who was seated at the desk in the back of the room, and her smile dimmed. At least he'd attended school for the entire week. But he'd been disengaged from everything. At recess she noticed him on the edge of the playground, instead of playing with the other boys as he'd done last week. She'd been so busy, though, that she hadn't had a chance to visit the Klines again. She hoped she'd have a chance to talk to them soon. She had some free time tomorrow afternoon. She made a mental note to visit Mr. Kline after school let out.

After the children left, Ruth sat down at her desk and didn't move. *Ah, silence.* The frenetic pace of the week had given her little time to enjoy quiet moments. It had also given her little time to think. But those times when she was able to pause, Zach was never far from her mind. Now, in the quiet of the classroom, he came into her thoughts full force.

He'd asked her to leave him alone, and she had complied, thinking he might come around. But he hadn't. Now she knew she had to be proactive. She wasn't finished with Zach Bender, God had made that perfectly clear. He needed her. He just didn't realize it yet.

Already her mind started to formulate a plan. First she'd have to convince him of the importance of reading. Then she had to figure out why it was so difficult for him. Ultimately she had to leap the biggest hurdle of all—getting him to accept her help. But she was up for the challenge. She had to help Zach. She cared too much about him not to.

She slipped on her reading glasses and went through the writing assignments in her students' notebooks. She had just finished reading her lone sixth-grade student's essay when she heard a knock at the door. "Just a minute," she said, not lifting her head. With a red pen she wrote an A+ on the top of the young man's paper.

"Ruth?"

The deep voice made her head jerk up. "Zach," she said, trying to hide her surprise. He stood in the doorway, and her stomach fluttered. How handsome he looked in his dark blue trousers, light yellow shirt, and straw hat. His hands were shoved in his pockets, his expression unsure.

"Is it all right if I come in?"

She nodded, rising from her chair. Seeing him made her realize how much she'd missed him. Truly missed him, like a part of her had disappeared in his absence. But this wasn't about how she felt. It was about helping him.

He walked in the door, his steps almost tentative. His hands still in his pockets, he looked down at her. "I owe you an apology. Again."

"Zach, I—"

"Ruth, I have to get this out before I lose my nerve." He took a deep breath. "I shouldn't have taken my anger out on you. I was mad at myself, not at you." He took a step backward. "All these years I've hidden the fact that I can't read. I didn't want anyone to think I was stupid."

"No one thinks you're stupid, Zach."

"I do. I don't get how to read. I never have. There's something wrong with me."

Ruth's heart went out to him. "How can you say that? Zach, you're so talented. Look at this place." She held her arms out wide. "A month ago there was a huge hole in the wall!"

"Which I caused."

"Accidentally caused. And you repaired everything almost exclusively on your own. You know how smart you have to be to do that? I've grown up around carpenters. I know what I'm talking about."

"Look, Ruth, I appreciate what you're trying to do."

She shook her head. "I don't think you do." She moved toward him. "I don't think you appreciate what I'm saying at all. I also don't think you appreciate yourself. Not like I do." The words slipped out, but instead of wishing she hadn't said them, she continued. "Let me help you, Zach. I can teach you how to read."

"You don't know what a tall order that is."

"I don't care."

He stepped away from her. "I'm fine, Ruth. Really. Things are going great for me at the shop and hopefully David can bring me on full-time.

I feel better about life than I have in a long time. I don't need to learn how to read."

But his words didn't jibe with the pain she saw in his eyes. She noticed something else too. At that moment she realized what held him back. "You're afraid."

His brows lifted. "Afraid? I'm not afraid of anything."

"*Ya.* You are." She stepped closer to him, and when he tried to move away from her, she put her hand on his arm. "You don't have to be scared, Zach."

He looked at her hand on his arm, and she started to pull away. Before she could, he covered it with his own.

His hand felt warm. Strong. She looked up at him through her glasses, still seeing the fear there. What could she do to reassure him? *Lord, help him understand that I'm here for him. That I won't give up on him, and I never will.*

"What if I can't?" he suddenly said in a low voice. His hand, still covering hers, tightened. "What if I never learn to read?"

She smiled at him. "You will, Zach. I promise you will."

"I wish I had your confidence."

"It's okay." Her smile widened. "I have enough for both of us."

* * *

The morning after her father's collapse, Deborah rose early, before Will woke up. She went into the kitchen where Naomi sat at the table, drinking coffee and reading the morning paper. Her sister didn't look up or acknowledge her as she entered the room. It was as if everything was back to normal. But things between her and her sister were never normal, and after yesterday, she didn't see how they ever could be.

Deborah pulled out a pot, filled it with water for oatmeal, and put it on the stove to boil. She added a little salt. While she waited on the water, she got two slices of bread out of the pantry and put a small amount of butter on each. Soon she had breakfast ready for her father and set it on a tray to take to his room. She turned to Naomi, who still had her head buried in the newspaper.

"Do you want anything?" At least she could try to be civil.

Naomi continued to ignore her. The only sound in the kitchen was the whispering of the newspaper page being turned. Deborah swallowed her ire and left the kitchen. When she reached her father's room, she knocked on the door with her elbow.

"Come in," she heard him say.

She walked in and smiled at him. "Breakfast! Thought you might be hungry since you missed supper last night." She still couldn't believe her father had slept for the rest of the afternoon and night. The sedative Dr. Williams had given him must have been powerful.

With weary eyes her father looked at the tray in Deborah's hands. "*Danki*, Deborah. But Naomi already brought me breakfast about an hour ago."

Deborah froze. Naomi had watched her make the food, and she must have known it was for their *daed* when Deborah put it on the tray. And still she said nothing.

"Everything all right?" He shifted to a half-sitting, half-leaning position on the bed.

Remembering what the doctor said about keeping her *daed's* stress level low, she said, "It's all fine." She set the breakfast on his dresser and walked over to him. "Do you need anything else?"

"*Ya.*" He held his hands out in front of him, gesturing to the bed. "I need to get out of this bed and back to work."

"You can't do that. Not yet. The doctor said—"

"I know what the doctor said. Naomi told me. Stole twenty minutes of my life giving me a lecture about eating habits and stress." He frowned. "That young doc means well but doesn't know what he's talking about. I didn't have no heart attack. I was just tired."

Deborah pulled up the oak rocking chair that

was in the corner of the room. "We want you to get plenty of rest. Naomi and I can help out. Whatever you need us to do, we'll do it."

He shook his head. "I know you will, but you have enough to do as it is. Plus you need to take care of my *grosssohn*. And I don't want to always depend on other people in the community to help me out. They have their own families to take care of."

"*Daed*, I know you like to do things on your own, but it's okay to accept help, especially from *familye* and *freind*."

"I know that." He leaned back against his pillow and sighed. "It's just…well, I ain't what I used to be. I can't spend the rest of my days depending so much on other people."

"Oh, *Daed*." She didn't want to hear him talk like this, even though those thoughts had entered her mind too. She needed to know for sure what he planned to do. "Stephen told me something the other day."

He lifted a gray eyebrow. "What?"

"He said you were thinking about selling the farm." She looked at her father, almost afraid to hear his answer. "Is that true?"

He shrugged, staring down at his lap. "Eventually, I might have to."

Her throat constricted. "But I know how much

you love this place. There's got to be something else we can do."

Her father stared straight ahead. "I don't know what." Then he looked at Deborah. "But I want you to understand, I won't sell to just anyone. The *mann* who buys this farm has to love the land like I do. I'm not handing over this farm just so some yahoo can put a fast-food place on it."

Deborah almost smiled. Considering they lived on a dirt road off the beaten path, there was no chance of that happening. But hearing her father say he would wait on the perfect buyer gave her hope.

"*Ya*, I'll need to find someone who will treat the land with respect. Someone like Stephen." He nodded. "He'd make a fine farmer. Never seen a *mann* take to farming like him."

"But he's a carpenter. He has his own business."

Her father tugged on his beard. "That he does. But maybe I could convince him otherwise."

Naomi's accusation against Stephen rang in Deborah's head. Surely her sister wasn't right. It had to be a coincidence that her father brought Stephen up. She couldn't imagine Stephen's generosity was just an act to get in their good graces. Or was it?

She stood up and kissed her father on the cheek, making sure not to reveal her thoughts.

"You don't have to think about that right now, okay? Naomi and I have everything under control. Promise me you'll rest and not worry about anything."

"But—"

"Promise?"

"All right," he huffed, leaning back. As he closed his eyes, Deborah picked up the tray of uneaten oatmeal and left the room, quietly closing the door behind her.

She walked into the kitchen to see Naomi wiping down the countertop. The dishes Deborah used to make breakfast had disappeared. Naomi had probably washed, dried, and put them away already. She set the tray on the kitchen table and sat down. She rubbed her temples, not wanting to bring up the subject of the farm with her sister. But after the conversation with her father, she knew she had to. Better to get it over with now. "*Daed* really is thinking about selling the farm."

"What?" Naomi spun around and faced her. "When did he say that?"

"Just now. I asked him."

Naomi threw the dishrag on the counter. "I knew it. I bet he's planning to sell it to Stephen Byler. Did he say anything about that?"

"He mentioned him—"

"I told you." She locked her furious gaze on

Deborah. "He's brainwashed *Daed* into selling to him."

She shook her head. "*Nee*. That can't be right." But even as she said the words, doubt slithered into her thoughts. Her judgment had always been bad when it came to men; trusting Chase was a prime example. And now she had trusted Stephen. After yesterday, her feelings toward him were clear. She cared about him, not out of loneliness or because her life was upside down, but because of the man he was. Or the man she thought he was. Her heart ached at the possibility of being betrayed by someone she cared about. "*Daed* hasn't made the decision yet. We just have to make sure it doesn't get to that point."

Naomi's expression softened a tiny bit. "What do you mean?"

"We can help him run the farm. It can't be too hard, can it? It's not like we haven't helped him over the years."

"Some of us more than others."

Her sister was right. During her *rumspringa*, Deborah had rarely been home to lend a hand. She had been too busy working at Mary Yoder's, hanging out with her friends, and having fun. She couldn't dwell on the guilt that accompanied that thought, however. She could put up with Naomi's digs if it meant she could get her sister's cooperation and they could keep the farm. "The harvest is in. The canning is almost done. We just have a few jars of green beans to finish. All we'll have to do after that is take care of the animals."

"And prepare the garden for the winter," Naomi added. "And what about the woodstove? We'll have to make sure there's enough wood to keep it going throughout the winter."

"But that's pretty much it."

"*Ya*, if you don't count laundry, cooking, cleaning, preparing for church service, which we'll be hosting in a month, plus anything else I can't think of at the moment."

Defeat dragged at Deborah. Couldn't her sister be positive for once? "Are you saying we can't do this? That we should just let *Daed* sell the farm without even trying?"

Naomi didn't answer for a long moment. "*Nee.*"

"Then we'll have to work together to make sure that doesn't happen. Can we do that?" She heard Will crying upstairs. She stood. "I have to *geh* get him." She glanced at the tray behind her. "I'll take care of that when I come back down."

Naomi picked up the oatmeal bowl from the tray and dumped it into the trash can without saying anything, keeping her back to Deborah.

Deborah shook her head. Her sister would never change. Not only did she have an uphill battle taking care of the farm, she'd still be fighting Naomi. She moved to leave the kitchen when Naomi called her name.

"What?" she said, turning around.

Her sister paused, glancing down at the floor for a moment. Then she looked up, the tight lines around her lips relaxing. "What do you think Will wants for breakfast?"

Chapter Nineteen

Zach pulled Maggie to a stop in front of the school, then tied her reins to the hitching post. He turned and looked at the familiar building in front of him. The students had already gone home for the day, and Ruth was inside, ready to give him his first reading lesson. But he was more nervous than a spooked horse. Ruth said she could teach him to read. Promised him. But he still wasn't sure if she could. Not because he doubted her. He questioned whether he could learn. He spent eight years in this *schulhaus* and he still couldn't read. What if he would never be able to?

He continued to stare at the schoolhouse. A little more than a month had passed since he'd driven into the back of it, and so much had changed. His relationship with his father had begun to heal. He had a steady job he enjoyed and his boss's respect. And his relationship with Ruth had grown into something beyond friendship. He cared for her more than he thought possible. Just thinking about her made him smile. Taking a deep breath, he walked toward the door. He let out a chuckle when he thought back to when he was a schoolboy. If someone had told him he would be spending this much time in a schoolhouse—without being forced to—he would have said they were crazy. But then again, he'd never had Ruth as a teacher.

She was at the blackboard when he walked in. The weather had turned a little cool, and she wore a long-sleeved dark blue dress with a white apron. She turned and smiled, her blue eyes twinkling behind her glasses. *So pretty.* He went to her and stood by her side.

Ruth looked at him. "I'm glad you're here."

"Hope you can say that after our lesson."

She lifted her chin, still smiling, still filled with confidence. "I know I will."

"I better warn you, though. I'm not the best of students. Especially around a pretty teacher." His comment made her blush, and he touched her heated cheek with his fingertip.

She looked up at him, but didn't move away. "I have a rule against buttering up the teacher."

"I'm not *gut* at following the rules, remember?" He chuckled as the color in her cheeks deepened.

The door swung open, and Zach and Ruth both turned to see Jacob Kline rush into the classroom. He skidded to a stop in front of her desk. "I forgot *mei* hat..." A puzzled look crossed his face when he saw Zach. "What are you doing here?"

Ruth glanced at Zach, then back at Jacob. "Zach's checking on the window he replaced. I thought I felt a draft this morning."

Zach frowned. Why was she lying to him? Then he understood. She had no idea Jacob knew he couldn't read. She was keeping his secret. He put his hand on her shoulder. "He already knows."

Her eyebrows arched. "He does?"

"Ya." He turned to Jacob. *"Fraulein* Byler is teaching me to read."

Jacob's eyes widened. "She is?"

He nodded. "You were right the other day, about not taking my own advice. So here I am. Ready to learn to read."

Jacob looked dumbfounded. "I can't believe you listened to me."

"Why wouldn't I?"

He looked away. "I'm just a *dumm kinn.* What do I know about anything?"

"You know a lot." Ruth came from the other

side of the desk and stood in front of him. "You're smart, Jacob. I've seen that in my classroom, and Zach has seen it too. I imagine your parents also know how intelligent you are. That's why it frustrates all of us when you make bad decisions."

"Like skipping school," Zach interjected.

"And not doing your work." She gave him a soft smile. "I'd like to see some changes in your behavior and work ethic, Jacob. I know you can do much better than you have been."

He looked doubtful, something Zach understood completely. "Hey, if I can change, anyone can. How about we make a deal? I'll learn to read, you stay in school and do your best."

Jacob smirked. "What's in it for me?"

"An *education*," Ruth said.

"And…a trip to my secret fishing hole." Zach grinned as Jacob's expression changed from doubt to curiosity. "I guarantee you'll catch twenty fish in one day."

"Twenty fish?" His eyes lit up. "We need to *geh* there now!"

He held up his hand. "Nope, not until you get your grades up, and I finish my lessons." He looked at Ruth. "Then we'll let *Fraulein* Byler decide if we deserve the fishing trip."

Stephen sat at the small picnic table outside the woodworking shop, his lunch spread out in front of him. His brothers sat with him, Tobias across and Lukas right beside. Most days they ate outside, except during winter. Stephen looked at his food—a club sandwich, potato chips, and three brownies. None of it appealed to him. As he had been since yesterday, he was preoccupied with Deborah and Moses.

Tobias and Lukas started talking about one of their regular customers who was being extra particular about an order. She had wanted everything done to perfect specifications and complained about every little thing, including price. "I have half a mind to tell her to take her special order elsewhere," Tobias said.

"*Ya*, but we don't want to lose her business." Lukas stabbed a piece of cherry pie with his fork. "She's bought a lot of pieces from us the past couple of years."

"But is it really worth the aggravation?" Tobias wiped a bit of mustard from his bologna sandwich off his mouth and sandy-blond beard. "It's not like she's our only customer."

"But she's a *gut* customer, one we want to keep. So we listen to her complain and do what she asks. If you don't want to deal with her anymore, let Stephen do it. He's always *gut* with the customers. Right, Stephen?" When Stephen didn't answer, Lukas nudged him in the side.

"What?" Stephen looked at his brother.

"You're not listening to us, are you?"

Stephen had to admit he only caught parts of their conversation. "You're talking about Mrs. Baxley?"

"Ya." Tobias grinned. "We decided you'll handle the customer relations with her from now on."

Stephen rolled his eyes. "I'd rather chew razor blades for the next twenty years."

"Ouch," Tobias said. He took another bite of sandwich as their father came out of the shop and joined them. He sat next to Tobias, and the three of them started talking about Mrs. Baxley again.

Stephen tuned them out. He couldn't think about a persnickety customer, not when his mind was back with the Coblentzes. He'd meant what he said to Deborah last night—he would come out twice a day if he had to. Knowing Moses, he'd ignore the doctor's advice and start working as soon as he could get out of bed. Deborah and Naomi would have their hands full taking care of him. They didn't need the added burden of trying to run the farm too.

"Stephen?"

Stephen looked into the face of his father. His beard, although liberally threaded with silver, was still mostly dark like the hair on his head, which was a little thinner than it used to be. There were creases beneath his eyes, and he wore bifocals, which he needed for close-up work. His father had been talking more and more about retiring, and Stephen knew the shop would eventually go to all three of them, with Lukas being in charge. Even though he would have an equal share in a thriving business, he wasn't sure he could see himself spending the rest of his life being a carpenter. And he'd been thinking about that more and more lately.

"*Sohn*, is there something wrong? You've been real quiet this afternoon. Like you're a million miles away."

He looked around to see that his brothers had already finished their lunch and gone back to work. His sandwich was untouched. He picked it up and started eating, wolfing down the food.

Joseph chuckled. "Slow down. You don't have to be in such a hurry."

"I have to get back to work." He picked up his glass of water and took a long swig.

"You've been working a lot lately. Not only for me. I noticed you've been spending a lot of time with the Coblentzes." He looked at Stephen. "You look tired."

Stephen felt tired. But it wasn't just from the physical labor. His feelings for Deborah and worry about Moses were taking a toll. Now he had something else weighing heavily on his mind. "Can I talk to you about something?"

Without his brothers around, this would be a good time to do it.

Joseph folded his hands and placed them on the table. "Sure. What's on your mind, *sohn*?"

"How did you know you wanted to be a carpenter?"

Joseph's bushy eyebrows lifted. He took off his glasses and set them on the table. "I suppose I've always known. My *daed* taught me how to build furniture. It was a hobby for him, but I loved it. Any spare time I had I was out in the barn, making something or trying to teach myself a new technique. I'd check books out from the library, or sometimes I'd just experiment with some scrap wood. I think I was younger than you when I decided I wanted my own shop."

"And you never had any doubts?"

Joseph shook his head. "Doubts about my profession? *Nee*. Doubts about my skills as a carpenter and a businessman? Of course, especially in the early years. But I trusted that God wouldn't have planted the passion in my heart or given me the skills unless He had wanted me to be a carpenter. The first years of the business were hard, but we have been blessed. Not only with a steady stream of work, but also with you, Tobias, and Lukas. I consider myself a lucky *mann* to have three sons following in my footsteps."

Stephen stared down at his half-eaten sandwich. A fly landed on the edge of the bread, and he swatted it away. His heart sank at the sound of his father's words. He didn't want to disappoint his *daed*, which would happen if he told him about his desire to become a farmer.

"Why do you ask?" Joseph leaned forward.

Stephen shrugged. "Just wondering."

"Oh, I think it's more than that. If there's something you want to tell me, go ahead. I'd like to think I raised my *kinner*, especially my *buwe*, to be able to tell me anything."

Pressing his lips together, Stephen took a deep breath. There was nothing else to do but tell his *daed* and hope he would understand. "I'm not sure I'm meant to be a carpenter."

Joseph looked surprised. "What makes you say that?"

"I feel I'm meant to do something else. I *want* to do something else." He picked at the crust on his bread, summoning the courage to say the words. He took a deep breath. "I want to be a farmer. Working with Moses these past couple weeks has proven it to me." He looked at his *daed*, willing him to understand. "It's not that I don't appreciate the opportunity I have here, that you've given me all my life. I've never wanted for anything, and I have to thank you for that. I don't think I ever told you how much I appreciate everything you've done for me."

His father swallowed and looked away for a moment, then faced Stephen again. "*Danki, sohn,* for saying that."

"That's why telling you this is so hard. I don't want you to think I'm turning my back on you or my *bruders.* That's not it at all."

Joseph looked at him squarely. "If you feel God is telling you to do something else, Stephen, then you need to follow the Lord's lead. The shop will be fine."

"But what about Tobias and Lukas? They'll think I'm *ab im kopp,* and that their little *bruder* doesn't know what he's doing."

"Oh, I think you'd be surprised. And even if they do have that reaction, you can't let them dictate what you're meant to do. If God's leading you in a different direction, then nothing any *mann* can say should keep you from the Lord's path."

Stephen nodded, appreciating his father's wise counsel. "I'm glad you understand."

"I guess I shouldn't be surprised. When you were *yung,* you always liked going to your grandparents' farm and helping out my brothers and uncles. I remember how I'd have to track you down at night and drag you inside. You were always in the barn or out in the field somewhere." He smiled. "You know, I was once in your position."

"You were?"

"*Ya.* Only it was just the opposite. I had to tell my *daed* that I didn't *want* to be a farmer. I come from a long line of farmers, and I think that's where you got your love for it. We all know how important farming is to the Amish, and turning my back on that legacy was hard. But farming wasn't where my heart was. My *daed* understood at that time. It would be hypocritical of me not to understand you."

Stephen's jaw dropped. "I never knew that."

"Telling your *mudder* was almost as difficult. We had already decided to get married, but I knew I couldn't marry her until I told her the truth and my plans for the future. I explained that not only did I want to set up my own carpentry business, but I wanted to move to Middlefield to do it. There were already a glut of carpenters in Holmes, and I thought the competition would be less here. Turned out it was." He looked down at his rough hands and laughed. "I was so scared the day I told your mother. I thought she was going to tell me I was crazy, or worse, break up with me."

"Obviously she didn't." Stephen leaned forward, marveling at how his situation and his father's paralleled each other. He'd never heard his father tell this part of the story of how he started his business.

Joseph's eyes grew glassy. "She supported me.

She said whatever I wanted to do, and especially whatever God was leading me to do, she would follow. Whether I failed or succeeded, we would do that together. She loved me, and she would go anywhere I asked." He looked at Stephen. "Your *mudder* is an amazing woman. She was willing to leave her family and come with me to Middlefield, where she didn't know anyone, because she believed in me and in my dream."

Stephen nodded, seeing his parents in a new light, especially his mother.

Joseph put his glasses back on. "So what are your plans? Have you already found some land?"

He shook his head. "*Nee*, I haven't looked. Right now I'm just trying to help Moses get back on his feet." He told his father about the heart attack. "I'll probably start looking for property in the spring. I'll need to save up my money until then."

"Sounds like you have it figured out." He stood up. "I don't think I've told you this, but I'm impressed with how you've helped Moses and his *dochders*."

"Anyone would have done the same."

Joseph shook his head. "Not the way you have." He reached out and patted his shoulder, then turned around and went inside.

Stephen let out a huge breath. He'd prayed about what his father would say, and his prayer had been answered. Now that he had his father's blessing, he could turn his attention toward his goal of having a farm. Except he couldn't think about anything other than Deborah and her family. Right now, they needed him even more than they had before. He just had to convince Moses—and Deborah—of that.

Deborah wiped her face with the back of her hand. Chopping wood was a chore she'd never done before, and it was tougher than she thought it would be. But the evening temperatures were starting to drop, and they needed enough wood to last them through the cold winter. She looked at the huge pile of cordwood that had been delivered last week. In order for it to fit into the small opening of the woodstove, each piece had to be chopped in half. But swinging an axe was difficult and awkward, not to mention physically taxing. She'd only split three pieces, and she was breathing heavily. She knew many Amish used coal stoves, but her father had never purchased one. Now she wished he had.

With the weather turning cooler, she thought of the cows. Had her *daed* ordered their winter hay? Once the snow came, the cows wouldn't be able to graze, and they would rely solely on the hay and grain. She would have to check on the feed supply for the other animals and prep the chicken coop for the winter. Although she and Naomi had forged a tentative truce, she couldn't rely on her sister for too much. She could ask Stephen for help—

She reined in the thought. Confusion warred within her. She still trusted him, but she couldn't shake the tiny doubt Naomi's accusation had planted in her. She didn't want to believe he had ulterior motives. But she couldn't be 100 percent sure.

She picked up a piece of wood and put it on the flat stump her father always used to split the wood. Right now she couldn't spend time trying to figure out what Stephen was up to. She had to finish chopping the wood. Raising the axe high overhead, she intended to slam it down on the wood. But the axe head pulled her off balance, causing her to stumble a few steps backward. She regained her balance before she fell completely backward. When she heard Will laugh, she scowled at him. "I don't find it funny at all."

She'd had to bring Will with her because Naomi had left for the grocery store and she didn't want her father to exert any energy watching him. Her father had slept most of the day, and she was glad he was taking the doctor's advice.

A buggy pulled near the barn where she was chopping the wood, but she didn't look up, thinking it was probably Naomi. She was glad; now

her sister could take Will inside. He was cor-
ralled in the playpen nearby, playing with a few
toys, and so far had been content. But she knew
it wouldn't be long before he'd start fussing and
want out. Taking a deep breath, she lifted up the
axe to make a second attempt at splitting the
chunk of wood in front of her. But when she tried
to bring the tool down, it wouldn't move. Looking up, she saw Stephen standing over her, grasping the handle in his huge hand.

"You shouldn't be doing this," he said.

"I'm fine."

He furrowed his brows. "Deborah, you don't
have to chop the wood. Take Will inside. I'm here
now."

"Maybe you shouldn't be." The words were out
of her mouth before she could stop them.

Hurt flashed in his eyes. "Why would you say
something like that?"

She tried to bring the axe back down, but he
held on tight. Her arms were aching, and her
body was twisted in a strange position. "Let *geh*
of the axe. I've got to get this wood chopped."

He let go, but the force of the weight of the
axe drove her forward. It flew out of her hands
and sank into the ground in front of her, part of
the blade exposed. She stumbled after it, trip-
ping over the stump. All she could see were the
ground and the blade coming toward her.

* * *

When he saw Deborah trip, Stephen reached out and grabbed her around the waist, yanking her toward him.

"Oh!" She cried out, then spun around in his arms. Her breath came in spasms as she looked up at him.

He was breathless, too, not only because he'd been terrified she'd land on the corner of the blade, which likely would have been a serious injury, even life-threatening, but also because having her this close to him, with his arms around her hips, made his heart dance.

She jumped back, looking away. She was acting strangely, and he had no idea why. "Deborah, what's going on? Are you mad at me?" When she didn't say anything, he moved toward her. "Please, tell me what I did wrong. I'll apologize. I'll fix it." He knew he shouldn't touch her, but he couldn't help himself. He cupped her chin with his hand. "I couldn't stand it if you were mad at me."

Her shoulders slumped as he pulled his hand away. "You haven't done anything. At least not yet."

"Not yet?"

"*Daed* is talking about selling the farm. He mentioned your name." She looked up at him, crossing her arms over her chest.

"He did?"

"Don't act so surprised. You're the one who told me he talked to you about it."

"It's not an act." Moses had never mentioned wanting him to buy the farm. And Stephen had never said anything about it either. He pushed his hat back and rubbed his forehead with his fingertips. "How did he know I wanted to have my own farm?"

Her eyes widened, filling with hurt and betrayal. "I don't believe this." She whirled around, her back to him. "How could you do this to me? To my *familye*!"

"Deborah, it's not like that, I promise—"

"All that talk about Will's legacy…" She faced him again, her entire face turning pink. "It was all a lie."

He went to her. "Deborah, I would never lie to you. Or hurt you." He clasped his hands behind his neck, bewildered by her accusations. "You have to believe me."

"Then why does he want to sell the farm to you?"

"Did he say that?"

"Not in so many words. But why else would he bring you up as a potential buyer if you two haven't discussed it?"

"I don't know." But he aimed to find out. He turned around and headed for the house.

"Where are you going?" she called after him.

He glanced over his shoulder. "To talk to your *daed*. I'm getting to the bottom of this."

"You can't." She ran after him, then moved to block his path. "The doctor said for him to rest and to not get upset."

"I won't upset him. I'm just going to talk to him."

"Don't!" She held up her hand.

It was almost laughable that she thought she could physically stop him. All he had to do was pick her up and set her to the side, then plow on through to the house. He wouldn't, though. He hoped she would come to her senses and let him pass.

Suddenly they both heard Will crying. He turned around to see the boy standing up in the playpen, his face red, his eyes soaked with tears. Deborah dashed over to him and gathered him in her arms. "Shh," she cooed, then sank to the ground, still holding him. "It's okay. It's okay."

Stephen went to her and stayed by her side, his heart breaking as tears streaked down her face. She was exhausted, anyone could see that. He crouched down next to her and took Will in his arms. She didn't protest.

"I can't do this," she said after a few moments. "I thought I could..."

"Do what, Deborah?"

"Handle everything." Her back slumped into a C shape. "The house. My *sohn*. I wanted to show *Daed* he didn't have to sell what he'd worked so hard for. But I didn't even last a day."

He sat down beside her, then settled Will in his lap. "You're right. You can't do it all, and you shouldn't have to. Let me help you."

She looked at him, her eyes wet with tears. "That's what I don't understand."

"What?"

"Why you're here. Why you want to help us. You've done more for us than any one person should. And there was only one reason that made sense."

Understanding dawned. "You think I'm here because I want to take the farm from you. Deborah, listen to me. And listen carefully. That never, ever entered my mind." He wanted to touch her, but he didn't dare. Not until she understood how he felt. "I've learned a few things about myself from working here. One is that I do want a farm of my own. God has shown me that." He looked at her, willing her to understand. "But not this farm. This is Moses's place. Yours and Naomi's and Will's." He glanced down at the child in his lap, who had slipped his thumb into his mouth, his chubby cheek leaning against Stephen's chest. "I would never try to take it from you."

Chapter Twenty

Deborah looked into Stephen's eyes. She saw no deceit, only honesty. And more than anything, she wanted to believe him. But the doubts wouldn't release her. She'd trusted before and had been hurt. She'd known Chase longer than she has known Stephen. They had worked together at Mary Yoder's restaurant. They had spent time at parties after work and on the weekends. He had said she was special. He'd even told her he loved her. But everything he'd said had been a lie. Then he'd rejected her and their son.

And here was Stephen, the most genuine man she'd ever known. She glanced at her son resting on his broad chest, nestled in the secure embrace of this gentle giant of a man.

"There's something else I've learned." He leaned forward, his voice low, the smooth timbre sending ripples down her spine. "I care about you."

Her heart tripped a beat. Had she heard him right?

"I care about Will too." A shy look entered his eyes. "That's why I would never do anything to hurt either of you." He kissed the top of Will's head, then handed him to Deborah. "If you still want me to *geh*, if it will be easier on you, I'll leave right now."

When he moved to get up, she put her hand on his knee. "Wait." A lump clogged her throat. She tried to process what he'd told her. He cared about her and her son. The words were too good to be true. But they were more than words, and as she looked into his eyes, any doubts she had about him disappeared. "I don't want you to *geh*, Stephen. Please, stay."

"Are you sure?"

She reached for his hand and threaded her fingers through his. "*Ya*. I'm sure."

He grinned and squeezed her hand.

They both looked up as a buggy came down the dirt drive. Stephen released her hand and helped her to her feet. She adjusted Will in the cradle of her arm, then reached for Stephen's hand again. Her sister would be angry to see her and Stephen together. But it didn't matter. Once she heard Stephen's side of the story, Naomi would understand.

Sure enough, when Naomi got out of the buggy, she stormed toward them.

"What's going on here?" Naomi glared at Stephen. "What's he doing here?"

"Clearing up a misunderstanding," Stephen said. "I was just telling Deborah—"

"I don't care what you have to say. You're a liar and a thief. Or at least you tried to be by stealing our farm from us."

"Naomi, that's not true. We were wrong about Stephen."

Her sister huffed. "I should have known you'd stick up for him. You'll believe anything a *mann* tells you. I thought you had finally learned, but I see you're still as *dumm* as ever."

"Naomi, you're not being fair."

"I'm not fair? You stand there holding your il-legitimate *kinn*, ready to lecture me about men? You think I don't know they're only after one thing? Then again, you found that out firsthand, didn't you?"

Shame filled Deborah. Her sister's words sliced into her, especially said in front of Stephen. Naomi made her seem loose, without morals. "I made a mistake."

"And now you're ready to make another one. What did he tell you? Did he promise to marry you and give your *sohn* a *daed*?" She scoffed. "Like that would ever happen."

"That's enough." Stephen stepped forward. "What Deborah and I talked about is none of your business. The only thing you need to know is that I'm not buying your *daed's* farm. I never intended to."

"Liar."

"It's true, Naomi. I thought the same thing, but he's right. *Daed* must have come up with the idea on his own."

"And you believe him?"

"I do."

"You can *geh* ask your *daed* if you want," Stephen said. "He'll back me up."

"Oh, I intend to."

Deborah watched as her sister charged toward the house. She looked at Stephen. "I'm sorry for what she said."

"You don't have to keep apologizing for her. You should *geh* after her though. She looks angry enough to snap."

"Sometimes I wonder if she already has." She glanced down at Will, praying her son didn't understand anything his *aenti* had said. One day she would have to tell him about his father, but she didn't want Naomi anywhere around when she did.

Stephen held out his arms to Will. "I'll take

him. We'll *geh* check on the cows, then I'll bring him inside. Hopefully by that time she'll have simmered down."

Deborah handed Will over to him, watching for a moment while the most special man she'd ever met took her son into the barn. Warmth flowed through her. No matter what happened with her and Naomi, just knowing that Stephen cared about her and Will was enough.

She went inside and walked toward her father's bedroom. She could hear Naomi's accusing voice outside the door before she opened it.

"He's got you both fooled," Naomi exclaimed.

"Naomi, you've got to calm down." Their father held his hands in front of him. "You're going to pop a vessel if you don't." He then looked at Deborah. "Will someone tell me what's going on here?"

"Stephen's here. He's in the barn with Will." She caught a glimpse of Naomi's glare out of the corner of her eye, but she continued on. "He says he's not going to buy the farm. He never intended to."

Daed lay back down against the pillow. "Of course he's not. Where did you get that idea?"

"You said you were thinking about selling it to him."

"I did?" He scratched his chin through his beard. "I don't recall saying that."

"Right after your heart attack, remember?"

"I told you I didn't have no heart attack—"

"You said you would try to talk him out of being a carpenter."

Her father frowned for a moment. Then his expression relaxed. "Oh, that's right. I did say something like that. And I still can't think of anyone better I'd want working this land. He loves it, with his heart and soul. Never hear a word of complaint out of him, always wants to do more, learn more." He looked at Deborah. "But I was just thinking out loud, Deborah. I wasn't going to sell it right away. I still have a few more *gut* years in me, and he still has a lot of money to save up before he can afford this place. If he even wants it. Might be hard for me to talk him out of being a carpenter."

Deborah knew differently, but she'd speak to her father about that later. Instead she looked at Naomi, who had finally settled down. "So you're not selling the farm?"

"Not yet," he said with a slight shake of his head. "But I have to be practical, *dochders*." He removed his reading glasses and set them on the nightstand, then looked at Naomi. "You're thirty years old and not married." Then he looked at Deborah. "You're still young, but you have, um, circumstances." He took a deep breath and then spoke. "I'm sorry to say this, but I can't depend on the two of you getting married. And I can't wait until Will is old enough to run things around here." Sadness entered his eyes. "I'd rather see the land go to someone who loves it like I do than see the farm fall apart."

Deborah nodded. She could see her father's logic, even if it hurt. She looked at Naomi, who hadn't said a word during the entire exchange. Her sister brought her hand to her mouth and suddenly fled the room.

Daed sighed. "I said the wrong thing. Again. Your *mudder* always said I must have a taste for shoe leather, I put my foot in my mouth so much. I should have never told you about my idea of selling the farm. I was feeling sorry for myself at the time. Things have been so hard around here without your *mudder*. She was the one who kept me going. Lately it's been hard to find the will to do anything."

Deborah sat down on the chair near the edge of his bed. She took his callused hand in hers. "Oh, *Daed*. I'm so sorry."

"I kept telling myself the next day would be better. But it never was. Then I'd end up in the pasture, staring at the fence that needed fixing, unable to bring myself to repair it. I'd think about your *mudder*, remembering the *gut* times we had, trying to forget the last couple months that the cancer took from us. Bless your sister, she kept everything going while your *mami* was sick."

"I should have been here." Tears streamed down her face. "Why didn't you tell me *Mami* was sick?"

"Because she didn't want you to know. Up until the end, she thought she had it beat." He wiped his eyes with his free hand. "She was a strong woman. Just not strong enough."

"What happened the other day? When you were in the pasture?"

"I don't really know. I'd been feeling poorly the past couple days, but I thought I was just tired. I hadn't been sleeping well since Martha's death. By the time I reached the back fence my chest felt as if it were on fire. The next thing I remember is Stephen standing over me when I woke up on the couch. If he hadn't found me when he did…" He shook his head. "I owe that *bu* my life."

Deborah nodded. "We all owe him so much."

Her father squeezed her hand and then released it. "*Geh* check on your sister. I'm worried about her. She's become so bitter over the years."

"Do you know why?"

He shook his head. "Your *mudder* and I could never figure it out. We thought it might be jealousy over you."

"Over me? She never wanted anything to do with me."

"When you were a *boppli* she did. But then when you turned two, you got very sick and ended up in the hospital for two weeks."

"I don't remember that."

He nodded. "Wouldn't expect you to, and it's not something we talked about. We couldn't bring Naomi to the hospital. She was only twelve, so several women from church came by and watched her, plus made meals for us. Their husbands took care of the farm for me. When we brought you home, you needed lots of care for several months. Naomi wasn't our priority anymore. You were."

Deborah now saw where her sister's bitterness stemmed from. "But that was so long ago. Why is she hanging on to it still?"

He shrugged. "I don't know. Maybe you should ask her."

Deborah looked away. "She won't talk to me."

"You won't know unless you try."

She'd been trying to get Naomi to talk to her since coming back to Middlefield. Deborah doubted she could reach her now. But she wouldn't tell her father that. She looked at him, seeing the weariness on his face. "I'll leave you alone now. You get some more rest."

He frowned, but his eyelids were only halfway

open. "That's all I've been doing. Are you *maed* going to keep me in bed for the rest of my life?"

She smiled, glad to see his feistiness returning. "*Nee.* But we will until you get better."

She walked out of her father's room, shut the door, and leaned against it. She thought about what he said. Was her sister bitter because of a childhood grudge? That seemed extreme, even for Naomi. Deborah suspected it had to be something else. She had to find out what it was, or there would be no peace in her family.

Deborah went into the kitchen to find Naomi. When she didn't see her, she looked throughout the bottom floor of the house. Then she went upstairs and saw that Naomi's bedroom door was closed. She knocked softly.

"What do you want?" Naomi sniffed.

Had her sister been crying? She couldn't remember the last time Naomi had cried. Her sister hadn't shed a tear at their mother's funeral. "Can I come in?"

"*Nee.*"

But Deborah wasn't about to give up, not this time. She turned the knob on the door and was glad it was unlocked. She eased the door open, then took a step inside. Her sister stood at the window, her back to Deborah, and didn't turn around. After a few seconds, Deborah went to Naomi. She expected her to walk away, but she didn't. They stared out at the barn and field in front of them, and just then Stephen and Will appeared from the barn, her *sohn* looking so tiny in Stephen's huge arms.

"I suppose you two will get married."

Deborah's brow rose with surprise. "What makes you say that?"

Naomi wrapped her arms around her thin body. "I see the way he looks at you. I see how he is with your *sohn*." She glanced at Deborah. "As usual, you get what you want."

"You think I want him?"

"You do, don't you?"

She looked back at Stephen, the image of them getting married and becoming a family suddenly becoming real. He said he cared for her, and she knew deep in her heart that she loved him. "*Ya*," she whispered as he headed toward the house. "I think I do."

Naomi walked away from the window. "*Gut* luck with your happy family, then."

Deborah reached out and grabbed her sister's arm. Jealousy and resentment emanated from Naomi. "Is that why you're angry with me? Because of Stephen? Because of Will?"

"You don't know how hard it is to want something you'll never have."

"Naomi, you can't say that for sure."

She turned away from the window.

"*Daed* told me about my being sick. I don't even remember it. You can't hang on to this jealousy—"

Her sister let out a bitter chuckle. "Of course you'd think this is about you. It's always about you."

"Isn't it?"

"Never mind. I don't want to talk about this."

"Naomi." Deborah went over to her. "We can't spend the rest of our lives angry with each other. It's not what God would want. We both know that. Please. Tell me what's wrong. I don't want us to fight anymore."

Naomi sat down on her bed and stared at her hands, her shoulders slumped. Deborah moved to sit beside her. Naomi didn't say anything for a long moment. Just when Deborah thought she wouldn't respond and was giving her the silent treatment, Naomi finally spoke. "I thought I was going to get married once," she whispered.

Deborah's eyes lifted in shock. "You did?"

"Don't be so surprised."

"But I had no idea."

"You were only eight, too young to know what was going on."

"But *Mami* and *Daed* never said anything about it."

"That's because they didn't know. No one did." She raised her head and looked at Deborah, then quickly averted her gaze. "I couldn't tell them I'd fallen in love with a Yankee."

"What?" Deborah couldn't believe what she was hearing.

Naomi nodded, still not looking at her. "We dated secretly for a few months." She glanced at Deborah. Her eyes were dry, but her chin was quivering. "He said he loved me, that I was special. That we should move in together. He even said he wanted to get married someday. And because I loved him, I believed him. But I was a fool. Everything he told me was a lie so he could get what he wanted from me."

Deborah's heart sank. She knew exactly what Naomi was talking about. Chase had said all the right things, too, and his rejection had hurt. But she hadn't been in love with Chase. She could only imagine the pain her sister had gone through.

"My friends had warned me about him. They told me he was no *gut*, but I didn't believe them. I was ready to give up everything for him, including being Amish. Then I found out he was seeing someone else the whole time we were dating."

"Oh, Naomi." Deborah reached out and touched her arm. "I'm so sorry."

"He manipulated me." A hard edge crept into her tone. "Just like Stephen's doing to you."

"He's not manipulating me, Naomi. I'll admit

that Chase did, but only because I let him. Stephen's nothing like Chase. There are *gut* men in the world, Naomi. Not all of them are like Chase or…"

"Trey. His name was Trey." She rose from the bed. "All my friends found a *gut* one. They married and have *kinner*. And I'm alone. I suppose that's what I get for sinning against God."

"I don't believe that. You can't judge yourself like this, Naomi. And you can't assume that God's punishing you for one mistake."

Naomi shook her head. "It wasn't just one mistake. I was willing to give up my faith. How could He forgive something like that?"

Things were starting to make sense. Her sister was pious to a fault, and now Deborah knew why. She still felt like she had to atone for the past, and she still carried around the hurt from Trey's betrayal. She reached for Naomi's hand. "Naomi, have you forgiven Trey?"

Naomi jerked her hand out of Deborah's grasp. "That's not any of your business. I should have never told you about him." She lifted her chin, her eyes narrowing. "I don't want to talk about this again, understand?"

"But—"

"I have to prepare supper. I'm sure *Daed* is hungry by now." She started for the door, but

Deborah tugged on her arm, trying to stop her. Naomi pulled away and walked out of the room.

Deborah sat on her sister's bed and scanned her austere bedroom. She closed her eyes, her soul filled with sadness for her sister. She'd had no idea how deeply Naomi had been hurt, or how she blamed herself for it. Nothing Deborah could say would help Naomi give up the pain she insisted on clinging to. Only God could change her heart, and she would pray every day for that to happen.

"My goodness, Deborah. He's quite a hottie."

Deborah looked at Aunt Sadie and laughed. Her aunt had arrived for a surprise visit the day before, and now they were sitting on the front porch, snapping the last of the green beans they had picked from the garden. Over near the barn, Stephen had set Will on his broad shoulders. He looked over at the women and waved.

"Yep," Sadie said, snapping a bean in half with one hand. "He's a fine-looking man." She glanced at Deborah. "And from all accounts, a very good man too."

"That he is." She waved back at Stephen and her son, then looked back at Sadie. "I'm so glad you're here, *Aenti*."

"Me too." Her bright red lips curved into a

smile. "Although I wish I had known about Moses before I got here."

"We didn't want to worry you, and he didn't want the attention." She picked up another green bean from the pile on the table and broke off the ends.

"I give you permission to worry me. I would have been here days ago if I had known." She glanced over Deborah's shoulder at Stephen again. "So what's going on between you two?"

Deborah kept her gaze on the bowl in her lap, but she couldn't hide her smile. "What makes you think there's something going on?"

"Oh please. I'm old but not senile. I know two lovebirds when I see them. So when's the wedding?"

"We've barely started to date, *Aenti*." Although she had to wonder that herself. Neither of them had brought up marriage, but Deborah couldn't imagine marrying anyone else. The more time she spent with Stephen, the more she fell in love with him.

"Fine, be coy about it. I'll make sure to keep my calendar open this fall, just in case."

Deborah grinned. It was great to be with her aunt again.

Stephen and Will headed toward them. When they reached the porch, Stephen lifted Will off his shoulders high in the air, letting him dangle there for a moment. Will burst into giggles as Stephen swung him down and set him on the porch. Stephen looked at Deborah, his blue eyes shining with warmth. Deborah could feel her cheeks heat underneath his tender gaze.

Sadie mumbled something about lovebirds, then set her bowl of green beans on the table and reached for Will. "Looks like this punkin's been having too much fun in the dirt." She rose from the rocker and took his hand. "Bath time for you, little man!"

After Sadie and Will walked into the house, Stephen sat down in the rocker next to Deborah and leaned his arms over his knees. "It's *gut* to see you smile."

She nodded. "I have a lot to smile about." And she did. Two weeks had passed since her father's heart attack, and he was gaining more strength each day. And even though Naomi was still distant, her attitude had softened toward her and Will. She even offered to watch him a few days ago while Deborah went to town for the first time. That spurred Deborah to pray even harder for her sister. She wanted Naomi to heal.

Stephen angled his chair toward her, his expression suddenly serious. "I need to talk to you about something. I hope you'll still be smiling after I'm done."

Deborah dropped the green bean she'd just

snapped into the bowl, alarmed. "Is there something wrong?"

"Nee." He reached for her hand. "Deborah, everything is right. It has been since I met you." He covered her hand with his other one. "I know we haven't known each other that long, so this might seem sudden. But it's the truth. I love you, Deborah. I want to be a husband to you, and a father to Will. But…" He looked away, swallowing.

She frowned. "But what?"

He met her eyes again. "I don't want you to think I'm marrying you because of the farm. In fact, I don't want it."

"You don't want to be a farmer anymore?"

"Nee. That hasn't changed. But if I thought for a minute you doubted my reasons for marrying you, I'd give up the idea of farming."

"Oh, Stephen, I could never doubt you. And I would never ask you to give up your dream of farming." She smiled, her heart swelling with love for this gentle giant of a man.

He let out a deep breath and squeezed her hand. "That's what I was hoping you'd say."

The front door opened and Aunt Sadie walked out, Will cradled in the crook of her arm. She looked from Deborah to Stephen, her lips spreading in a fat grin. "Now, now, don't mind us."

From the satisfied look on her aunt's face,

Deborah knew her aunt hadn't just appeared. "You were eavesdropping again," she said as Stephen dropped her hand and leaned back in the chair. His cheeks reddened.

"Absolutely not. I was casually listening. There's a big difference." Sadie glanced from her to Stephen. "Don't stop on my account. I just came out here to get Will's toy. He kept asking for that wooden horse of his. There, I see it." She went to the opposite end of the porch and picked it up off the floor. Then she turned back around and walked inside. "Carry on," she said before shutting the door.

"Well," Stephen said, still looking a little embarrassed. "That wasn't exactly how I expected my proposal to *geh*." He rose from the rocker and stood in front of her, holding out his hand. "But it doesn't matter. As long as you say you'll be my wife."

Deborah took his hand and stood. "I'd be honored to be your wife."

Smiling, he leaned down, giving her a soft, quick kiss on the mouth. Then he drew her into his arms.

She closed her eyes and leaned against him, marveling at how God had brought them together. He knew what they both needed and wanted, even before they realized it themselves. He had known it all along.

Epilogue

One year later

"Zach, what are you doing?" Ruth glanced over her shoulder as he grabbed her hand and led her to the other side of Lukas's house. When they were shielded from her entire family, he let go of her hand. She leaned against the white siding of the house and put her hands on her hips. "Well? Are you going to answer me or not?"

He grinned, putting both hands on either side of her face, then drew her mouth to his for a lingering kiss. "How's that for an answer?"

Breathless, she nodded. "*Gut* answer." Then she shook her head and regained her senses. "You can't do that here. What if my family catches us?"

"I'm a troublemaker, remember? I have a reputation to uphold."

"Sorry, that reputation has been shattered for months." She smiled at the joy on his face. He had come so far in the past year learning to read. He hadn't been exaggerating when he said it would be difficult to teach him. Through her research, she discovered he was dyslexic, and it had taken several months and a lot of determination on his part to succeed. Witnessing his drive had made her fall more deeply in love with him, and they would be getting married in mid-November, which was only three weeks away.

As much as she wouldn't mind spending time alone with him right now, they both knew it wouldn't be appropriate. "We better get back before anyone misses us."

"I think they're all too busy to notice." He leaned forward again, but she put her finger to his lips. He smiled against it and stepped away. "All right, you win. This time."

She laughed as they went back around to where the rest of the family were gathered. She could only imagine what he meant by that. Zach had changed a lot in the past year, but he hadn't lost his impulsiveness. And for someone who never liked surprises, she didn't mind his at all.

"Where did you guys *geh* off to?" Ruth's mother asked when she and Zach joined her at the picnic table. Lukas had set up several of the tables in his spacious backyard. One table was devoted completely to food where, not surprisingly, she saw Stephen piling up his plate.

"We took a walk." Zach looked at his future mother-in-law, his eyes wide with innocence. Ruth had to look away before she started to laugh.

Emma peered at him over her eyeglasses, but didn't say anything. "Did you two get enough to eat?"

"*Ya*," Ruth said, sitting next to her mother.

"I doubt there's any left if we didn't," Zach added, joining them. "I see Stephen's hit the table pretty hard."

"I heard that."

Ruth turned and saw her brother a few feet away. He grinned as he sat down with them. "Where's Deborah?" she asked.

"With the *kinner*." He gestured with his thumb to the sandbox several yards away. Deborah, Elisabeth, Moriah, and Rachel were sitting near it, keeping an eye on the children. He took a bite of potato salad, then wiped his bearded chin with his napkin. He and Deborah had married in January and were staying at the Coblentz farm with her father and sister until he built a house of his own.

"Stephen! Zach!" Lukas's foster son, Sawyer, called out from the other side of the yard. His dark brown hair lifted in the cool fall breeze.

"Get over here. We need two more players to make the teams even."

"Just a minute." Stephen wolfed down a couple more bites of food, then handed his plate to Ruth. He trotted over to Sawyer, who was conferring with Tobias, Lukas, and Aaron. The men wore baseball gloves, and Aaron was tossing a baseball up and down in his right hand.

Zach looked at Ruth, eagerness in his green eyes. She nodded and he took off running toward the men.

Once Zach left, she heard her mother sigh. She turned and looked at her. "Are you okay, *Mami*?"

"*Ya*. I'm perfectly fine." She smiled, but her eyes shined with tears. "It's hard to believe how fast the time goes. I remember when the six of you used to form your own team."

"And Stephen always struck out." Ruth laughed quietly. Her brother was talented at many things, but he had never gotten the hang of hitting a baseball.

"Now look at all of you. Moriah and Gabriel have three *schee maed*. Tobias has a *wunderbaar frau* in Rachel, and his Josiah is as mischievous as he is." Emma chuckled. "Lukas and Anna opened their hearts and home to Sawyer, and soon will have two other foster children. And Elisabeth, she'll be a *mudder* by Christmas. Stephen and Deborah have a fine *sohn* in Will. Then there is my youngest." She swiped a finger under her eye. "You'll be married soon."

Ruth looked at her siblings and their families. Her nieces and nephews playing in the sandbox and on the swing-set, her sisters and sisters-in-law close by. She saw Elisabeth place her hand over her swollen belly, remembering how giddy she had been when she announced she and Aaron were expecting.

Her gaze traveled to the men, who had already chosen teams. Stephen, Aaron, and Tobias stood by the old baseball mitt that served as home base while Lukas, Zach, and Sawyer formed the other team. Her father and Gabriel stood by, their arms crossed over their chests as they talked.

"The Lord has blessed us mightily," Emma said. "He has given us a *wunderbaar familye.*"

Ruth nodded. "*Ya, Mami.* He certainly has."

* * * * *

READING GROUP GUIDE

Guide contains spoilers, so don't read before completing the novel.

1. Because of decisions Zach has made, he often feels like a failure. Have you ever felt like you failed at something? How did God help bring your confidence back?

2. Ruth doesn't like surprises, yet during the story her plans don't work out the way she expects them to. Discuss a time when your plans didn't coincide with God's. What was the result?

3. Deborah worries about the community not accepting her and Will because of the circumstances of his birth. However, she does believe God accepts her no matter what. Give an example of a time where you felt God's acceptance and how that affected your life.

4. Stephen is unselfish and loyal in helping the Coblentz family take care of the farm. Is there a person in your life who has demonstrated these qualities? In what ways?

5. Zach is ashamed that he can't read, and he is afraid he'll never learn how. Think about a time in your life when you were afraid. How did God help you overcome that fear?

6. In the story, Ruth learned that first impressions aren't always accurate. Have you ever formed an opinion about someone, only to change your mind after you got to know him/her? What happened to make your rethink your opinion?

7. Naomi still harbors the pain of her past. If you could give Naomi advice, what would you say to her?

8. Do you think Stephen should purchase his own farm or take over the Coblentz farm? Explain your answer.

9. How important was it for Jacob to see Zach accept Ruth's help? Describe a time where admitting personal weakness has benefited someone else (you can use a Biblical account or personal account as an example).

10. Stephen showed unconditional love when he accepted Deborah and Will into his life, in spite of her past. Discuss a time when God specifically showed you His unconditional love.

Acknowledgments

I'd like to thank my wonderful editors, Natalie Hanemann and Jenny Baumgartner, for helping me bring *A Hand to Hold* to life. They continually teach and encourage me, and I couldn't have written this book without them. Thanks to my agent, Tamela, who's not only a great agent but a dear friend. A big thank you and hug to my children, Mathew, Sydney, and Zoie, for being the best three kids in the world. A special thank you to my friend Maria for reading over the manuscript and giving me her invaluable feedback. And most of all, thank you, dear readers, for your support and encouragement. I'm so glad we made this journey to Middlefield together.